a Promise Kept

a novel

anissa garcia

A Promise Kept

Cover Design: Regina Wamba with MaeIDesign.com

Editor: Erin Noelle

Formatting: Jeff Senter with Indie Formatting Services

ISBN: 978-0-9975430-1-8 (Paperback)

ISBN: 978-0-9975430-0-1 (Ebook)

For Melissa and Marla – Thank you for helping me every step of the way and believing in me even when I couldn't find a way to believe in myself.

"Only by joy and sorrow does a person know anything about themselves and their destiny."

JOHANN WOLFGANG VON GOETHE

Chapter One

"Lead with your head, not your heart." That was the motto thirty-two-year-old Grace Lynn Clark was told to follow by her father. After years of growing up with that saying, along with the constant *"Why can't you be more like your brother?"* line, she thought she would have eventually found a way to comply with her old man. Instead, that was the opposite of what she had done when it came to her career.

Grace chuckled darkly under her breath and puffed away a stray lock of hair that fell out of her messy bun. It was because she followed her heart that she was now standing outside her new neighbor's home waiting to evaluate a leak under the kitchen sink. Not all authors had great contracts, not all of them hit the bestseller lists, and only some of them had the opportunity to make writing their only profession.

Grace's folks had moved away from her the moment she entered college, but the weight of their judgment still lurked. Thoughts of inadequacy couldn't be helped when she had to ask a family friend for a job. And the *"Why can't you be more like your brother"* line? Well, that had stopped soon after Nathan passed away, although she sometimes wondered what it would have been like if she had gone to law school instead of getting her degree in English.

At least this occupation gave her more time to write than her customer service gig at a makeup counter at the mall. Plus, she had worked as a property manager long enough by now that everything ran smoothly. Until this particular afternoon. The timing couldn't have been more wrong, but she hurried her way over, having to abandon a very rare opportunity to have her own book signing at one of the local bookstores.

Grace shifted the heavy toolbox from one hand to the other, her patience starting to wear thin. The door swung open, and every thought escaped her brain. She swore her heart stopped beating as she stared at the strikingly large male specimen who stood before her. She would have taken the time to slowly roam over every inch of chest, arm, and torso muscle hugged by black cotton, or would have gawked at the way those dark jeans hugged his narrow hips, but instead, her eyes widened to the size of saucers as she focused on a face that was completely recognizable.

"You must be Grace." The smooth tone of his voice wrapped around her ears as he held his hand out and introduced himself. "Evan Matthews."

Grace quickly gathered her wits, as the personal lump of gray matter that was her brain began to function again. "I...wouldn't have guessed." Luckily her sarcasm was taken in stride with a warm smile. She ignored the instant shockwaves the large, warm, and callused hand sent throughout her body when he shook hers.

"You live here?" This wasn't Hollywood, and although movies were sometimes filmed in the capital of Texas, it wasn't a typical occurrence running into an A-list actor. Especially one who lived next door.

"For the next six months, according to my lease. I'd figure my property manager would know that already." His cerulean eyes gleamed mischief. She had just met him and he was already teasing her. The thought gave Grace a slight thrill, then she remembered who this was. He was Evan Matthews, star of the multi-billion-dollar franchise *The Ending Series.* He was a charmer, most definitely.

"Funny, you looked a lot like a man named Zach Collins when you signed the paperwork a few weeks ago," she quipped.

"Yeah, he's my stand-in."

Grace chuckled. Zach looked nothing like the gorgeous hunk in front of her. Evan's body was drool-worthy. His muscle mass alone flashed a superhero status. The light brown stubble on his strong jaw demonstrated an edge, which was different from the clean-cut character he was most famous for playing on the big screen. She could almost say he looked handsome in a familiar sort of way—a way that made him amenable. A young Paul Newman, perhaps. She hoped a sigh didn't escape her mouth as she thought of Brick from *Cat on a Hot Tin Roof.*

"Come on in." He held the door open as she passed, and without warning, he seized the toolbox she held in her other hand. Instant relief hit her arm from the released weight.

She strolled inside the tidy townhome. It was modern with neutral tones, black furniture dispersed throughout. The living room showed signs of being lived in with papers, scripts, and books scattered across the coffee table.

"I was expecting Zach to be here since he's the one that called," Grace commented as she approached the kitchen sink.

He followed and stood near her as she bent low, opening the cabinet and peering inside. "He's my assistant."

"He mentioned he had a roommate. I didn't realize it would be Captain Drew Abrams." God, could she be more awkward? Bringing up his movie role was probably a great way to alienate her tenant.

The beautiful film star crouched beside Grace and reached forward, ignoring her statement. She caught a whiff of something heavenly, and as he stretched toward her, she decided it was the perfect mixture of sandalwood, amber, and a hint of mandarin.

"Right there's where it's seeping," he explained, glancing over at her. "I'll try to tighten the screw, but I think the pipe needs replacement. It might be a tear. In that case, you'd definitely need a plumber out here to sweat-solder it in place."

"Okay, well, I can try to tighten the screw right now, and we'll see what happens."

Evan stood after her and watched her movements. "We can try to flush the pipe. You want to flush my pipe, Grace?" His eyebrow cocked up, joy evident in his verbal banter.

God, he was such a flirt. It was a bit of a turn-off because she knew he probably spewed sexual innuendos left and right to all women he encountered. Having just read the latest issue of *US Weekly*, she was well aware of Evan's appetite for women. In fact, he had just recently dumped reality star Rachel Smith, his flavor of the month. *Get a grip and stop gawking over him, Grace. He's not for you.*

She opened her toolbox, the clang of the lid echoing against the countertop, and a hearty laugh escaped his mouth. She glowered at him. "What's so funny?"

"Pink-colored tools?"

Grace swore her cheeks flushed the same hue, but gave him an artful grin. "What's wrong with pink-colored tools?"

He shook his head and stepped back, giving Grace the opportunity to reach for the pipe wrench. "Absolutely nothing. It's cute, actually." As he gazed at her, she knew what he was looking at—a petite brunette in her early thirties dressed in yoga pants, a plain shirt, and Nike running shoes. The look didn't scream sexy, but after Zach stated the leak made a huge mess, Grace thought it best to change into clothes she didn't mind getting dirty.

"What exactly are you planning to do there?" His voice trailed off as Grace turned on the faucet, bent low, and twisted the valve, allowing the water supply to turn on.

"I'm checking the leak–"

"Shit, I wouldn't do that…"

Grace yelped as water drenched her face. Trying to stop it, she wrapped her hand around the pipe, which only made the water spray in different directions. She tried to reach for the valve, but lost her balance and fell forward. Two strong hands clasped around her waist and pulled her back. Evan easily shut the supply off, letting the water dissipate to a small trickle. "Way to go, Ms. Fix It," he chuckled.

Grace wiped her eyes clear of water and nodded with a feigned confidence in her assessment. "Looks like a tear in the pipe."

"Clearly." Evan's body reached full height, and his hand extended to assist her, but she avoided touching him. She pulled herself to standing position as he offered her a dishtowel. Embarrassment washed over her as she patted her skin dry. A smile played across his lips in amusement. "It was a nice attempt. At least I got you all wet."

She huffed and crossed her arms over her chest in defense. His gaze followed the movement, lingered on her breasts, until his eyes met Grace's with impact. She cleared her throat as she tried to push away any thoughts of attraction. "You know, Zach told me this was an emergency, but with the valve turned off it's not that bad."

"Zach over-exaggerates."

"He said he needed it fixed immediately." Annoyance began to creep in and overshadowed the excitement of standing in front of Mr. Hollywood.

"He's always been dramatic." His toothy grin remained as his eyes roamed toward her lips. Discomfort was beginning to set in, along with frustrated lust.

She planted her hands on her hips, her mouth

scowling. "I was in the middle of a signing. I had to leave for this."

"Signing?" The curiosity in his voice perked up. "Signing for what?"

"My book." Grace pulled the top of the toolbox off and began to dig inside the lower compartment. "I had to leave early, and for no reason."

"You're an author?"

She found the roll of magic tape and began to unwind it. "Never mind that. I'm kind of pissed off now."

"How long have you been managing properties?"

Grace's eyes narrowed as she looked at Evan in confusion. He blatantly disregarded her bubbling anger. Writing was her life. It was her livelihood. It was the most important thing in the world to her. Sure, she didn't know him, but it was just the type of behavior to expect from a movie star. He only cared about himself. "A while, but did you not just hear what I said? I'm upset. My signing was important to me."

"And how long have you been writing?"

"A long time." She bent under the sink again and wrapped the magic tape around the pipe repeatedly to properly cover the affected area.

"So, I could go to Book People right now and buy your books if I wanted?" he inquired, curiosity evident in his tone.

"If you're into historical romance, then yes."

The task at hand was complete. She took the time to wipe the water under the sink, then straightened to find Evan standing way too close. He grabbed the towel from her hand as he towered over her. The brushing of his fingers over hers made her legs wobble. An electric current ran throughout her body.

"Thanks for wrapping my pipe."

They were both quiet for a moment, staring at each other longer than necessary. The tension between them was growing, and Grace had to quickly shut off that part of her brain. He was dangerous, a serial womanizer, a playboy. "If you'll excuse me, I should go. I have a deadline to meet."

"What are you working on now?" he asked casually as she shut and locked her toolbox more violently than necessary.

"Do you always ask this many questions?" Her tenor was semi-teasing. A ringtone blared, and she excused herself as she dug into her pocket and glanced at the screen. "I need to answer this."

He nodded as Grace spoke with force and determination to the plumber on the other end of the line. Hearing that he wasn't available until late afternoon the next day did nothing to placate her. "Unacceptable. I need you here earlier. If you can't make it, I'll go with another company." The man made another excuse and Grace growled, her voice firm. "It's a crack in the pipe, and I don't just happen to have plumber's putty hanging around my house."

Grace knew the tape would hold over for a few days, but this plumber only got the job done when she held steady and gave him a scare. Most of the time men thought her helpless, and then revealed surprise when she took care of things herself. "Alright then, I'm calling

Al's Plumbing. Thank you." He sputtered what she wanted to hear. "Okay, on the dot." After ending the call, she slipped the phone back into her pocket and saw Evan look at her in a daze with his head tilted in interest. "Plumber will be here first thing tomorrow morning. Nine sharp."

"You're a bit of a badass, Grace."

"It's a gift," she joked, tugging the toolbox from the countertop, the weight pulling her shoulder down a notch.

"I like it." His voice sounded raspy and gritty.

Evan did well in keeping stride with her as she walked toward the entrance, disregarding his compliment. Something caught her eye near the door.

"That baseboard has a gap."

Evan shrugged. "Is that bad?"

"Well, it can negatively affect the energy efficiency." Leaning over, she saw it had a small fracture in the corner. "It needs to be sealed. I'll figure something out with it," she quietly muttered and made a mental note. Her to-do list was growing longer than she had expected.

"Not only do you fix my leak, but you're gonna caulk my crack too?"

Looking back to him, she saw his eyes crinkling as he chewed on his lip. No longer able to hold back, they both burst out laughing. "Are you always this ridiculous, Mr. Matthews?"

"Maybe." He continued to give her a studied look. His stance was confident and calm. It was sexy as hell and making her nervous. "So, what do you do when you're not writing or property managing, Grace?"

"Fighting crime in my invisible jet, of course." *Don't get too personal,* she warned herself.

"And when you're not busy saving the world?"

She shifted the burdensome toolbox, gripping it with both hands and holding it in front of her. "Regular stuff, I guess. Go out with friends. Go to the bookstore. There's a lot to do in this city, if that's what you're trying to get at. The film festival is next week. You're not attending?"

He shook his golden brown head. "No, I'll be filming most days."

"What are you filming?"

"The last *Ending* movie."

"Oh." That was a big deal. She'd heard some rumor awhile back that he was retiring from acting. If that was so, it would be his last film. The urge to ask him more about it was instantly buried. "Well, the nightlife is diverse. There's 6th Street, lots of cool bars and restaurants."

His eyes kept to hers and she knew she had to get out of there. Fast. The water had doused her, but it didn't alleviate the heat that was stirring between the two of them. Her libido was usually kept under control, but he was making her question whether she could resist his charms.

Grace cleared her throat. "I need to go. Like I said, I have a deadline looming."

Evan held the door open for her, following her outside as she passed. "I'll walk you back," he insisted. Then without warning, he hauled the toolbox from her.

There was that damn spark again as their hands brushed. It shot through her and made her tingle. She'd have to avoid that. "What's your favorite restaurant, Grace?"

"I can't choose one."

"Well, how about we hit up one of your favorites this week?" he proposed, hope dancing in his eyes. "You and I. We could go out for drinks or lunch."

Grace stopped and looked at him with an uncertain glare. She was rarely caught off guard, but he baffled her into silence. Was he actually asking her out? He continued, "I hear they have great shops down Congress. And I heard Lady Bird Lake is really gorgeous at sunset."

It was way too often that guys like him tried to work that undeniable charisma on her, and she was used to always resisting. But with a man like Evan Matthews? Grace might let herself cave into this beautiful man. No, she would not give in to that temptation. *Kyle Erikson,* she reminded herself. That guy wormed his way into her heart years ago, then misled her. *Never again.*

"Thanks, but I'm not available," she burst out and spun around, walking away from him hastily.

"Ever?"

"No."

"You've got a boyfriend?"

"Nope."

"You're single?"

"Yes."

"But you're not available?"

Grace shook her head and turned back to him when

she reached her door. He studied her as if she was a mystery to be solved. She took the toolbox back, careful to not let her skin touch his. "Excuse me. I have a deadline."

A smile broke out over his lips. "So you said. I'm sorry about your book signing, Grace."

He was apologizing for Zach. The sincerity reached his eyes, and she let herself relax for a moment. "It's okay. It wasn't your fault. It was nice meeting you, Evan. Let me know if there are any issues with the plumber."

His eyes remained on hers as he smirked. "Change your shirt, Grace." He winked before heading off.

As Grace looked down, she saw the drenched cotton plastered to her thin laced bra, her nipples fully visible. A mortified gasp released from her throat. She heard his chuckle as he strolled back to his place. She rolled her eyes and slammed the door, and wondered exactly how she was going to resist the glorious appeal of the movie star guy next door.

Chapter Two

Evan Jonathan Matthews ambled his way over to his living room and sat on the couch, eyeing the mountain of scripts that beckoned him. He picked one out and tried to concentrate on the story, but found himself reading the same page over and over. His attention was pulled elsewhere. The remnants of his neighbor's scent lingered in the air. Was it strawberry? Whatever the fuck it was, it washed over his brain like a tidal wave and was drowning him.

God, he adored women. Evan knew he had an effect on the opposite sex. He grew up around females, understanding what made them tick. Being raised alongside two sisters by a loving mother had definitely made him appreciate the beauty of women. Sure, he hadn't matured into his body and voice until senior year of high school, but he grew up well-liked thanks to his older sister's popularity. Leaving Boston gave him free reign to meet and date all types of girls. Elsewhere, he was someone other than just Katie's younger brother. And since then, he had his fair share of some of the most beautiful women in the world.

He tried his best not to break hearts and attempted to remain a gentleman. His intentions were always clear with his short-lived flings. One would never call him close-minded to the girls he had dated in the past, but none had jolted him in such a strong way like Grace Clark just had. Well, there was his ex. But he was so young, it seemed…different. And that mess was so long ago that it was almost a faded memory.

There was something extremely appealing about the attractive property manager that just left. Thinking about her made his nerves tingle, among other things. Brown hair knotted on the top of her head, bright chocolate eyes full of reticence and mystery, and a body with soft curves in all the right places, he was intrigued.

He wondered if she had a lover. Many admirers perhaps. She was insanely beautiful. But more than that, she was the type of woman who knew exactly who she was, what she wanted, and how she wanted it. She exuded confidence, and that was attractive as hell. Well, those perky nipples that showed through that lacy purple bra were pretty damn sexy too. Thank God for white shirts and broken water pipes.

Thing was, he had put his flirt on and she'd shut it down, immediately. The usual attempt at banter seemed to do well at first, but then as if a light switch turned on, she changed her tune. He had a feeling she held some type of secret locked up in the recesses of her heart.

What the fuck are you even talking about, Evan? Romantic bullshit crept up in his thoughts, and that never happened. Thank fuck for the interruption when the door that led to the garage opened. Zach, Josh, and Hank made a ruckus as they strolled toward the kitchen.

"Hey, Evan, did the pipe get fixed?" Zach asked as he lugged bags of groceries.

"No, it needs to be replaced." Evan moved over to help put the items away. "You told Grace it was an emergency."

"It was. Sort of." Zach was his childhood pal. Evan was never in need of constant around-the-clock care, but it was nice being able to have things organized when he didn't have time to do everything himself. Zach gave him a hand, and had great managerial skills, which included helping Evan pick his projects. He liked having him around, even if he could be a dick. "Did she snake your drain?"

Evan rolled his eyes as he emptied the contents of the recyclable bags. "Uh, how about *not yet*? She was a bit pissed off. You interrupted her book signing."

"Shit, I forgot she had that going on today."

How the hell did Zach know about it? His thoughts were interrupted by a pulling on his jeans. "Hey, Hank," Evan bustled as he bent low to wrestle with the energetic rescue boxer that vied for his attention. "How's Josh treating you, buddy?"

Josh McKenzie was Evan's personal trainer, and had become a close friend and confidant since the filming of *The Ending Series* had begun eight years prior. He pretty much traveled with him wherever Evan went when on filming locations.

"He met a lady companion a few houses down. A small dachshund," Josh specified in his Southern London accent. Hank began to wag his tail and run around the living room in excitement. Josh had found the beat up stray in an alley a few years ago. He took the time to nurse him to health, and they all had an affinity for the loveable dog.

"Oh, getting his flirting game on?"

"She wasn't having it."

Evan laughed, thinking of the woman next door. "I feel your pain, Hank."

"Speaking of lady companion, what'd you think of Grace?" Zach asked, immediately making Evan wonder if Zach was crushing on her.

If that was the case, Evan knew it would be an instant hands-off situation for him, which would be really unfortunate. Sure, Evan was considered to be the good-looking one, the charmer, but Zach was funny and had that whole sensitive, hot-geek-vibe that chicks dug. Zach grabbed a couple of Sam Adams bottlenecks and passed them to Evan and Josh.

"We're training, mate," Josh declined, giving him a scolding look as he watched Evan grab the beer and twist off the cap easily. "Evan, don't-"

"Just one, bud." Evan took a swig and gave a satisfied sigh.

"Calm down, Pops. It's light beer." Zach tried to validate the choice, but then shut his mouth. Evan grinned, knowing Zach was intimidated not only by the amount of tattoos in view on Josh's upper arms, but because of his size as well. Despite Zach being taller than them all, he was sinewy and lean, where Josh was hard and strong. Impressive with eyes like ice. "Just one beer, Evan," Zach muttered softly.

"So, who's this Grace?" Josh inquired, grabbing a can of mixed nuts and popping them open. He set out a serving for both him and Evan. "Here, eat that."

"You my nutritionist now too?" Evan teased, reaching forward and popping an almond in his mouth, thankful for the reminder to eat. He needed the bulk. His body was an accomplishment. It was months of extensive physical training, and was one of the hardest parts of his job. The results, however, were inspiring thanks to Josh and a slew of others who helped him train.

"You ignoring the question?" Josh asked.

A whimper released from Hank's mouth as he jumped onto the couch and circled several times before rolling into a comfortable ball. Evan watched, wishing things could be that simple for him. "She's the property manager. The plumber will be here tomorrow. Nine in the morning. She wrapped some type of tape over the pipe so it should hold over tonight."

"She's a sexy little thing." Zach began to search the fridge, taking out thawed chicken and a Tupperware full of broccoli. "I tried to flirt, but much like that dachshund, she just wasn't having it." *Good*. Zach was one to give up quickly, not wasting his time on a woman who didn't instantly throw herself on him. Grace was not Zach's type at all.

"She's unavailable," Evan promptly revealed.

"Is that so?" Josh smiled slyly as Evan avoided both guys and turned his back to them. *Shit.* He just gave himself away.

"Someone shot down the great Evan Matthews?" Zach laughed as he finished packing the cupboard with food.

"I'm convinced the world will now end," Josh

followed.

"Shut your pie-holes." Evan sat beside Hank on the couch and stroked his dark brown fur. He ignored their continued jabs as he put his beer down and picked up another screenplay in the piles he needed to go through. His last project he had directed and produced hadn't been widely received by critics, and he was searching for the perfect job to tackle next.

"Did you read that action one I told you about?" Zach began to prep the dinner for that night.

"I did, but you know I don't want to take on something that big. It'll only be my second film."

Lately Evan had been feeling the need to learn new things, take on a new challenge. He wanted more than just being in front of the camera. Stepping behind it had always been an interest, and it wasn't until just recently that he began to do it. But the right script, the right project, was everything. He didn't want to mess up by taking on more than he could handle.

"That other flick did well enough," Josh stated grasping the remote and turning on the television as he plopped on the lounge chair. "Do another one like that."

"No, I want something different, Josh. I need something I can really sink my teeth into. Right, Hank?" Evan heaved a sigh, closing the script. He handed it to Hank who clasped it with his teeth and began chewing on it with vigor. The sound of ripping paper filled the air. "Yeah, see? Hank doesn't like this one either."

"Always trust the dog, mate," Josh declared.

Evan grabbed his beer and took a long swig of it, wondering when he'd see Grace again. How would he break through her reserve enough for her to agree to a date with him? He'd have to use his resources and figure out a way to win her over.

Chapter Three

Grace had clasped the phone in her hand, grappling for only a short moment of whether to press the send button in a group text. When she did, she knew the response from her friends would be instantaneous.

Grace: So, I may or may not be living next to an A-list actor.
Jaime: Who????
Marla: Yeah, then you woke up.
Grace: Captain Drew Abrams!
Jaime: Nah-uh!!!!!!!
Marla: You lie.
Grace: I'm serious. He's my neighbor.
Jaime: We need to go over…now. Grace, bring out the binoculars!
Marla: Agreed. Seeing is believing, after all.
Grace: We are NOT spying on my tenant.
Marla: Then what's the point of you texting us?!
Jaime: It's so happening.

Jaime Caldwell entered the room haphazardly, throwing her purse on the antique hall tree Grace had refurbished with a dark cherry finish. "Nice to see you too," Grace spoke as she picked up Jaime's giant mom bag and hung it up on one the gold hooks.

Jaime plopped down on the couch in the living room and moaned as she stretched her feet out in front of her. "I needed to get away," she sighed as her dark strands of straight hair splayed out on the sofa cushion. "Please just tell me all about hunky Evan Matthews and help me escape the two boys at home who just dragged mud onto my expensive Persian rug."

"Ouch. Jake's grounded, I take it?"

"So is Dean. From any physical activity with me. He knows better."

Jaime and Dean met a year after she had finished college. They grew up in the same neighborhood, and even had mutual friends, despite Dean being a few years older than Jaime, but it wasn't until one night when the girls had decided to go to Stubb's BBQ for a show that he introduced himself to her. They'd been inseparable ever since. Perhaps some things were just meant to be.

For instance, Grace knew these women were somehow destined to be in her life. She couldn't explain how, but it felt like her brother had led them to all be connected. Marla was her roommate freshman year of college and Jaime lived across the hall in the dorms. They were her family and they helped her move past the crippling devastation she felt when Nathan had died two years before.

The doorbell chimed and before Grace could answer, Marla Sullivan sauntered in grasping her recyclable tote bag. "I skipped yoga and got some snacks. We're ready to see a movie star tonight."

"I don't consider tofu cream cheese and kale chips an

actual snack," Jaime teased. "And I might be too tired to stalk hottie next door."

"I brought a veggie tray. I'm trying to be good."

Grace peeked in the bag and clasped the most important items—two bottles of wine and held them up with a huge smile. "Good, huh?"

"They say drinking a glass of red wine is like going to the gym," Marla disputed.

"I'm sure they didn't say that about this." Grace took out a chocolate bar and let it swing from her fingers.

"I said *trying* to be good. Besides chocolate has antioxidants," Marla reiterated. "How was the book signing, Grace?"

Grace shrugged. "It went okay. It was mostly curious people passing by, asking where the restrooms were located."

"Lies. She had a group of loyal readers there. I saw them myself." Jaime stood from the couch and joined the girls in the dining area. "I only stayed a little while though because Jake had swim lessons."

"I would've been there, but I had a meeting that I couldn't get out of. I'm sorry, Grace." Marla was a marketing coordinator at a small creative agency located downtown. She was extremely A-type personality at her job, but when away, she was the most relaxed and chilled out of the three women. Sometimes.

"It's okay. I got called away from my own signing with the broken pipe debacle. Evan's assistant told me it was an emergency. Which he lied about."

"First name basis with the movie star already, huh?" Marla began to meticulously set out the veggie tray on the table, which sat conveniently beside the window. "Where are the binoculars?"

"We aren't stalking my neighbor." Grace fumbled through the kitchen drawer, finally locating the wine opener.

Jaime's gaze fixed on Grace. "Okay, Miss Elusive. Tell us exactly what happened. From the beginning. Leave no word out, nothing unsaid."

"It's the house on the right? The lights are on and I see movement." Grace moved to where Marla stood and slapped her hand away from the blinds. "Ouch! Hey, that hurt!"

"Guys, please let's not make a big fuss. He's a dude who's just like every other prick out there trying to get his hands on any woman he can."

Marla smiled, her voice lilting. "Oh, so, he tried to hit on you?"

Jaime ambled to the table and frowned at the colorful arrangement of healthy food in front of her. "Of course he did. There's something wrong with him if he didn't." Looking over her shoulder at Grace, she grinned. "Got any real food, Grace? Like chips or cookies?"

"I made cookies yesterday. They're in the pantry."

"Oh, let's order Home Slice!" Jaime exclaimed. The popular pizza spot was located in the heart of downtown Austin.

"We'd have to pick it up," Grace reminded her.

"I wish I had thought about that. I could've brought my organic flour. We could've made the pizza ourselves. That would've been so much fun!" Marla's bright brown eyes smiled in excitement. There was nothing Marla loved more than to bake and cook from scratch.

Jaime scoffed. "Um, yeah that's a negative. I get away from the boys so I don't have to cook. I'm ordering Home Slice. There's a company that can deliver. And then you can tell us all about your new boyfriend, Grace."

"Boyfriend? Never." Grace knew a man like her new next-door neighbor was not for her, and she definitely wasn't for him.

Marla laughed as she ate a carrot and moved toward the hall tree. "Please. Like you'd deny someone like Evan Matthews? Get real, Grace. I know you're strong, but you're not that strong." Maybe it was a good thing Grace didn't tell them about turning him down earlier that day. Marla opened a drawer and reached inside. "Are we doing poker, bananagrams, or catchphrase?"

"Poker. And Jaime, you order the pizza. No pineapple!" Grace grimaced inwardly at the thought of fruit on pizza.

"I'll pay for the pineapple pizza. I never get what I want with Jake and Dean."

Marla set out the poker chips and cards on the table. "Because nobody likes pineapple on their pizza but you."

"Lots of people do. That's why it's an option." Jaime protested, looking up the delivery app on her phone. "I'm ordering two pizzas. I don't care what you say."

Marla rolled her eyes. "Like we could stop you. Just hurry up and order. I wanna hear about Captain

Abrams already."

Grace wasn't looking forward to reliving her encounter with Evan Matthews. Soon after having left his place, she took a long look at herself in the mirror and drowned in embarrassment. Mascara dripped down her cheeks in long gray lines from the water that had hit her head-on. Wisps of hair had fallen from her loosened bun and had curled in a frizzy state over her face. And her choice of shirt that day hadn't been wise at all. In most cases, Grace never cared what people thought about her casual look. She loved her laidback style. But when her nipples showed through the material of her white shirt and Evan Matthews was on the receiving end of it? Well, it was no wonder he wanted to ask her out. Grace wasn't an easy target, and Mr. Hollywood would not be capturing her interest when millions of other women fell to his feet.

"I see someone!" Marla gasped as she held a wooden blind up and peered between it. She then huffed, "Ugh, it's not him. Some beef-head is standing outside."

"I wanna see!" Jaime cried and moved toward the window just having finished ordering the pizza. "Is he hot?"

"Eh. He's alright," Marla responded. "God, he has like fifty million tattoos."

Jaime held her side of the blind up. "What is wrong with you, Marla? He's sexy! And it's not like he has tattoo sleeves. He has just the right amount."

"Get away from the window, please. You're embarrassing me."

The girls hummed their compliance as they stared at

the man outside. Grace couldn't help but take a peek. He was sexy, whoever he was. With his arms crossed over his chest, and his tall stature, this man was a monster. A gorgeous one. However, something about him didn't stir her insides the way Evan did. She hoped whatever that feeling was, that tangible spark, left her brain as quickly as it had entered.

All three girls gasped when icy blue eyes caught them peeking out and watching him. They immediately turned back. "Shit. You guys, now he's going to tell Evan he has a bunch of stalkers next door. Thank you!"

"Crap! Sorry, Grace." Jaime laughed with little remorse.

"Like he'd notice. He looks a little slow on the uptake. All the steroids probably," Marla stated matter-of-fact.

Grace chuckled at her friend's preconceived notion. "Geez. A little harsh there for someone who's so Zen, Marla."

"I don't like those beefy-type guys. All they do is spend time at the gym and take selfies in the mirror."

"I'd selfie with him so hard. He needs to be selfied with. Did you see those lips? If I wasn't happily married…"

Grace chuckled and sat down, grabbing the deck of cards and shuffling them expertly. One of the many things she learned from her brother—how to play a mean game of poker and of course, how to ward off womanizers like Evan Matthews.

Within minutes, Grace was already winning the first round of their game. It might've been the fact that Jaime and Marla were too busy trying to glance next door to see if anyone was exiting or entering the house.

"Pay attention!" Grace demanded and reached over to close the blinds. "We're playing a game here, not checking for the idiot next door."

"Fine. But I still want to meet him. You have to have some type of get-together and invite him over," Jaime suggested.

"No."

"What did he smell like? Was he as pretty as he is on screen?"

Grace tried to hold back a grin but she couldn't help it. She gave a slight rise of her shoulders. "He smelled… good."

"Good? That's it?" Marla asked. "Bullshit, you're so trying to be coy, Grace Lynn Clark. Tell us now!"

The doorbell rang and Grace hopped up to answer. "Pizza's here."

"You're not getting off that easily, dearie. You're giving us details!" Jaime called as Grace turned back.

"Why don't you just go over and you can sniff him yourselves?" She swung the door open and instead of the delivery guy, there stood the dreamboat neighbor she just couldn't seem to get out of her head, along with giant icy-blue eyes.

Grace's own eyes bulged and her stomach churned as if a storm was beginning to brew. She heard yelling from inside her house. "Give the delivery guy a good tip!"

She blinked several times to make sure she wasn't hallucinating. Evan stood in front of her with two boxes of pizza. "Someone order pizza?"

"What-"

Before she could continue, Evan sauntered in. "Delivery guy got the wrong address, apparently. This is Josh."

Grace said hi and shook Josh's hand. She then looked over to Jaime, who kept her eyes on her cards. Her poker face was total shit. "Jaime…"

"Whoops," Jaime looked up with a smile. "I always get the numbers of your house mixed up. I'm so glad the neighbor was nice enough to bring the order over." She stood and stretched her hand out, her eyes wide as she took in both men. "I'm Jaime. Hi. Sorry about that, I didn't know the house number, and I took a wild guess, and um, well, I didn't expect you to come over. I mean, I sort of expected this Mr. Muscles guy to come over…" Grace tried to hide her laugh as Jaime continued to ramble. "Not that I did it on purpose, but I mean… never mind. I'm shutting up."

The smile from Evan's face was radiating, his eyes crinkling at the corners in amusement. "Evan. Nice to meet you, Jaime." He let his gaze move to Marla as they introduced themselves. Grace grasped the boxes balancing in Evan's hand and set them on the table.

"I'm so sorry about this, Mr. Matthews." Grace shook her head. Jaime had gone too far, and Grace didn't want her neighbor to feel like he was being stalked. Strangely, he didn't seem to mind.

His hands rested in the pockets of his jeans and his face remained open and friendly. "Don't be." His smile turned into a sly and knowing grin. "Josh told me you girls were having a little party."

Josh's expression said everything and Grace's cheeks instantly flushed. "You saw my friends peeking out the window, didn't you?"

The guys laughed. "I promise we won't hold it against you," Josh stated with his voice soft as silk. It was completely contradictory to his tough exterior. The smooth, British sound of it was lilting.

Evan continued, "Although, that looming deadline excuse? That one I might hold against you." He winked at Grace and she felt her insides flutter. God, what the hell was he doing to her, and why was the effect so instantaneous?

She stood staring at him, trying to figure out why he didn't just send Zach over with the pizza. But she knew the answer. It was because he was appeasing her friends. He knew they wanted to meet him. Grace defended herself. "We're just hanging out for a little while. It's not a party."

"We're playing poker. You gentlemen can join us!" Jaime exclaimed with no qualms, and Evan laughed.

"I love playing games," Evan smirked at Grace then took his seat.

"I'm sure you do," Grace muttered under her breath. How the hell had Evan Matthews ended up in her dining area? And how was she going to resist him when he was attempting to stick around?

Evan couldn't help but be curious when Josh had told

him that several sets of snooping eyes kept peeking out of his neighbor's window. Zach urged him to go see what Grace was up to when he couldn't convince the guys to go out bar hopping with him on 6th Street. The pizza getting sent to his house was a deliberate move on her part and the perfect excuse for him. In most cases, he'd be bothered, but he had to confess that he was looking forward to seeing Grace again, even if it was twice in the same day.

And now that he saw her, he knew it was a good decision. His heart sped up the moment she'd opened the door. Grace looked adorable in her hip-hugging jeans and loose shirt. It had an outline of Texas on it stating, "Y'all" in white letters. A pair of pristine white Converse adorned her feet and her hair was once again knotted on the top of her head.

Her surprise of his arrival instantly alerted him that the pizza mistake hadn't been her strategy, and he soon figured out Jaime was the one to blame. At least he knew Grace had talked about him. And that was key. Yeah, he definitely wanted to know this girl better.

He promptly felt warmth radiate from her home when he walked in. Something about the decor and the atmosphere made him feel embraced and peaceful. As though he took a step into a different era. It felt personal, creative, and fearless. Swing band music played from an antique record player that rested on full bookshelves, and he could see himself spending quite a bit of time there.

Grace's friends stood as he made his way toward the table where a deck of playing cards, poker chips, glasses of wine, and snacks were set out. Evan could sense each of the women were down-to-earth and fun. Josh sensed it too. If he wasn't comfortable he would have left immediately. That was Josh. He didn't take shit from anyone.

"I want in on that poker action." Evan scooted a chair out and sat down easily. "Josh, you in?"

"Yeah, why not?"

"Where's Zach?" Grace asked as she moved to the kitchen.

Why the hell did she care where Zach was? Was she into him? He moved that idea aside. "He went out with some of the crew to 6th Street."

It was only a moment before Marla began to chat with him. "Have you been to 6th Street before, Mr. Matthews?"

"Not really my scene." Evan shrugged as Josh agreed. "And call me Evan, please." He picked up a carrot and dipped it in the hummus. "I just got here last week, so I haven't had much of a chance to explore."

"I'm sure work keeps you busy," Jaime chimed in, fiddling with her poker chips. She was obviously nervous, but it began to subside the more he talked to her.

"I have some long days scheduled, especially at the beginning, but it won't be as bad toward the end."

"Don't tell me you die in the last one!" Jaime exclaimed with worry.

"Grace said you're filming the *Ending* movie here." Marla served more vegetables on her plate and chewed on a celery stick.

He ignored Jaime's question, not wanting to give spoilers. "The last one. Ben and Kara are flying in this weekend to start filming. Right now, I'm rehearsing some action scenes with the stuntmen."

Evan heard Jaime give a small whimper. He sensed she was trying to keep herself calm. "Ben, as in Benjamin Taylor? Will he be living nearby too?"

Evan laughed and wondered if Jaime would pull the pizza delivery trick with Ben as well. "Yeah, he's renting out across the street."

"So, he'll be my tenant too?" Grace seemed more excited about that than about him, and the thought of her liking Ben irritated him. *Getting jealous already?* He had just met her.

"I'm guessing so. These gated townhomes were recommended to us by the studio. I was surprised there were any available since they're so close to downtown." Evan grasped the deck of cards in his hand and squinted his eyes in concentration as he shuffled them. It was difficult keeping focus. He was more concerned about how he was going to get Grace to go out with him.

"They're leased month-to-month. My friend Stephen owns a handful of them, but doesn't allow college kids to rent anymore, even though the universities are nearby." The girls all grabbed a slice of pizza and Grace held the box open. "Evan? Josh? Would you like pepperoni?"

"Or pineapple?" Jaime asked.

"Nobody likes pineapple," Marla and Grace spoke simultaneously.

"No, I like it. I'll take a pineapple," Evan piped up.

"See? I knew I liked you, Evan Matthews." Jaime smiled at him as he grabbed a slice.

"Evan, don't." Josh's voice became harsh. "You already had a beer."

"Come on, man," he whispered under his breath, cursing the diet. He hated the damn diet. "One slice." He dug into the piece and reveled in the delicious taste.

"I will not go easy on you tomorrow. Neither will Joe." Evan knew his stunt trainer would learn about this and wouldn't be happy.

"Lighten up, he looks amazing." First impressions were never what they seemed. Evan had taken Marla to be quiet and shy, but the redhead had a feisty nature that was beginning to emerge as she defended him against Josh. "Besides it's only one slice of pizza…with fruit on it."

Josh rolled his eyes at her and crossed his arms. "Fine, one slice, Evan. Tomorrow, you'll be sorry."

"Til I puke," Evan stated, knowing the drill.

"Ugh," Marla groaned in annoyance with the man who sat across from her. Evan tried not to smile, but he saw the flash in Josh's eyes as they zoomed in on the spirited woman. Oh, Josh was interested in this girl.

Everyone sat cozy and chatted as Grace took out napkins, wine, and cookies. She took her seat beside Evan and he caught a trace of her scent. Whatever she wore, it had that strawberry aroma that was starting to drive him nuts. He gave her a little nudge with his arm to grab her attention. Her smile seemed to be tentative as he spoke. "So, what's your new book about?"

"I'm actually in the process of writing two books. One's for my publisher. The other one, I don't think they'll want it."

"Grace is writing a memoir," Jaime blurted.

"A memoir?" He focused in on her with curiosity. "That's intriguing." His voice was huskier than he intended, but he really was curious to know more about this guarded woman. "Would you be willing to let me read it?"

Grace looked at him skeptically, a huff escaping her pretty pink lips. "Um…well, it's not finished yet."

"So?"

Grace diverted the subject. "Let's play some poker."

"She hasn't let anyone read it," Jaime whispered to Evan.

He grabbed a cookie from the tin and took a bite. Without meaning for it to happen, a groan escaped his mouth. "Damn, these cookies are amazing."

"Evan…" Josh grumbled trying to get him to stop eating.

"Grace made them." Marla gave a sly grin. "You should try one, Josh. They're actually protein cookies."

Josh's gaze was taut. "No, thank you."

"Seriously? Wow." Marla hitched a discerning brow at him. "It's one cookie."

Josh reached over and tried one. He nodded as he chewed, his whole body seeming to relax as he gave in to the pleasure of sugar. "These aren't healthy cookies."

Marla's honeyed voice rang out. "No, they aren't. But they're delicious, right?"

Evan was certain Josh would give Marla an ugly

look or leave on the spot. Instead, his taciturn nature shifted and a small smile played on his lips. "They are."

Evan would have to tease him about that later. He grabbed a second cookie and let the perfect flavor sit on his tongue. "So, you made these, Grace?" He looked up into her chocolate eyes and she nodded slightly. "I might have to marry you."

She laughed heartily at the insinuation until she realized how determined he seemed. She shifted uncomfortably as he stared at her with admiration. "These rival my mom's recipe, believe it or not."

"Thanks. I'm sure Nestle Tollhouse would appreciate the sentiment," Grace joked as she grabbed the deck from Evan and began to deal.

They soon got lost in the game of poker. Evan stared at his cards and glanced at Grace. "Fold." He stated and threw his hand down.

Josh set his cards. "Call it. Two pairs."

Grace nodded and smiled, placing her cards out. "A straight. Read 'em and weep."

"Never fails. How the hell do you always win?" Marla sighed as Grace took all the chips.

"It's called practice, dear friends," Grace retorted with a victorious grin spread wide across her face.

Evan's gaze was focused on hers. Shit, she was his dream woman come to life. How the hell did she even exist? He then straightened as she piled up her chips in neat stacks.

"Let's play another round," Evan suggested. "And this time, if I win, you have to let me read your memoir —as is."

Grace chuckled as he heard Jaime gasp under her breath. "And if I win?"

"I have to go out with you." He tried to hide his smirk.

Her laugh grew louder, but her friends stared in awe. He knew he was making a fool of himself, but he had to find a way to get this girl to go out with him. "That's not really a win for me."

"Damn, that's harsh," Marla teased.

"Okay, fine. I'll cook you a meal." He wanted to somehow find a way to spend time with her, and he knew she wasn't an easy win. He was bringing out just a taste of how big he could go.

Grace scoffed, "I'm still not sure that would be a win for me."

"Hey, I'm a great cook," Evan contended. "I'll even wash the dishes after."

"No, if I win, you have to help me refurnish a desk I have waiting for me in the garage." Grace smiled. "It's heavy and difficult to move."

"Deal," Evan agreed. That couldn't be too hard, right?

"And what if I win?" Jaime claimed boldly.

Marla laughed. "Really? We both know neither one of us has a chance in hell against Grace."

"Shut up. I could totally win," Jaime asserted.

"Okay," Evan began, "if you win, what?"

"If I win, you have to come to my son's sixth birthday party. In costume."

"Deal." He put out his hand and shook Jaime's. "I didn't know you had a kid, Jaime."

"Yeah, my husband wanted one. I guess I did too." She winked playfully at him, and Evan began to really like these women.

"What if I win?"

"Seriously, Marla?" Jaime countered. "You just said we couldn't win."

"Well, we might as well all state what we want."

"Then tell us what you want," Grace said as she shuffled the cards.

"I want dinner at Uchi."

"Whoa, nice one, but expensive," Grace chuckled. The sushi place was one of the best in the city, and quite costly. But worth every dime.

"Fine, I'll change it. Loser has to go to a yoga class with me." Marla then pointed to Josh, "But you'd have to eat a slice of pepperoni pizza."

"Never," Josh laughed, shaking his head. "If I win, loser has to take a training session with me."

"Ew." Jaime grimaced and then smiled. "I mean, uh, cool. Yay, to exercise."

"Let's get this done." Grace began to deal the cards, and they launched the game. Evan had to hand it to Grace, she knew what she was doing. He could've sworn she was bluffing, but he didn't know her habits well enough. He looked at his hand and scowled. Marla and Jaime had already folded. Evan waited for Josh to look at him, then kicked his foot.

Josh growled then shrugged. "I fold."

Evan's eyebrow raised and he cleared his throat. "Okay, I'm raising. If I win, you have to not only let me read your memoir, but you have to go on two dates with me."

Grace craftily grinned. "I see your two dates, and add a homemade dinner – dishes washed after."

"I'll see your bet, and raise you a trip to Boston." His face was serious, but his eyes were alight with mischief.

Jaime and Marla stayed completely still watching the two of them in shock as Josh sighed in boredom. Grace sniggered. "I can't afford that."

"We didn't talk about a pot-limit, darlin'. You gonna fold?"

Grace shook her head. "I'll find a way." She placed her hand down and smiled. "I call. Four of a kind."

Evan chortled under his breath and shook his head. "Shit. You're good." He held onto his cards and leaned back on his chair. "Looks like I owe you a refurnished desk, a couple of dates, a homemade dinner with dishes washed, and a trip to Boston."

"What did you have?" Jaime asked him as Grace yelled in triumph and gave Marla a high-five.

"I am the master," Grace sang as she got up from her chair and did a little dance that made Evan's heartbeat rise. "Gotta use the little girl's room. I'll be back in a bit."

Josh followed Marla to the kitchen as Evan set his cards back into the deck. He noticed Jaime's large hazel eyes staring at him. "Why didn't you set out your cards, Evan?"

"I was bluffing. Didn't have a good hand."

Jaime looked at him skeptically. "Then why didn't you let us see your cards?"

She was undeniably on to him. "Um, I was

embarrassed?"

"Is that so?" She crossed her arms and cocked her eyebrow at him. She wasn't going to let it go. "You were winning, weren't you?"

He lowered his head and chuckled. "You can't prove a thing."

"All I have to do is tell Grace, and she'll believe me over you."

Evan groaned. "Okay, Jaime, I'll go to your son's sixth birthday party if you don't tell Grace I had a straight flush."

Jaime gasped, "I knew it! Oh, if Grace finds out..."

"But she won't know, right? Think of your kid and that birthday party, Jaime. Poor…"

"Jake."

"Poor Jake won't get Captain Abrams at his party."

"Fine." Jaime smiled and shook his hand with strength. "You'd better not back out on me. His party is November 14th."

"I'll be there. You can have Grace remind me."

"Why Boston, by the way?" Grace strolled in. Wavy wisps of hair caressed her skin and Evan had a craving to push them out of her face then grab that hair tie and yank it off, let his hands tug through the thick, wavy locks. She sat beside him and he tried to keep his eyes off of her. It wasn't working. "I mean, can I pick another location? And is it all-inclusive? Because, I really think it should be. Although, I have no idea what I'd do in Boston."

The females around him were all fascinated by his answer. "Boston's my hometown. I was hoping to get a free flight from this little wager."

"Like you can't afford it?" Marla ridiculed as she sat down with a glass of wine and piece of chocolate. "Those *Ending* films made billions of dollars."

These women didn't miss a thing, did they? Evan shifted in his seat. "It's always nice to go home and visit the folks."

"But I don't have to go to Boston, right? I mean, why Boston? And I can take a guest, right? Marla, you up for a vacation?" Grace asked again as she grabbed a cold slice of pizza and yanked a piece of it with her teeth.

"Well, I didn't mention it, but you gotta take me with you." He smiled at her slyly as he saw tension climb into her body.

"You can't change the terms of the bet." Grace's voice sounded suspicious.

"Why not? You're trying to change the terms of the bet by asking to change the location and getting me to pay for the hotel and food," Evan countered.

"Forget it. Let's just pretend this game didn't happen." Grace dismissed him, dropped her leftover pizza on her napkin and began to put away the chips in their case.

"Hell, no. I owe you help with a refurbished desk, two dates, a homemade dinner plus clean up, and a trip to Boston."

"It's not like this game was serious. Why would I ever want to go to Boston anyway?"

"Are you joking? Why wouldn't you?" His voice climbed with incredulity. "Boston is amazing. It's gorgeous there, there's history, places to go antique hunting."

Grace quickly glared at him. "How do you know I like to go antique hunting?"

Evan sat back with his hands in the air. "Um, it's pretty obvious. Your house looks like an Anthropologie catalogue."

Tension crept into Grace's body as she straightened, her brow furrowing. "My stuff isn't from Anthropologie," Grace declared defensively as she grabbed the cards and placed them back in their box. "I bought most of my furniture from estate sales and restored them. Everything's authentic."

"I didn't mean it as a bad thing, Grace. I like your home."

"So, what's the whole point of this little argument?" Marla asked as everyone became silent.

Evan wanted Grace to stick with this bet. It was the only way he could get to know her better. "I'm just saying, I should go with her. She could see the best places by someone who knows that city inside and out."

Grace argued, apprehension sneaking through her, "That wasn't included in the terms of the bet though."

"We didn't discuss the terms and conditions, so anything goes," Evan demurred.

"Like changing the location and the person I go with?" Grace flitted her eyelashes at him and he growled.

Evan had never come across a woman so determined to avoid him. "No. I specifically stated Boston, and we were the ones wagering."

"Well, then maybe the whole bet should be called

off. Play another game?" Marla suggested.

Grace nodded, overly eager to change the outcome of her winnings. "Yes, and none of this traveling and dates stuff. We should've set a pot limit and kept to the poker chips."

"Nah, I gotta go." Evan stood and stretched, then looked at his Omega watch. "I have an early call time tomorrow."

"You have an even earlier workout session, mate. You have to burn the food you ate tonight." Josh strolled with Evan toward the door. "It was lovely to meet you ladies."

Evan reiterated Josh's statement. "Yes, really nice spending time with you. Thanks for the pizza." He lagged behind as Grace walked with him toward the door. He gently leaned over, and placed his lips near the shell of her ear. "I'll get in touch with you for our first date."

Evan detected her inflexibility, her body straightening and moving away from him. "In your dreams, Mr. Hollywood."

He walked out the door, with the hopes that he stimulated his unassuming neighbor. "A bet is a bet, Gracie Lynn." He glanced back and saw her confused expression, no doubt caused by the fact that he knew her middle name.

As soon as they entered the house, Josh quickly punched Evan on the shoulder. "Could you be more of a pussy?"

Evan punched him back. "What the fuck, man?"

"What are you thinking?" Josh asked as Hank ran up

to him and grabbed the leash near the entrance with his mouth. "Letting her win? Making those bets? You barely met this girl and you want to take her to Boston?"

Evan moved toward the living area and plopped onto the couch. Hank left Josh's side and jumped into Evan's lap, dropping the leash and making himself comfortable. Evan stroked the boxer's fur softly and shook his head. "I don't know. I like this girl."

It had been so long since he'd spent time with a woman where he actually enjoyed her company for more reasons than just getting her naked. Grace was smart, funny, cautious, and not one to fall for his charms. He wondered if it was the challenge that was captivating him more than anything else. He honestly didn't know what he was thinking when he bet that trip to Boston. But he could see Grace spending time exploring the city with him, and for some odd reason he wanted to make her genuinely happy.

"Evan, you've known her for a few hours."

"I know," Evan covered his face with his hands, "I know, but I just have this feeling about her. She's different, somehow. Am I going crazy?"

"Yes. Why don't you just drink your glass of Riesling now and listen to your fucking Adele CD as you weep dressed up in your leggings?"

"Shut the fuck up."

"Wanker," Josh laughed. "Look, she's nice. She just doesn't seem like…"

"A fuck-her-and-leave-her-type girl?"

"Exactly, Evan. Girls like her? You don't mess with.

You don't break a heart like hers."

Evan nodded. He had to be careful, and he needed to make sure his motives were in the right place. Was she a challenge, or was she the real deal? Either way, girls like her were not easy to find. "What if this chick is the end of me? God, she could so mess me up."

"You let her. Then attempt to drink her away."

"I shouldn't go there, man, but she's…" He thought about her and sighed. What the fuck was happening to him? "That face, that body."

"You've always had a thing for the girl-next-door type," Josh laughed as he whistled for Hank. The dog approached him and he bent to put his leash on.

"Girl-next-door? Did you see her body? It's all curvy and lush under those baggy clothes." Evan gave an astute grin. "Oh, I guess you were too busy noticing Red."

"Fuck off."

"Yeah, I saw you staring at her cute friend."

The fact that Josh ignored his comment made Evan wonder if Josh too felt differently about this Marla girl than others he'd met. "I'll come by, six a.m. sharp. Straight to the gym, Evan."

"I hate you," Evan grumbled as Josh left him in the house alone. Picking up another script from his table, he attempted to read, in hopes of finding that next great project. Instead, all he could think of was ways to get Grace to trust him. He would have to take it slow, get her to open up, and let her realize he'd be the best thing that ever happened to her.

Chapter Four

"Sweet tea?" Zach handed Grace a glass filled with the refreshing beverage as she sat on the floor of his living room. She'd gone to Lowe's to get the items needed to fix the wooden baseboard and then headed toward Evan's house. She was partly relieved he wasn't home, although that hadn't stopped her from thinking about him since the night he'd come over and made that ridiculous bet.

"Thanks." She rested the caulk gun on her leg and put the sponge back in the bucket that sat beside her. The hopes for a great glass of iced tea quickly went down the drain as she took a huge gulp. "Ugh," she grimaced, "sorry to tell you, Zach, but this tea sucks."

Zach laughed as he retrieved the glass from Grace. "Sorry about that. Too much sugar?"

"Way too much sugar."

"I'll get you some water."

"Yes, please." Grace picked up the caulk gun again along with the putty knife. She focused in on the wall as she spoke animatedly to Zach. "Glad they fixed that pipe up."

"Me too."

"How long have you been Evan's assistant?"

"Since he's needed me. So, almost ten years," Zach called out bringing Grace a bottled water. He set it down beside her, then rested on the arm of the lounge chair. He crossed his long arms as he watched her work. "His family took me in when we were kids, so I'm more like his brother than anything else."

"That's cool." Grace kept her eyes on the wall and held back sadness that always came with the mention of brothers and how she always ached for hers. "It's important to have people you trust around you."

"It is. We have a no bullshit tolerance."

Grace looked at him and saw his forest-green eyes keenly focused on her. She nodded in understanding. "I'm sure he's had his fair share of leeches."

"He's discerning, most of the time. Sometimes he can get a bit clouded in his judgment though. Especially with women." Grace turned toward him and rested her forearms on her knees, giving her back and neck a small break from the pressure of working on the wall. She studied Zach's demeanor and gathered that he was trying to be protective of his friend.

"What is it you're getting at, Zach?"

He shifted, running a hand through his tousled dark hair. His posture relaxed as he gave a small smile. "I'm just looking out for him, Grace."

"You gonna ask what my intentions are?" She smirked as she picked up her bottle of water and twisted the cap, taking a sip and letting the coolness soothe her throat. He looked impressed with her sass as she continued. "Don't worry, I really don't think I'm his type."

He slyly grinned, "Oh, you're exactly his type, Grace. That's the problem."

"I'm a problem?" Grace stared wide-eyed at Zach, worry breaking through her reserve. She gulped and finally looked down, closing her water and setting it aside. "I'm not interested in him, Zach."

She picked up her tools again and turned toward the wall. He snickered. "I'm not sure if you're lying to me or to yourself." Shit, this guy didn't hold back. And Grace knew she was trying to convince herself not to want Evan the way she did. "It doesn't matter, Grace."

Once again, she glanced over her shoulder at him. "Why?"

"Because I think you might be good for him."

"You're talking as though Evan and I are dating. We're not and we won't. I told you, I'm really not his type." A grin played across his lips, which cracked to a full smile. She wanted to reach over and smack him. "What?"

"Nothing, Grace. It's just that you're a lot more modest than I thought."

"And you're a bigger jackass than I thought."

He gave an energetic laugh. "Guess you don't take bullshit either."

"You'd guess right."

He moved toward the kitchen as the silence suffused her senses. It allowed her to think of all that was just discussed and what it meant. Had Evan told Zach about the bet? It wasn't like anything would be cashed in on, no matter how much Evan would try. But the feeling of his warm breath touching her ear when he whispered he owed her a date? She felt tingling from the top of her head to the tips of her toes.

She couldn't deny that part of her wanted to indulge in getting to know Evan. It had been so long since she liked someone and Grace forgot how good it felt. Good and horrible at the same time. Her mind reeled in reliving the way his serious eyes had taken her in when they'd played poker. The smoothness of his face along with the strong jaw entrenched her memory; she knew she couldn't be stupid about the lust that ran throughout her body.

Evan Matthews was not a good prospect for her. He was well-known for being a philanderer. Models, actresses, and singers walked in and out of his life. He was an accomplished flirt, and he knew how to get what he wanted. Then why had she let him get under her skin? Sighing, she stopped thoughts of what his lips would feel like on hers and studied the wall instead.

"I really do need help with this iced tea thing. I can't seem to get it right!" Zach shouted from the kitchen.

Grace smiled as she reached for the sponge in the bucket and squeezed out the excess water. "You can't steep the bags too long, it gets bitter. And easy on the sugar."

"I love me some sugar, Grace. I can't help it." He joked as he kept busy in the kitchen.

"Don't drink his tea, Grace. It's a trap." The familiar voice carried over to her and she straightened before she looked up. Only he could cause butterflies in her stomach. She listened as Evan entered the house and set his keys on the table nearby.

Finally her eyes drew to his, and she felt as if her breath was being smothered. She tried to look away but was captivated by him. The scruff that had been present on his face was now shaved clean. His dusky, golden brown hair was perfectly styled, and he wore a plain shirt and jeans that would look boring on the average guy. Evan was far from the average guy, however, and Grace knew she was in trouble.

Clearing her throat, she gave half a smile. "Too late. I thought I was going to fall into a sugar coma after one sip."

"Again, Zach? Don't even try anymore, man." Evan moved to Grace and sat down beside her. "You caulking my crack, Grace?"

She held the gun in her hand and pointed it at his head, trying to stifle a laugh. "Don't say caulk. You make it sound dirty."

"Exactly." He smirked as she ignored him and grabbed the sponge. He laughed, "You're wiping my caulk now, I see."

"Shut up, Matthews," she chuckled and pushed him with her elbow. "I'm almost done here."

"Don't fuck up her concentration, Evan."

Grace saw Evan's features turn dark, as if his happiness had buried and turned into something else. *Jealousy?* "Zach, Josh needed you to get Hank from his place. He's staying on set late."

"Now?"

Evan turned back to him, his eyes like lasers, and his voice stern. "Now."

"Damn dog. I love and hate him at the same time," Zach groaned.

"You'd give your life for that dog."

"I would," Zach agreed. Grace stayed focused as she worked with the putty knife but smiled at the idea of these guys going soft over a pet. Zach huffed, "Fine. I'm going. See you later, Grace."

She looked over to him and nodded. "Thanks for the tea, and the talk, Zach."

Before he reached the door, he grabbed a set of keys. "Hey, Evan, invite her to the Halloween party."

"Yeah," Evan mumbled as Zach left.

Grace stayed quiet as she turned her attention back to the wall. What was she going to say to him? She hoped to be done with all this before he got back, but unfortunately, that wasn't the case. His body heat radiated from him, and he looked and smelled amazing. Women the world over would love to be in her spot at this moment, and here she was, sitting next to *GQ's Man of the Year*, one of *People's Sexiest Men Alive*, and yet, she tried to stay away. Why? She knew exactly why. *Remember the promise,* she thought to herself.

"Look at me, Grace." Evan's voice was rough, masculine. Slowly, she turned toward him, and saw his electric blue eyes urge her to speak truth. "Are you interested in Zach? If you are, then tell me now. If not, then I'm definitely asking you out on a date."

A surge of emotions welled inside of her. She couldn't let down her defenses. The strategically-placed wall around her heart needed to stay put, but she struggled as she stared at his mouth and wondered what his lips would feel like on hers. He stayed still beside her as he waited for her answer. She tried to keep it light. "The bet didn't mean anything, Evan. It didn't count."

"Bullshit, Grace. It counted." She pushed herself up from the floor and he followed. His tall stature hovered over her and he clasped her wrist before she could move away. "You like him?"

Grace felt her pulse drumming and heard her heart pounding in her ears. She lifted her chin and roamed his faultless face. "Gracie?" He breathed her name with a husky sound that made her insides melt.

She tried to gain her balance and focus on the initial question, but could only stare at his beautiful soft mouth. "Yeah?"

A crinkle appeared between his eyes. "You do?"

"Do what?"

He backed up and the spell she was under quickly dissipated. "You like Zach?"

"What? No. I don't like Zach. I mean, not like that." She moved away and began to gather her things. "Look, um, I gotta go. I have a-"

"Deadline. I know." He smiled that mega-watt charming smile at her, and she tried to keep her calm. "I'll help you take your things." He picked up the bucket with water as she grabbed the rest of the items she had brought with her and tucked things in the pockets of her paint-stained overalls.

They walked outside and he dumped the contents of the bucket over his lawn. Her mind began to function properly again and she recalled the last time they had said goodbye. "Hey, Matthews, how did you know my middle name?"

He grinned. "You didn't think I would Google you?"

Her face reddened as they reached her doorway. "You Googled me?"

"What? You didn't Google me, Grace?"

"Why would I Google you?"

"Ouch." He playfully placed his hand over his chest. "You're breaking my heart, Gracie Lynn."

Grace tried to pretend that Evan saying her name didn't have an effect on her, but that was far from the truth. "All the dirt on you is in *US Weekly*, Matthews." She opened her door and rested her tools on the hall tree then turned to grab the bucket from him, but he had already settled it near the entrance.

Evan stood watching her with a purposeful gaze. "Don't believe everything you read, Grace." He stayed put, but surprised her when he reached over and tugged on a strand of hair that hung out of her bun and pushed it behind her ear. "We're having a Halloween cast party at Old School Bar and Grill. You and your friends are invited."

"I'll see what we're up to." Grace shuddered as his finger grazed the plane of her cheek. She moved away from him. "I can't guarantee we'll make it."

"I'd really like you to go, Grace." His voice was suave and she felt her insides clench at the thought of him whispering sweet things in her ear.

"Would it count as one of the dates?"

"No. That'll be later."

"I still don't think the bet counts at all."

"Stop trying to get out of it, pumpkin. I'm taking you out." He winked as he began to leave. "See you later, Gracie."

Was he trying to destroy her? After years of terrible dates and unsatisfactory men, Grace had given up hope of finding someone who would make her feel all these crazy sensations she had only ever written about in her books. The romanticisms she thought of as only fictional were beginning to stir within her like a vortex, and she was being pulled in. How would she fight against this man who was the essence of perfection? She had to stay strong, remember what was important, and not let herself get lost in a fantasy world she knew couldn't exist with Mr. Hollywood.

Chapter Five

A strong weight pressed on Grace's chest. Her breathing was restricted, airflow cut off by gushes of water entering her lungs. The heaviness of her clothes towed her under as she attempted to tread her way to the surface. Something grabbed her ankle and pulled her further down. Looking above, a hand broke through the water and reached for her, but it was no use. The hand was too far away. She couldn't breathe…

Grace sat up in bed, gasping for air. A sheen of sweat covered her and her heart pounded violently inside her chest. The nightmares were rare. For years they lay inactive, but ever since she started writing her memoir about Nathan they had emerged. The guilt monster would come roaring out, telling her it was all her fault. Years of therapy had trained her to recognize that it wasn't something that could have been controlled. That she wasn't to blame, no matter what her brain noise made her believe.

Grace reached for her phone and checked the time. She let her body fall back down on her pillow and tried to steady her breathing. Five in the morning was way too early to be awake, so she attempted to get a few more hours of rest before starting the day.

Later that day movie star Benjamin Taylor would be moving in across the street from her. She needed to make sure all the paperwork was taken care of and the place was properly organized for him. Evan's co-star was tall, dark, and handsome, and on the verge of becoming the next Hollywood heartthrob. She wondered if he was as self-assured and cocky as Evan was.

It had almost been a week since she'd last seen him. Perhaps he'd met another girl who was easier to charm. Guys weren't willing to be patient with her. At least in her experience. She tried to clear her thoughts of him as she tossed and turned in her bed. She grabbed her phone again and sighed. There was no way she was falling back asleep. Reluctantly, Grace got out of bed and changed into her workout clothes.

Grace hated that it was still dark outside when she left home, but the cold air felt great in her lungs as she rolled down the window of her car and drove over to the gym. She didn't go as often as she should, but every now and then she liked to get a workout in. A nice go on the elliptical would clear her mind and her raging hormones from the effect of the hunk next door.

Within the hour, Grace was working up a sweat as she huffed and puffed on the treadmill. The gym was full of morning people who used all the elliptical machines, which was an unexpected and annoying revelation. She grumbled to herself as she picked up speed and let Bruno Mars blast in her ears.

She slowed after half an hour and grabbed her towel to wipe her forehead. Her peripheral vision caught a man walking toward her and she did a double take. *Oh, Jesus, help me.* Grace tugged her earbuds off and slowed her pace as Evan approached the machine and rested his sweaty forearm against it.

"Good morning, Gracie Lynn." He stood before her with his damp hair hanging over his forehead and his white shirt clinging onto his chest. She could see every cord of his neck muscles as he steadied his breathing. "You stalking me?"

The length of his physique stood out—trim, well-defined, and unflawed. He was so confident and masculine. Even with sweat trickling down the side of his temples he looked absolutely delicious. It just wasn't fair.

"You wish, Matthews." She tried to force her mouth to remain straight as she reached for her bottled water and took a sip. "What are you doing at my gym?"

"Getting tortured for the sake of art."

Her laugh couldn't be held back as she stopped the treadmill and jumped off. She glanced over and saw Josh with a few other guys all pumping iron. "Well, you play your role very well."

"So you're saying I got a rocking bod?" His smile grew as he followed her. "Wait til you see me without my clothes."

"God, that ego," she teased. Grace noted several women looking in their direction. Some of them gaped, trying to get themselves under control. Others tried to give Evan seductive looks in hopes he would return them. He was hard to ignore. She wondered if any of these women would be brave enough to approach him.

He was probably used to being stared at and hit on all the time. It seemed like second nature to him. A pang of jealousy suddenly hit Grace and she tried to let the emotion pass as quickly as it had appeared. These feelings were beginning to creep on her, more so when she was around him.

"Don't say you wouldn't appreciate it," Evan joked.

"Looks like blondie over there appreciates it." Grace smirked, pushing her chin toward big boobs on the elliptical. The woman was basically eye-humping Evan the moment she had spotted him.

"You jealous, Gracie? I only got eyes for you, doll."

"Sure you do, Matthews," she chuckled as she reminded herself to take it to the friend zone. Stopping, she forced herself to look at Evan and caught him observing her carefully. Her skin prickled and she suddenly felt vulnerable. Heat surged between their bodies and she was aware of how close he was getting to her.

He leaned in toward her, hovering, the largeness of his body towering over her small frame. "I'm taking you to breakfast, Gracie."

His smooth demand caressed her ears making her forget that friend zone thing. "O-okay," she stammered, fighting for breath. "I-I-need to just…" She tried to move away from him as she pointed toward the ladies' room. "Um…I need to shower."

"Me too," he chuckled. "Look, I'll meet you at your place in twenty minutes."

Grace nodded in compliance as she walked away completely at a loss of how she was going to stop herself from giving in to this gorgeous man.

~

Evan knocked on Grace's door and tucked his hands inside his blue field jacket. He lowered his Red Sox cap and kept on his aviators as the sun was beginning to peek out over the horizon. Texas skies were beautiful, and the weather, although a bit more humid than Los Angeles, was pleasant.

Grace stepped out and locked the door. Her hair was wet and bunched up in a clip and her porcelain skin was makeup free. She looked perfect—even in a sweatshirt, jeans, and those clunky UGGs girls loved wearing. "Magnolia Café?"

"I haven't been."

"It's good. We'll go there," she announced and headed toward her car, then paused. Turning back to him she scrunched her nose. "Maybe we should take your car."

The old, white Honda Accord was riddled with chipping paint and small dings from years of use. He laughed and took his keys out of his pocket leading her toward his rented Lexus. "Your car's acting up?"

"The Freon leaks and I can't use the AC. I'm constantly having to fill it."

He opened the passenger door for Grace as he made his way to the driver's side. "You need a Freon with sealant, so it closes any holes it might have in the hose. I can take a look at it and see what else it might need."

"You know about cars?" The surprise in her voice didn't pass him.

"I do. My Uncle Bill was a mechanic. On days when my mom needed a break, she'd send us kiddos over to her brother's place. My sisters, Katie and Hilary, would spend the day playing makeup with my Aunt Sharon, and I'd spend it out in the garage restoring old cars."

"You're going to take a right on Congress." Grace gave directions and seemed to relax as he began to talk more openly. "And your dad?"

"Dad and Mom divorced when I was in middle school. It was for the best, but my Mom was pretty heartbroken. She hasn't dated or remarried. Instead she kept her focus on us. Dad married soon after the divorce and has three kids."

"Wow. Are you close with them at all?"

"I see them on occasion, but he's got his own life going on now. How about you?"

He sensed tension and hesitance in her voice. "My parents moved to California after I graduated high school. We're not close."

"No brothers or sisters?"

"I had a brother. He died when I was sixteen."

"I'm so sorry, Grace." He kept his eyes focused on her as they waited for the light to change. "It couldn't have been easy dealing with that loss. I can't imagine losing one of my sisters."

She avoided looking at him. He wanted to dig in deeper, find out everything that happened, but he didn't want to scare her off, so he stepped carefully. "What was his name?"

"Nathaniel. Nathan. November 7th is his birthday."

"That's right around the corner."

"Yeah. He would've been thirty-four this year."

"My age."

She smiled nostalgically, but melancholy filled her

eyes. She then looked over to Evan. "Light's green."

He snapped out of his trance and looked forward, a comfortable silence settling between them for the remainder of the drive. They arrived and Evan laughed when he saw the signage leading into the café. "*Sorry, We're Open*?"

"Yeah," Grace laughed. "They have it on their menu too. I personally like getting the *Sorry, We're Pancakes* dish."

"Keep Austin weird," Evan muttered the city slogan as they walked in.

Luckily, the wait for a table wasn't long. Evan fidgeted with anxiety, hoping nobody would interrupt their meal. His fame could sometimes be a hindrance and he wasn't certain how Grace would handle the attention. At the gym, he was well aware of people staring, and Grace had caught on. He hoped it wouldn't detract her from wanting to know him.

Their waitress greeted them with a friendly smile and set down silverware on a tabletop covered in an owl print. She had a short, pink pixie haircut and tattoos covering almost every inch of her body. Evan wondered if she would recognize him, and kept his head tucked down. After taking their coffee order, she leaned in. "Don't worry, just keep your hat low. I'll tell the hostess to be aware of who they seat around you." She winked and smiled, turning to Grace, dynamically offering her the specials.

Evan was aware of the fact that she took care of Grace first and was grateful. Too many times the company he kept got pushed aside while he got the attention. It made him deeply aggravated when that happened, and hoped it wouldn't ever be something Grace would have to put up with.

He began to unwind and noticed Grace gazing at him. The look in her eyes indicated she was definitely interested. He didn't mind that at all. What he couldn't figure out was why she was denying that lust and trying to push him away? He was a perceptive guy, could read almost anyone, but she was a bit more mysterious.

"So, what were you doing exercising at an ungodly hour today, Gracie?" he asked casually once the waitress was out of earshot.

She dumped what must have been twenty creamers into her coffee and about four packets of sugar and shrugged as she methodically stirred the piping hot beverage.

"I woke up and couldn't go back to sleep," she replied. "Figured I'd let off some steam."

"Running away from nightmares?" She flinched and her eyes grew wide, leaving no doubt in Evan's mind what the answer was. "Want to talk about it?"

She shook her head and took a sip of her coffee. "Just a lot on my mind."

"Your deadline?" She nodded. "I read your stuff. I like it."

A small upturn of her lips and the flush on her cheeks gave him the pleasure he was hoping for. "You read one of my books?"

"I did. I'm on your third book, and so far I'm really interested to find out if Lady Sarah Thompson ends up with Duke Nicholas Elliott. I think she should end up with bad boy Bow Street Runner Jack Shipper though."

Grace laughed and he felt his stomach jump to his throat. To hear her laugh forever might probably be the best thing he could ask for. "Well, you'll have to read the rest to find out."

"Oh, I intend to, Gracie. I'm not much of a romance-genre type of reader, but my curiosity was piqued. I need the other books, and I already have *I Married a Duke,* which I think is the latest one, right?"

"Right. I'm almost done with the next one. Just going through some editing and re-writes." She sipped on her coffee and added another sugar packet.

"What's the title?"

"I'm deciding between *The Duke's Lust* or *Waiting on Lust*."

"Anything with the word *lust* in it is pretty much a winning title for me." They both laughed as they then placed their food order.

He watched as she pressed her lips together. She seemed more comfortable when talking about her books, so he continued. "So, why historical romance?"

"I've always been interested in the past. I like the whole idea of the way things worked back then. The civility and the manners. For example, women and men were usually required to wear gloves. If you think about it, just the touch of a bare hand could be the most sensual, intimate thing. It was so polite in those days, there were rules for everything."

"Now it's just a big mess?" Evan smiled as he was getting more insight to the woman he was determined to know.

"Exactly." Her face was lit up, and her passion was sparking something within him. God, he really liked that about her. "Nowadays nobody knows what to do. Even greeting someone is a bit awkward. Do you hug? Do you shake hands?"

"I say you and I French kiss when we greet. Mandatory rule."

Grace rolled her eyes, but it hadn't stopped her from smiling. "I mean, social media has ruined everything. Nobody talks to each other in person, instead they stare down at their phones. People don't even court anymore."

"Sorry to point this out, Gracie, but nobody's courted in a very long time. I think that went out of style in the 70s." Once again, they both were laughing.

He watched the way her skin blushed as she spoke. "You know what I mean. Dating is just a different ball game now. Everyone texts, nobody talks. It's amazing you and I even became friends."

Friends. So, she was trying to friend-zone him. If she wanted to be courted, he could deal, but there was no way he was staying in the friend zone. "So what's your favorite era?"

She hummed a moment in thought. "Too many to choose from. But I just love the 1940s. The music, the hairstyles and fashion."

At that moment, two girls came over and fumbled asking Evan for his autograph. For once he had been so caught up in talking that he had forgotten his life, the life where he was constantly trying to hide.

Embarrassment rushed through him and he hoped nobody else saw the girls making a ruckus as they squealed about what big fans they were.

He was grateful to them, and loved what he did, but he wondered about the woman with him and how she would react. He smiled politely, signed a few papers and looked over to Grace who seemed entertained through the whole encounter. He was even more shocked when she spoke. "You girls want a photo with him?"

They excitedly handed their phones over to Grace who got out of her booth to take several shots and angles on each phone. She even had the audacity to tell Evan to smile more and attempted to make them all laugh. She had definitely succeeded too. The girls thanked the both of them and left.

The waitress returned with their meals and apologized profusely, but at that point it didn't matter. Grace had made it all okay, and nobody else seemed to be remotely interested in the commotion that just took place. He stayed still for a moment as he watched Grace dig into her pancakes. She ate vigorously and then glanced up at him. "Aren't you hungry?"

"Yeah," he prepped his eggs and potatoes with salt. He promised Josh he'd be semi-good.

"You don't like the fame stuff, do you?"

"Not always." He chewed his food and watched her nod; however, he wasn't sure she understood his reasoning. "I know what you're going to say. *You're an actor, and you asked for it. You accepted the part, you made your bed, now you gotta lay in it."*

"I wasn't even thinking that." Grace cut a half a piece of one of her pancakes and placed it on Evan's plate. "Here, you have to eat this. It's too good not to." She picked up the syrup and poured it on top for him. "I won't tell Josh, I promise."

Evan laughed and didn't hesitate to try it. "Shit, these are delicious."

"I know, right? No need to be sorry about these pancakes at all." She finished another forkful and then ripped through a sausage link and cut a piece, setting it on Evan's plate. "Try the sausage. Anyway, I was going to say that I don't think anyone could get used to what follows when fame hits. Your privacy is taken away. It's a scary loss of control. I'm sure that has to be strange for you to deal with."

"I just had this idea that I would be a character actor. Make independent movies for most of my life, eventually make my way into directing."

"But then the *Ending* movies came your way?"

He nodded in response, not having discussed this with many people, especially not with a woman he had barely met. But something about Grace made him feel comfortable. As if his secrets would stay with her and his feelings were safe. "I thought about it a long time. Really weighed my options. I even said no the first time they offered it to me."

"They asked you again?"

"Yeah, I said no a second time. By the fourth time they asked I realized that maybe it was..." Evan trailed off, almost uncomfortable of sounding clichéd.

"It was meant to be. You were meant to take that

role, Evan. Nobody could play that part but you."

He smiled wide, pausing and enjoying the moment. Acting was a very internal art. He was fascinated in human behavior, studying why people conducted themselves the way they did. At this moment, he was speculating why Grace's lips parted and her breathing became restricted. Was she feeling the same effects that he felt around her?

He thought he'd die if he couldn't ever feel her mouth on his. He longed to know if she tasted like strawberry the way she smelled of it. He wanted to take her to his bedroom and strip her of those baggy clothes, let his hands roam every single inch of her sexy body and make her wet with desire. He wanted to know exactly what would make her moan, which spots would set her off as his tongue explored her sensual figure. But more than anything, he wanted in on all her secrets that she seemed to lock away. He wanted that access to her more than he had ever wanted with any woman. It was both exhilarating and terrifying.

She cleared her throat and broke their intense stare. "I'm sure it's something you're glad you said yes to."

"Of course. Looking back at it, I'm really happy I did. It's afforded me so many incredible opportunities. Nobody would have given me a shot to direct my first film."

"And look how happy you just made those girls. They'll remember this encounter forever." The waitress refilled their coffee cups as they continued to chat about his movie. "So, do you like acting better or directing?"

"I like both. I really am looking for a great movie to

direct next. I need a great script so I can get backed by other producers and studios, actually. I want to get better at it, you know? Continue to grow and challenge myself."

Grace nodded. "I know what you mean."

"Yeah? You going to keep writing that memoir?"

Grace took a deep breath before speaking. "I've asked my publishing company about it. They don't seem to be interested."

"I'm interested. Can I at least know a little about it?" He looked at her with expectant eyes. He saw her lips part in hesitation, but he stopped her. She wasn't ready to talk about it. "It's okay. I don't want to push. But please, keep me in mind."

The waitress brought the check and Grace reached for it. Evan quickly snatched it from her hands and gave the waitress a big bill. "No change needed and thanks for your help."

"I was going to pay my part," Grace disputed as they got up to leave.

"Outrageous. Women never pay, Gracie. I thought you of all people would know that rule, Miss Manners."

Grace laughed. "There are no rules anymore, remember? It's a mess."

Evan opened her car door and placed his hand on the small of her back. He wished he could keep it there forever and pull her against him. "It doesn't have to be a mess, Grace," he whispered leaning over her. "Sometimes the easier it is, the more it's meant to be."

He felt her body shiver as she lowered inside the car and he closed the door behind her. They drove back listening to the radio, chatting about the upcoming festivals going on in the area. It was too soon that they were back home.

"Thanks for breakfast, Evan."

"You're welcome, Gracie Lynn. What are you up to the rest of the day?"

"I have to meet with Benjamin Taylor. Make sure his paperwork is squared away and go through his house."

Evan nodded, slightly annoyed she'd be spending time with Ben and not him. It wasn't like Evan would be home anyway, but he still wanted to be the one taking her time. "How many homes do you manage?"

He walked with her across the yard and to her door. "Mine, plus four more. It's an easy job most of the time. Stephen is a friend of my father's. He's always traveling and needed someone to look after all the small things he can't."

"Gives you time to write?"

"Yes, definitely. And I get discount on my rent. He and my dad are close, so he didn't hesitate to help me out."

"Well, I'm glad I rented this place. And that my pipe leaked." He watched her body tense up as she turned to unlock her door. "The cast party is on Friday night. I'm renting a small shuttle to come pick us up."

"A shuttle?" She stepped partially inside before turning.

"Yeah, so everyone can party recklessly but get home reliably. Besides, who wants to find parking and drive in downtown traffic, right?"

"Smart move."

"Be sure to wear a sexy costume, Grace."

"I don't do sexy." Grace placed her bag on the hall tree and turned back toward him. "And one date down, one to go."

"You are sexy. And today was not a date."

"Says who?"

"Me."

"See? If this was in the old days, we'd define this as a date."

He laughed and stuffed his hands in his pockets. "It's not the old days, honey buns."

She crossed her arms and continued. "So what, in your opinion, defines a date, Mr. Matthews?"

Evan grasped her arm and tugged her forward. Their bodies were so close, and he could feel himself stir as he breathed in her scent. His hand brushed her cheek, and his lips drifted near hers. She didn't push him away, but he knew if he got any closer she would. "When I get to kiss you at the end of it, Gracie. And I will eventually kiss you, doll." He winked at her and walked away, letting her settle with that notion and knowing he was getting closer to winning her over.

Chapter Six

Training was fierce for Evan that morning, and by afternoon, he was looking forward to relaxing with a good movie. He knew what he needed to do was find a damn script he wanted to work on. His agents and partners were beginning to pressure him, and he wasn't enjoying the repercussions of his procrastination.

His phone chimed and he glanced at it quickly as he drove up to the community mailboxes to retrieve a package he had been sent. Zach asked if he wanted to go to a bar downtown, but Evan really was getting tired of that scene. It hadn't interested him in years, but he kept it going for the sake of meeting women who were there for the exact same reason he was. Hooking up was easy, making it last was less so.

Evan responded to Zach and grabbed his mail. He smiled when he saw the handwriting on the package he retrieved. He missed his family. Boston beckoned him, and he wasn't one to go long without a visit. Now, to convince Grace to go with him was another thing entirely.

Reaching the driveway, he exited his car and watched Grace and a little boy walking to her door. Her laughter filled the air as she grabbed the young boy's cup. "I'll give it back to you when we get to the kitchen."

The little boy reached up with both hands and pouted. "But I can carry it. I won't drop it."

"Remember what happened last time you said that? You spilled it everywhere." She juggled her keys and a pizza box, placing the two Styrofoam cups on top of it.

"Here, I can help." Evan found himself approaching hastily, offering his assistance. He quickly observed the boy to see if he looked like her. "Hi, big guy, how's it goin?"

"Aunt Grace took my snow cone."

Aunt Grace? Did she have another sibling she hadn't told him about? He noticed the boy was around his own nephew's age. His brown hair was spiked up stylishly, and he wore an Incredible Hulk t-shirt, cargo shorts, and Vans Star Wars shoes. His big brown eyes looked up at Evan in sadness. "I told her I can carry it. I won't drop it."

"Bud, how about I hold it for a little while, and I'll guess what flavor you got?" Grace gave him a relieved glance as she unlocked the door.

The boy eyed Evan hesitantly and then nodded. "I bet you can't guess. But don't taste it, then you'd be cheating."

"I promise I won't cheat." Evan passed her as she held the door open. "Hello, Grace." A loose, white button-down shirt and dark cropped jeans styled her body with her signature white Converse decorating her feet. Her hair was still bunched up on the top of her head.

His smile was returned with a twinkle in her eyes. "Hi Evan. Okay, Jake, take off your shoes at the door please."

Jake. "Oh, Jaime's kid?"

Grace nodded as Jake began to take off his Vans. "Excuse me, guy, you have to take off your shoes too." Jake pointed to Evan's Nikes. "You can't get the floor dirty."

He grinned and shucked off each shoe. "Gotcha, bud."

"Now, guess what the flavor is. You won't guess."

Evan began to call out random flavors for the green-colored shaved ice as they walked inside. He called out spinach, broccoli, celery, and boogers as Jake yelled out things like, "sick," "no way," "disgusting," and "gross."

As they made their way into the kitchen, Jake interrupted one of his guesses. "Excuse me, you can give it back to me now, guy."

Grace spoke as Evan placed her snow cone down on the kitchen island. "Jake, this is Evan. Do you recognize him?"

"Yeah," Jake said, grabbing his cup and spoon tightly and sitting at the dining table. "He's your boyfriend."

Evan laughed and watched Grace's cheeks turn a shade of pink. "Where did you hear that? He's not my boyfriend, Jake."

"That could change," Evan smirked as he set down his mail on the kitchen counter nearby. Grace handed him the pizza box with paper plates and napkins above it, disregarding his statement.

"Take that to the table, please, and you're more than welcome to join us for dinner." She moved to the refrigerator and took out a pre-made salad and dressing.

"Mommy said he was your boyfriend," Jake announced with a mouthful of ice. "When I saw him on TV, she said that."

Evan was getting a kick out of the situation, and it also gave him something he needed. Hope. "I see you and Jaime have been discussing me?"

She brought the salad, dressing, and utensils to the table as Evan passed out the plates and napkins. "I think that discussion was held between her husband, Dean, and her, if anything. I don't spend my days pining over you, Mr. Hollywood."

Sitting next to Jake, she continued, "Your mommy is making that up, Jake. He's my next-door neighbor."

"Is he your friend?" Jake peered up at Grace and she hesitated before gazing over at Evan's eager eyes.

"Yeah, we're friends," she answered with a smile.

"And he's a boy, so he's your boyfriend," he said matter-of-factly as she opened the pizza box from Home Slice Pizza and served him a piece. Jake grabbed at it quickly, ripping through it, forgetting his snow cone. "Mommy said when you were fighting the aliens on TV that aliens aren't real. But I was still scared and Mommy turned it off. You don't fly, anyway. Superman can fly. He's cooler." He took another big bite of the pizza, the pepperoni hanging out of his mouth as he tried to chew.

"Jake, that's not nice," Grace scolded. "Batman can't fly."

"I don't like Batman either. I like Superman."

"Don't talk with your mouth full, please." Grace

served herself a slice as Evan began putting the salad on each of their plates.

"Well, to be fair, I'm just a space captain," Evan clarified as he grabbed the dressing. He was surprised as Grace pushed her snow cone toward the middle of the table offering to share. He scooped up from her spoon and ate what appeared to be strawberries-and-cream flavor.

A flash let him imagine kissing her and tasting it on her lips, but he focused instead on Jake. The kid was honest and funny. He loved that about children. They didn't take bullshit from him. Then again, neither did Grace.

Jake continued, "But they say on the movie that you're a superhero." His big eyes studied Evan a moment before blurting out, "You look different in real life."

"Well, I have to color my hair lighter and I have cool costumes on in the movies, not gym clothes." He began to eat his salad as Grace served him a slice of pizza.

"My mommy colors and cuts hair. She colors Aunt Grace's and Aunt Marla's and all these people who live here. She's in magazines for Austin and wins awards." Jake took to licking his fingers and Grace quickly grabbed a napkin, helping him clean up. "Maybe she can cut your hair too."

Evan grinned. "Maybe she can. Watermelon. You got a watermelon snow cone, didn't you?"

Jake nodded his head, then started to talk about how he was spending the night. He then rambled about his birthday party, but Evan decided to not tell him he would be attending in full costume.

"Excuse me, guy, where do you work?"

"His name is Evan," Grace interrupted.

"Okay, excuse me, Evan, where do you work?"

"I work in different places, but usually in Los Angeles. Do you know where that is?"

Jake shook his head up and down, "Disneyland. I went there last year." Evan started on the pizza but reminded himself to only eat one slice. "Evan?"

"Yes, Jake?"

"Can you spend the night?"

He and Grace both chuckled and looked at each other, Grace answering for him, "Evan has his own house next door."

"But he's my new best friend. He can stay here." Jake pouted.

"He has to stay in his own house," Grace said, finishing her slice and wiping her hands and mouth with a napkin.

"But you can share a bed with Aunt Grace, and I can sleep in the other room." Jake was animated with a hopeful look on his face.

Evan couldn't stop grinning as he gazed over her. "That sounds like a great idea to me, Grace. We could spoon, ya know."

"In your dreams."

"Aunt Grace, you don't like Evan?"

"Yeah, you don't like me, Gracie?" He pouted his lip and watched as her body began to tense up. Rising from the table and grabbing the empty plates, she headed to the kitchen.

"Jake, he's not spending the night," she stated tensely as she rinsed the silverware and put them in the dishwasher.

"Pleaaaaaaase," Jake began to mope.

"Not til later, sport," Evan winked at him. "When Aunt Gracie is ready." Obviously he was still being friend-zoned, and that would have to change soon.

Grace was beginning to feel edgy by Evan's expectations. And Jake's comments weren't helping keep him at a distance. What would she have to do to get the point across that she wasn't interested in starting anything with him? Mr. Hollywood wasn't the relationship type, and she wasn't one to have a fling. Grace was used to flat-out telling a man she wasn't interested. This was more challenging with Evan. The biggest reason being that she felt herself attracted to him beyond measure.

Evan began to help her clear up the rest of the table as Jake moved toward the living room. On his way, he stopped and Jake called out, "What's the box?"

Evan looked back at the boy. "It's a package from my mom."

"Your mom sent you a present?" Jake asked curiously as he skipped over to it. "She doesn't live with you?"

Grace watched their interaction and smiled. *Well, crap. A package from his mom? How freaking cute was that?* No, she couldn't let herself be charmed by him. It didn't matter that he was close to his mom. Or that he was really nice and funny. Or that he looked so damn gorgeous with his hair spiked up today that she wanted to run her hands through the top of it and tug it while he licked the space between her neck and shoulder. Nope. None of that mattered.

He took the box and moved it toward the kitchen island, asking Grace for some scissors. She couldn't stop looking at him as his big hands gripped the box, his large forearms and chest flexing, the content look on his face as he smiled—he was worth staring at. Grace found herself thinking about him all the time, and that was scaring her. She had to be vigilant and had to keep her guard up. A promise was a promise, after all.

Inside the package was a Tupperware container full of homemade brownies, an envelope with photos, and a letter. He stuffed the letter inside the pocket of his track pants and opened the plastic container, handing a small square toward Jake. "These are the best brownies you will ever taste."

Jake bit into the chocolate goodness and smiled. He handed one to Grace, his blue eyes bright. Evan studied her as she bit in. The chocolate melted on her tongue, the richness overcoming her taste buds as she sighed. "I need this recipe in my life."

He shook his head, eating his own brownie. "Nope, not happening. My mom keeps her recipes safe, all in her head. She won't even give them to my sisters."

Jake asked for another brownie, but Grace refused more sugar intake, and got him to calm down by putting on the old Superman movie for him. When he was finally settled, she joined Evan in the kitchen again. He had been reading his letter with a look of tranquility. She felt like she was intruding as he stopped and regarded her. Smiling, he folded the paper and placed it back in his pocket. "My nephew Jonah is in Kindergarten, and my mom takes care of him after school. She says he's even more hyper than I was."

He handed her a photo of a woman who looked exactly like Evan as she stood with a blond-haired, blue-eyed boy that hugged her tightly. Grace smiled at the crazy resemblance between them all. Their eyes were all the same shape and color. "He's adorable."

"He's Katie's. She's a drama teacher, married to James. And Hilary is a blogger and perpetual student."

"How many degrees does she have?"

"I think she's on her third? Maybe fourth? Can't keep track."

Grace was impressed, moving about the kitchen and motioning toward a bottle of red wine. He took the bottle and opener from her, and proceeded as she grabbed the glasses. Checking on Jake, she saw he was in his own world, so she allowed herself the chance to relax with Evan. He poured the wine and handed her a glass. She sipped and felt it trickle down her throat. "Are you the oldest?"

"Middle. And I took every opportunity I could to tease the both of them when we were growing up. I drove them crazy." His eyes were reminiscent as he spoke.

Grace could sense how important his family was to him. Something she wouldn't have gathered from the playboy. Her heart felt that twinge of longing for love and acceptance from hers. She couldn't help but yearn for that. "You seem close to them."

"I am. I miss them a lot when I'm away. But I have a place in Boston so it gives me an opportunity to be with my family more than not." He strolled toward her bookshelves and she followed. "And your family, Grace? You don't talk to your parents at all?"

She stood beside him and shook her head resolutely. "Not really. When Nathan died, they pulled away. I wasn't the golden child, that was more his role."

"They don't call you? Visit?" His blue eyes focused on her and she was afraid to see pity from them. Instead she saw an urgency to know more.

"Sometimes they text, but it's a quick hello, doing okay, still alive type thing." Grace focused on her bookshelves instead and tried to remind herself she wasn't at fault, even though her parents thought so. She took a gulp of wine, hoping it would lessen the tightness in her throat. "They haven't even come back to visit his grave. They left everything behind. Including me."

"How did he die, Grace?"

His voice was soft, understanding, and it seemed effortless to want to tell him everything. Or perhaps her want of a companion was stronger than she thought. Loneliness was something she had gotten so used to, it could be said it was her best friend. That kept her from confiding completely in this man. *Keep it short and to the point, Grace.* "He fell and broke his neck."

Evan's eyes widened in shock and she knew her

abrupt answer required more of an explanation, but she wasn't ready to give it yet. "That's awful. I'm sorry."

"Accidents happen," she added that more for her own comfort at the moment than for his. He wasn't questioning any further, so she said no more about it. There was always that awkward feeling of what someone was to say after something like that, so she spared him and changed the subject. "So, your mom likes to bake?"

Sensing the shift, Evan nodded with a smile. "Yeah, she always had homemade oatmeal chocolate chip cookies for us. We'd get home after school and that was our comfort food."

Grace liked hearing as he told her stories about how he would tease Hilary and tell her she was the adopted weirdo. "You probably scarred her for life," she laughed.

"She came out alright," he chuckled then perused her shelves. "I like these books, Grace. I see you have a lot of poetry stuff."

"Yeah, I like poetry."

"Me too. I took an acting class where I had to memorize poems instead of monologues. I got hooked," Evan shared as his finger grazed along the spines of her books.

Grace realized there was much more to Evan than she initially thought. "This one's my favorite." She tugged out a frayed copy of a book and handed it to him. "Goethe's *The Sorrows of Young Werther*. I know it's a bit dark, but the way he loved her was beautiful."

His demeanor had instantly shifted. She watched his

eyes gloss, as if his mind were somewhere else as he grasped the book slowly.

"Did I say something wrong?"

He looked at her with tenderness as he gently lifted his lips to a smile. His voice was soothing. "Not at all, Gracie Lynn. Goethe's my favorite too."

She gave him a doubtful glance before turning away and broaching another topic. Before they realized it, the sun had gone down, and Jake was asleep as Superman had finished saving the world. Evan insisted on picking Jake up himself and carrying him to her room. Grace allowed it, and followed Evan as they both tucked him in.

Grabbing his box from the kitchen, he handed her another brownie. "For tomorrow."

"Thanks," she giggled and took it from him.

"Thanks for the pizza." She walked him toward the door and he turned, his midnight blue eyes focused on her. He tugged on a curl and ran his finger over her cheek. "I'll see you Saturday night."

The moment would've been perfect for Grace to tell Evan that she didn't want to date him. The problem was, she wasn't so sure of that fact anymore. Evan Matthews was a force to be reckoned with, and for the first time in her life, she was questioning that promise she had made long ago and whether she'd be able to keep it much longer.

Chapter Seven

Grace ran her hands over the top of her high ponytail and tugged it tighter at the base. The dark, shiny locks fell down and she knew she'd be in for a scalp ache at the end of the night. Nervously, she yanked on the short black skirt and turned back to see if she was close to showing her ass. The tall, black, platform boots were going to give her a hell of a time walking down the uneven sidewalks of 6th Street.

"Don't second guess yourself, Grace. You're hot." Marla walked into Grace's bedroom and stood in front of the antique full-length oval mirror, pushing her aside to get the entire view to herself. "You wearing panties under that thing?"

"Of course. Difference is mine aren't showing and yours definitely are," Grace teased with a laugh.

"They aren't panties."

"More like hot pants?" Grace snapped the waistband of Marla's blue polyester shorts with white stars.

"Jaime didn't tie the corset tight enough. Can you fix it?" Marla placed her hands on the wall in front of her as Grace tugged and pulled tight at the strings.

"Will you be able to breathe?"

"I'm Wonder Woman. I can do it all." She then let out an exhale and pressed a hand to her stomach. "Okay, are you trying to kill me? Let the ties out a little bit."

Grace rolled her eyes and adjusted the red and gold corset for her. "Where's your headband?"

Marla stopped in her tracks and stared at Grace with her jaw to the floor. "Excuse me, it is not a headband. It's a tiara that doubles as a boomerang."

Grace shrugged. "Sorry, geez."

"What makes Wonder Woman so wonderful is that her accessories are not only fabulous, but they also serve a purpose."

Grace laughed at Marla's dry delivery. "You're cracking me up."

"Fine. I'm glad I made you laugh, but I'm serious." She paused a moment, then cracked a smile. "And I saw Jaime trying it on Dean's big noggin."

"It looks good over his Batman mask." Jaime sauntered in wearing a black leather Cat Woman outfit. On top of her head was the Wonder Woman tiara/boomerang. "Looking sexy, Grace!"

Grace fidgeted with the skirt and put her black leather jacket on over her olive-colored shirt. A smirk crept up on her lips as she thought about what Evan's reaction would be to her character choice tonight. "Let's see if I survive the night wearing these ridiculous boots."

Marla countered, "Let's see if you survive the rage of Captain Abrams once he sees your costume."

"You think he'd care?"

"Oh, he'll definitely care."

Grace suddenly felt worried. "I don't even know why we're going to this stupid party."

Marla and Jaime gasped. Jaime approached Grace and shook her as Marla exited the room. "Don't be an idiot, Grace. A party with the stars of the *Ending Series*. Evan Matthews? Benjamin Taylor? Kara Jones? I want to meet all these people."

"You're just nervous. Here, have some of this." Marla passed around shot glasses filled with liquid amber.

Grace grabbed one and sniffed at the contents. "Did you just bust open my bottle of Glenlivet?"

"Like you were going to drink it anytime soon." Marla held her glass up and the three girls clinked them together. "To a night out. Finally!"

The three girls gulped down the whiskey, and Grace winced at the burn her throat felt. So much for the celebratory "you-finished-your-memoir" bottle she bought herself. Marla poured them all another round. Grace had to be careful. She had been too caught up to get a chance to run to the grocery store earlier, so dinner had been set aside. Perhaps there would be food at the party.

"So, Grace, tell us about Ben Taylor. You haven't spilled since he's moved in," Marla probed when she finally took the tiara off of Jaime and adjusted her auburn hair over it.

"He's nice." Grace finished the last touches of her makeup by adding extra mascara and setting everything with powder. "He sort of reminds me of Nathan a little bit."

"Oh, then not interested in dating him, huh?"

"Ew. That'd be weird." Jaime made a face as she

adjusted her costume.

"He's super beautiful though. Can't you overlook it?"

"Um. No, I can't." Grace laughed at the notion. Benjamin Taylor was courteous and dashing, but she instantly took to him in a platonic way that she wished she felt whenever she thought about Evan.

"Speaking of beautiful, how about Mr. Matthews? Jake can't shut up about him. You know, the teacher called to tell me that he was lying to his friends saying that Captain Drew Abrams was his new buddy. I think she was in shock to find out it was true. The woman won't stop sucking up to me now. She even booked a haircut with me. Have you guys gone on one of your dates yet?"

"He's fine, and no. But what I want to know about is if Marla's still talking to that Cameron guy from work."

Marla grumbled. "The idiot won't leave me alone."

"Hah, so you have been talking to him," Jaime teased Marla and luckily forgot about Evan.

"I keep telling him it was a one-time thing. The guy keeps trying to convince me otherwise."

"I think that's sweet," Jaime laughed. "He's got a crush."

"I think it's bordering on harassment, actually," Grace chimed in, swigging the rest of her drink. She'd better pace herself. Last thing she wanted was to lose control around Mr. Hollywood. It was difficult enough when she was sober.

"You girls ready yet? The shuttle's here," Dean announced after waiting patiently in the living room for the girls as they got ready.

Grace couldn't help but chuckle at the black smudges around his eyes. "Did that Batman mask get a little hot, Dean?"

"Yeah, I'm sure that place is gonna be packed too. I'm almost wishing I was a woman so I could wear a skirt."

"You could've played a highlander and worn a kilt, babe." Jaime smiled and gave Dean a kiss. Grace watched with a twinge of sadness tugging on her heart. Their relationship was something that Grace longed for, but she had started to believe that it didn't exist for her. Cynicism was starting to take over, the dream being lost long ago.

"You two are repulsively cute. Let's get going," Marla sneered as she grabbed her cash and pushed it inside her bra. "Bring the whiskey so we can drink on the shuttle, Grace."

"You owe me a new bottle."

"You said you just sent your manuscript to your editor. The Glenlivet is for celebration."

"It was for the memoir celebration. Not the historical romance one."

Marla shrugged. "Whatever. It's still an accomplishment, Grace. Now, pass the bottle around. We're drinking and partying."

"I need to eat something," Grace mumbled, reminding herself to stay in control.

The driver smiled as they filed into the swank privately-owned shuttle. Grace sat down, settling her purse on the edge of the seat. Screw control. When was the last time she had fun? She would let herself unwind and enjoy her evening. She got to put on a sexy outfit, go out with her girlfriends, and see a hot man who just so happened to play a space superhero. She was ready to have fun and mingle.

~

Over my dead body. That was the first response that shot into Evan's mind earlier in the day when Ben talked animatedly about his gorgeous property manager to the other guys at work. Evan might've let his elbow get a little too close during stunt training and accidentally clipped Ben a few times in the face. *That's right, asshole, stay away.*

Damn, how was he letting a woman affect him in this way? There was no doubt that Grace was a sexy woman, and she did everything to stir up feelings of lust, but he wasn't the type to get caught up in thinking long term. Long distance relationships never worked. He had to think of ways to keep this light, have a fun few months with her, and part as good friends. It always worked well with others, but she was so different and he was having trouble figuring out how he would ever let her go if he even had the opportunity to catch her.

He checked his watch again, his leg bouncing on the barstool in anticipation over Grace's arrival. She had texted him letting him know they were running late, so he had sent the shuttle back to get them despite her protests. He wasn't going to let her get away that easily.

Josh sat beside Evan and scratched under the stethoscope that hugged his neck. "I fucking hate Halloween," Josh groaned as he drank from a bottle of water.

Evan smirked as he kept his eyes roaming the crowded bar. "Well, at least you made a little effort, Doctor McKenzie."

"I'm not one for flash."

"No shit, really?" Evan snickered. He tugged on the gear of his SWAT uniform he had borrowed from their props department. The camouflage pants and military green shirt were fine except for the heavy ballistics vest he wore. There was still no sign of her. He leaned over and nudged at Josh's arm. "Listen, if you see Grace around other guys, keep an eye on her."

"Other guys?"

"You know, just take care of her for me."

Josh smiled slyly at Evan. "Shit. Zach was right, then."

"What? I was actually right about something?" Zach approached with a drink in hand and gave it over to Evan.

"I'm not sure. What exactly is he right about, Josh?" He sipped on his Old Fashioned slowly.

Josh shook his head and pointed to Evan with his thumb. "This guy just asked me to keep an eye on Grace."

"Boom! You owe me a crispy, new one hundred dollar bill, you fucker!" Zach punched Josh's shoulder.

Evan stared in confusion. "You going to tell me what this is all about?"

"Zach said you had it bad for the little romance author next door. I just assumed you wanted to sample and get her out of your system. Didn't think you were actually serious about her."

"I'm not *serious,* guys," Evan contended, trying to contain his embarrassment.

Zach grinned. "You'd never care if it was just someone you wanted to get *out of your system*. Right?"

Evan sighed. "Guys, it's not like that. Grace is a nice girl. I don't want dickheads like Ben and Ryan bothering her all night."

"Sure."

"You're one to talk, Josh. You still obsessing over Red?"

"Don't call her that," Josh grumbled, pointing to Zach with an intimidating look.

"You let Evan call her that."

Josh puffed out his chest, crossing his arms. "Because I know he's not lusting after her the way you are."

"Dude, I haven't even met her, you prick."

"What woman doesn't Zach lust over, Josh?" Evan chuckled as he put down his empty glass on the bar and stood up. "Anyway, just look after her, guys. I might be pulled away and I don't want idiots bothering her."

"Like they're bothering her now?" Zach tipped his chin to the other side of the bar. "Grace's been here at least twenty minutes. I thought you knew that though."

Evan looked up to see Grace talking with the two guys he knew would be swarming around her like bees to honey. Benjamin Taylor and Ryan Dane were chomping at the bit to get to her. She was too gorgeous not to have men want her. That skirt was the shortest thing he'd seen, and her legs were creamy and shapely. Those platform boots were something else, and he wanted nothing more than to have them wrapped around his body.

He'd be damned if he was going to let Ben or Ryan get their hands on her. Sure, she was stunning, but his interest in her was more than that. He appreciated Grace in a way those twats never would. She twisted his insides, tested him not only physically but intellectually. She seemed attentive to who he actually was, what he had to say, and how he said it. Which was more than any other woman wanted from him.

"She doesn't look all that bothered, Evan," Josh muttered.

"What's she doing talking to those assholes?" Evan grumbled as he watched Ryan give her a drink. He cursed under his breath as Ben touched her forearm. Evan's hands had already curled into fists, his nails digging in almost to the point of drawing blood. She turned, her ponytail brushing over her shoulder. Ryan clasped a lock of her hair and felt it between his fingers.

Evan then saw Grace push his hand away as she knocked back the alcohol in a flash. He felt his heart pounding in his ears, and swore his blood pressure was climbing. Brazenly, he skyrocketed toward her and put his arm around her shoulder. "There you are, sweetie pie."

"Evan, hi! I'm talking to Ben and Ryan. They're so nice."

"Guys, I'm stealing my date for the night. If you'll excuse us." He swept her through the crowd, and felt her push away unsteadily.

"Date? So tonight's a date?"

"No. I told you it's a date when I kiss you, babe."

"Then let's kiss twice and get it over with."

He caught her as she swayed. "Whoa, you drunk already, Gracie Lynn?"

"I'm not drunk. Just a little buzzed. I thought there would be food here so I didn't eat." She waved her hand in dismissal. "Anyway, I was talking to them, Evan. Don't try to stake your claim on me tonight if this isn't a date. I'm here to let loose and have fun."

"You don't party often, do you?" He kept his arm around her, craving to have her near.

"Why?" She looked up at him and teetered on her shoes, her body leaning into his.

"Because you should always make sure the drink comes directly from the bartender. What if the guy buying you the drink put something in it? Party safely, Grace."

She chuckled, pressing her face into his chest, "Okay, Dad." Oh, Jesus, she was definitely on the way to getting sauced. Her giggles kept coming and her speech was slightly incoherent. "Ouch, that vest is hard." She rubbed her forehead and looked him over. "You look hot in that SWAT getup, by the way. What do you guys do? You think to yourselves, 'What costume could I wear to make myself look even hotter than I already am? Oh, I know! Let me dress like a SWAT guy and BOOM - sexy.' It's not really fair, you know that?"

He smiled at her confession. "You girls do the same exact thing, Miss Clark. Your little skirt and those shoes almost gave me a…"

"Raging hard-on?" She laughed and stumbled in his arms, her face achingly close.

"I was going to say heart attack." She wasn't wrong though. He could feel her body pressing against him, and she was so lush and warm. She also smelled like whatever flowery perfume she spritzed on that delicate, white skin and looked like a—

"What the fuck are you wearing, Gracie?" He eyed her olive green shirt and stepped back. He pushed her leather jacket aside and pointed to the symbol near her shoulder. "Are you kidding me?"

Her thick, black eyelashes fluttered at him innocently as her lips smirked. "What?"

"You dressed as Captain Kirk?"

"Live well, and prosper, fool!" She threw the Vulcan sign up and snorted a laugh.

"You dressed as the wrong Captain, pumpkin."

"I can't help it. That Chris Pine guy is hot. Do you know him? Can you introduce me?"

Evan growled, hating the idea of her crushing on someone, anyone, else. "You did this on purpose, Grace Lynn Clark. Just to piss me off." She continued to laugh, his frown suddenly breaking into a wide grin from the sound of it.

"Okay, okay, I might've dressed this way to rile you up. It totally worked, didn't it?" Her chocolate eyes looked at him brightly as she chewed on her bottom lip. Her legs wobbled and her body kept pressing in all the right areas. It was making his brain malfunction.

"In more ways than one, Gracie." He thought about that hard-on she mentioned earlier. Her skirt was torturing him as his mind pictured the treasures that lay under it. He contemplated whether she went commando or wore bikini bottoms, perhaps a thong. His eyes felt hungry as he stared at her lips.

"That's Captain Kirk to you, Captain Abrams." She gave him a mock salute.

"Captain Kirk doesn't wear a skirt, baby cakes, and he's not my type."

"Neither am I, Evan." She hiccupped as her friends made their way over.

"Grace, there you are!" Jaime called as Dean and Marla followed.

"Where the hell did you go?" Marla asked, her hands resting on her hips. Evan chuckled knowing the pose wasn't on purpose, but all she needed was to twirl and the look would be complete. He contemplated asking about her invisible jet.

Grace instantly held herself up and roamed her hands over the edge of her skirt to make sure nothing was on display. "I was talking to those hotties, Ben Taylor and Ryan Dane, but SWAT guy here interrupted us."

"He totally cock-blocked her," Zach proclaimed, walking up with drinks in his hands. He passed one to Evan, but his friend declined, more interested in keeping his focus on Grace. They all said their hellos and were introduced.

"I wanna meet Ben and Ryan!" Jaime yelled as Dean

gave her a glare.

"Only if I can meet Kara Jones," Dean replied.

Jaime rolled her eyes then looked to Evan. "Think you can get the whole cast to Jake's party? We'd love you forever."

Evan laughed. "Don't know about that, but I'll see what I can do."

"See? I just like this guy, Grace. He's so cool!" Jaime tugged Grace to move closer to Evan. He knew Jaime's maneuvers, and wasn't objecting to her plot to hook them up. "So, when is Evan's and Grace's first date happening? Evan, you know, Grace hasn't been on a date in—"

"Subject change!" Grace held her hands in the air, interrupting Jaime's revelation that Evan was more than curious to hear. "Zach, I'll take that extra drink, as long as it's not your iced tea."

"Done, babe. Here you go." Zach handed her the glass and winked. Evan shot him an odious glare discerning Grace didn't need more alcohol.

"Gracie, watch your intake," Evan warned.

"Oh, that's right, I forgot." She shimmied to Zach and held the glass up to him. "Take a sip first, Zach."

"Why?"

"Because Dad over here told me to get it straight from the bartender in case it was laced with something from the guy who bought me the drink. So, my question for you Zach is—are you trying to poison Evan?"

The group laughed as Marla looked over to Josh. "He has tried before," Josh joked.

"With what? Carbs?" Marla smirked as Josh eyed

her up and down. "Did your super-strict trainer over here not allow for drinking tonight, Evan?"

"He's not that bad. There's an exception for Halloween."

Evan saw Josh's eyes flash with irritation. "I'm not that much of a dick, Supergirl," Josh growled toward her.

"I'm Wonder Woman, Doc. I see your costume took no effort whatsoever." She glanced to his plain white lab coat and stethoscope, then to the bottle in his hand. "Water? No mean green juice tonight? Protein shake?"

"He had that earlier along with his chicken and broccoli," Zach teased as Josh kept his eyes on the bold woman in front of him.

Grace turned her head to his friend, eyeing him up and down. "What exactly is your costume, Zach?"

"One that wouldn't piss Evan off, Grace," Zach answered, knowing her tactic.

"You're Justin Timberlake, right?" Dean guessed, pointing to his outfit. "The suit-and-tie bit."

Zach straightened his gray tie against his crisp white shirt. "No, I was going for Christian Grey."

The women groaned, and Marla pointed out. "Seriously? You did it all wrong, Zach!"

"I thought this suit was slick." He ran his hand through his wavy dark hair. "No?"

Grace stood before Zach and handed her drink to Jaime. She reached up and began to adjust his tie. It took all of Evan's will to not wish he were Zach at that moment being undressed by her small hands. More than that, the thought of Grace reading the erotic novel made his skin prickle with thoughts of what they could do together. "First, let the tie hang a bit like that. Second, you should've brought a riding crop, handcuffs, and a blindfold as props. And third…"

Her hands began to muss up Zach's hair. "You've got awesome hair, you just need it a little more tussled. Unfortunately for you, he had copper-colored hair, and yours is dark." She bit her bottom lip as she worked on him, undoing his top shirt button. She stepped back. "Okay, so you look more like Jim Halpert from *The Office*, but a girl might just be drunk enough to fall for it."

Everyone laughed, including Evan. She swayed a bit and Evan stepped beside her, holding her steady against his body.

"You shouldn't have brought that bottle of whiskey on the shuttle," Jaime scolded. "You're getting so plastered, Grace."

"I'm not drunk, guys. Besides, Marla told me to bring it."

Marla dismissed her with a shake of her hand. "You're such a tattle tit."

She took her drink back in her hands from Jaime and swigged the rest of it. "I need another one. I'm celebrating."

Josh asked, "What are we celebrating?"

"Grace finished *Waiting on Lust*," Marla answered.

"Why would she wait on lust? You have to act on that, Grace," Zach tried to joke.

"Her book, moron," Evan corrected him. "Congrats, Grace!" Everyone in the group cheered.

"I think that calls for dancing!" Grace yelled as they went toward the small stage set up with a local band playing. She dragged Evan behind her as they all went toward the packed dancefloor.

She stumbled and he reached out, his hands clasping her hips as she turned. "Seriously, SWAT man, I'm okay."

He smiled, letting his arms wrap around her. He pulled her against him and let his lips touch her ear. "You can't walk for shit in those boots, Gracie Lynn."

The music was so loud it was difficult to hear and all he wanted was to be in an intimate spot with her, kissing her, hearing her whimper in pleasure. He could feel the silk of her hair brush against his cheek as he leaned down. Her arms wrapped around his neck as she let their bodies grind to the music.

He could feel every inch of her pressed against him, and it was heaven and hell combined. His hands roamed her body, one moving to the small dip of her back as he tugged her closer to him. Their legs entwined as the beat picked up and the lights twirled. He was getting lost to her until she almost fell. His hands held her up.

"I'm dizzy!" she yelled near his ear.

He nodded and told Grace to wait as he strode to Marla and informed her he was taking Grace back home. Marla looked to her friend and nodded, giving a thumbs up as she danced with Ryan.

"Come on, Gracie. We're heading home."

"Why?"

"Because you're drunk."

"So?"

They careened through the crowd and made their way to the shuttle as he texted Zach and Josh. "Slow down, daddy long legs, I said I'm dizzy."

"Sorry, babe. How much did you have to drink anyway?" he asked as he held her against him.

She shrugged her shoulders. "I don't know. Twenty."

"Twenty drinks?"

"Ounces. Possibly. Is that a lot?" She joked as he led her toward the shuttle. "Honestly, I don't really know what I'm saying."

He helped her sit and grabbed a bottle of water that they had purposefully stocked. "Here, drink this."

"You're so prepared, agent." She grinned as she attempted to twist the cap off. "I can't do it." She threw the bottle at him and laughed as he easily opened the top for her. "Thanks. You're so strong. And manly." He watched her with his eyes alight as she gulped the water and then continued. "Do you purposefully wear those tight shirts? Like so you can show off those hunky muscles?"

He froze as she ran her hand over his bicep. He loved feeling her touch and couldn't imagine it ever stopping. "I don't think about what I wear most of the time. I have clothes that get sent to me."

"Pshhhh…lucky bastard. You have money to shop but get everything free." Her wandering eyes moved from his eyes to his mouth. She gently let her fingertip trail over his bottom lip. "And you're really handsome, but you must be told that all the time. All those women chasing you."

His smile grew as he grabbed her hand and kissed her palm. "It's nicer when it's said by someone you care about."

She drew closer to him, her breathing amplified as she stared at his lips. "You always know what to say, Mr. Matthews. So suave, so perfect."

He had no words, because she was on him in a second when she grasped the back of his neck and pulled him close. Nothing existed around him except her. Not the music that filled the busy streets, nor the rattling of the engine that drove them home. God, if he were drunk this whole situation would be fair. They'd both be inebriated and chalk it up to a crazy night. But this wasn't just anyone. This was the girl who had invaded his every single waking thought for the past month.

Her mouth roamed his, and for a moment, he got caught up; her soft lips tasting of whiskey and honey. The sweetness invading him was something he couldn't begin to compare. His body was beyond aching for this woman as her hands traveled over the nape of his neck, but he knew this wasn't the way he wanted it to be. This meant more to him than it should. Finally, he found his raspy voice as she parted for just a second to catch her breath. "Gracie, not this way, honey."

"Yes, this way." She whimpered against his lips and he drew back. It felt beyond torturous and unnatural to pull away from her. He let his hands cup her face, his thumbs brushing against her cheeks. Her skin was like rose petals, softer and even more beautiful than he had imagined. He caught her pouting as she tried to jerk away.

"Grace, no. Look at me."

"I'm not your type, Evan." She twisted her body to look out the window and rested her forehead on it.

It had been twice that night that he heard it from her mouth, and it upset him that she thought so. "Yes, you are, Grace. You're precisely my type. That's why I don't want to continue kissing you when you're not fully coherent."

Stillness pervaded the space as he exhaled. "You have your stuff here?" He rose and looked around to the seats nearby and spotted a brown leather bag. He knew it had to be hers, it was just her style. He picked it up and moved back, sitting down beside her again. "Grace, is this your purse?"

He waited for her answer. Great, she was playing the silent game with him. "Grace." He shook her shoulder, and realized she was fast asleep. Sitting back, he studied her and laughed under his breath as he then dug inside the purse for her keys. This woman was just too much for his heart to handle.

Chapter Eight

Grace attempted to pry her eyes open, but they instantly shut again, feeling heavy and dry. Her throat was on fire, and her nose was stuffy. She gave a slight cough, but groaned as her throbbing head informed her how that was a mistake.

"Shit," she creaked and shifted her sore body. The muscles felt tight as she twisted and turned, trying to tuck the pillow behind her neck. Sleeping forever seemed like the perfect solution for her hangover from hell.

"Morning, cupcake."

The deep voice startled Grace and she sat up way too quickly. "Ouch, fucking hell, shit-fuck." Clasping her head, she stared at the man who sat in the corner of her room on her recently reupholstered lounge chair. His feet rested on the footstool she matched to it. He rested with a book in his hands and looked positively delicious. *Did he look that great last night too?* Grace barely recalled.

She tugged on the ponytail holder that had kept her hair in place and yanked it out along with stray strands of hair. Her hands worked through her aching scalp as all of it tumbled down. She groaned and fell back. "What are you doing here, Matthews?"

"Making sure you wouldn't vomit in your sleep,

Captain Kirk."

"Shit." She grimaced in humiliation. "God, it feels like Thor is hitting my head with his fucking hammer." She propped herself up in a sitting position against her headboard. She'd never fall back asleep now. "Did you see me throw up?"

"You didn't throw up, Grace." Evan moved beside her and pointed to the nightstand. Grace grabbed the water and gulped. "But you sure kept me entertained."

"What? Why?" Her mind swirled, trying to figure out what happened. "Did we? We didn't…"

"We're still clothed, doll."

Grace shut her eyes in relief. "Thank God!"

"Don't sound too relieved."

"Well, that's the last thing I'd want to happen."

"You do wonders for my ego, you know that?" He kept his eyes on her, a smile playing over his lips like he had a secret. "Never seen your hair down before, Grace."

She closed her eyes, not wanting to imagine if she looked as horrible as she felt. "I don't give a flying fuck if I look like shit right now, Evan, so go ahead and make fun all you want."

His husky laugh still did things to her body even though she wasn't up for any type of silly banter. "You've got a dirty mouth on you, Gracie. Who knew?"

"Only when I feel like dying. What happened? Where is everyone? Where's my phone?" She glanced around and noticed her boots sitting neatly near her dresser. He had taken them off of her? Took care of her. A wave of degradation coursed through her body. She never lost control, especially around a man, and not one like him. She prayed she hadn't said anything stupid, but judging from the look on Evan's face, something must have happened.

"It's here." He handed it to her from the nightstand and Grace blushed at the oversight. She needed coffee to get her brain working properly. "Don't worry, I've kept up with Marla and Jaime."

"How?"

"They came back to the house after I put you to bed. They left when I promised I'd watch over you."

"Bed?" Grace tried to reconnect the dots slowly. "I passed out?"

"On the bus." They remained quiet as she tried to think back. For some reason she had flashes of Evan's lips—of a kiss—but she hadn't wanted to assume that they actually shared something that passionate. It had to have been a dream. "What do you remember, Grace?"

She shook her head as she tried to grasp at memories. "I remember talking to Ben and Ryan. I think Ben was supposed to call me for something."

"Yeah, let's not worry about him," Evan said, trying to change the subject. "What else?"

"Oh, you were pissed off because of my costume. And was Zach dressed as Christian Grey?"

They both laughed, but Grace felt a surge of nausea hit. "I might be sick." She fumbled from the covers and ran toward her master bathroom, barely making it to the toilet.

Evan rushed over, standing beside her, and pulled her hair back as she heaved out the contents of her stomach. God, she was puking in front of Evan Matthews. "Sorry, shit."

"It's okay, you'll probably feel better now." He rubbed her back then handed her a wet wipe from the case on top of the toilet. He waited, holding her hair as she wiped her mouth. A few minutes passed before he spoke softly. "Can you stand?"

She nodded as he pulled her up with firm hands. "I'll get you some fresh clothes and you can take a bath. Is it alright for me to go through your dresser, Grace?"

Grace sat on the edge of her tub and nodded in exhaustion. She heard him rummaging through her dresser, but at this point she didn't care. Her body felt feverish and she wanted to just feel normal again. He walked in and set a pile of things near the sink. He started the water in her claw foot tub and checked the temperature. "Shout out if you need something."

She nodded again, feeling enough energy to muster a small grin. "Thanks, Evan."

He closed the door behind him and Grace stared at the running water and bubbles. *He added bubbles.* Butterflies were instantly being blamed on her current stomach issues. Grace approached her sink, reaching for her toothbrush. Glancing up, she gasped in fright. Smudges of mascara painted her lids black, making her look like a raccoon. Her hair was a teased and ratted mess, and her pallid complexion made for one hell of a scary post-Halloween look. She brushed her teeth and tried to construct all that happened, and for some reason the taste of Evan's lips kept coming to mind.

Grace took her time in the bath, dunking her head in

the hot, sudsy water and letting her muscles unwind. A light knock took her out of her secret daydream. The one of a delicious kiss she couldn't stop envisioning with the very man who opened her bathroom door.

"Hey." Evan stood with a cup in his hand. "Can I come in?"

Grace gave a hesitated nod, hoping there were enough bubbles to cover her body. He lowered himself to the edge of the tub. His eyes were a beautiful cobalt, and she focused on those instead of that mouth she kept lusting over. He still donned the tight green shirt and camo pants from his costume last night, and scruff covered his perfect jaw.

"I brought you some ginger tea."

Reaching up, she brushed her wet hand against his and felt that familiar jolt in her stomach whenever their skin touched. Despite how awful she felt, those sensations of craving him hadn't subsided. "Where did you get ginger tea?"

"I asked Zach to pick some up."

"Oh, God, he didn't make it, did he?"

Evan laughed and shook his head. "I hope not."

"Making him work for his money though?"

"I'm supposed to pay him? Oops."

She chuckled, but felt the throbbing in her temples and winced.

"Yeah, you had quite a bit to drink last night, little one."

"Never again." Upon opening her eyes, she caught him grazing her legs that peaked out of the water. Clasping her thighs together was the immediate response, along with making sure suds covered the proper places. She slowly moved more of her body back under the water and tried to push away the instant heat beginning to creep between her lady bits.

He moved his eyes away and Grace saw him swallow as he shifted his body. "I'm going to head home, but I want to take a look at your car and work on it today."

"You don't have to, Evan." The tea instantly made her stomach settle, and she took another sip in appreciation.

He leaned over and brushed his lips on her forehead. "Rest up, Grace. Eat something. Toast and eggs. That'll help."

Relief came flooding over her as he shut the door behind him. Grace could exhale the oxygen she held in her lungs. *A kiss on the forehead?* What was she, twelve? That was it. Whatever attraction Grace assumed Evan held toward her, it all fled out the window like a gust of winter wind. How could he possibly be attracted to a woman who not only got completely trashed, but also barfed in his presence?

Wasn't that what she wanted though? She kept nudging him over to friend territory. He had finally caught on and took it. Of course, she busted him staring at her legs, but he was a typical man. There wasn't a doubt in her mind that he'd want sex. But that was something Grace was unwilling to give him. She should've admitted that from the start. Been upfront with him like with all the others.

The concern was that she enjoyed his company more

than she had anticipated, and that selfish part of her wanted him to stick around. If she confessed to him what she always told other men, he would do exactly what they always did. Drop her like yesterday's newspaper and never look back. No matter how much she prepared for that to happen with Evan, the action of it would hurt much more than the idea.

~

Grace felt renewed after her bath and eating some food. She walked over to the window and peeked between the open blinds to see Evan hunched over the engine of her car. He looked gorgeous, his hair gleaming in the late afternoon sun that broke through the gloomy sky. Muscles moved tautly through his plain white shirt, and his jeans sat low on his hips. Big hands moved around the engine with expertise as he shifted tools around with precision.

Grace grabbed a bottle of water and walked to him, watching as he poured in windshield wiper fluid. Even though the temperature had dropped a little, beads of sweat had formed on his temples, and she let herself gaze at him with awe. He really was quite handsome. Part of her wished she had the guts to tell him that.

"Enjoying the view?" He looked up at her with a slight smirk.

She held out the water as he stood straight, wiping his hands on a small towel. "It's alright, I guess."

"Not what you said last night." He winked as her eyes popped open and he grabbed the bottle.

"What did I say last night?"

He ignored her question. Evan began to gulp down the water quickly, and Grace stared fixedly as his throat bobbed. She could see dampness on the corded muscles of his neck, and she suddenly wanted to lick him. She trailed her eyes down his shirt, abs showing slightly through the material.

"I fixed some issues with the air conditioning. Hopefully the sealant will keep the holes in the hose closed for a while. I replaced the spark plugs and PCV valve. Put some new windshield wipers and some fluid in there and changed your oil."

"Is that all? I mean, I was expecting a new paint job too."

Evan gave a boisterous laugh as he lowered the hood. "That's tomorrow, doll." He handed the keys to her and leaned against the car. His arms bulged from the sleeves of his shirt and she couldn't help staring at him. "Glad you're feeling better, Gracie."

She looked away and tried to hide her smile. "What did I say last night, Evan?"

"You complimented my big guns." He raised both arms up and flexed making her burst out with laughter. "You did. Totally serious."

Her small hands squeezed his biceps. "Hmm. I must've been pretty wasted if I thought these were worth praising."

"You're so full of shit right now, Grace." He grabbed her wrists and tugged her forward letting his hands wrap around her waist as she braced her palms on his broad chest. Her eyes stayed down, looking at the fabric that separated them from the sexual tension that overwhelmed her senses. She could feel his breathing pick up, her hair ruffling from the gentle breeze. Every receptor was heightened as her skin prickled with awareness.

When her gaze met his, she felt something familiar. "Evan?"

"Yeah?" His lips were getting dangerously close.

"Did this happen last night?"

A gentle smile played on his mouth as he pulled her closer. He bent forward and Grace shivered in anticipation. Should she let this happen? Who was she kidding? There was no way she could stop. So much for the friend zone. Closing her eyes she awaited his kiss.

Instead, his lips touched her ear as he whispered, "I'll never tell."

Grace pushed herself off of him, rolling her eyes and headed toward her door. "Goodbye, Mr. Matthews. Thanks for fixing my car."

"You're welcome, sweets. I'll see you later."

She turned and gave him a final salute. *Keep that promise, Grace.*

Chapter Nine

The cold and rainy November day proved to be daunting for the cast and crew of *The Ending Series*. The weather fit the scene that was being filmed—the cloudy exterior, the consistent rainfall, and the muddy terrain—but it made for a grueling shoot. Evan's fight scenes were extensive and brutal.

He was aching and tired, and was constantly trying to hide the semi hard-on he had whenever he thought about Grace. She was driving him senseless. He even felt a consuming need to have her all for himself. Ben and Ryan had asked if he was dating her, and Evan had no idea what to say. What he did know was he didn't want her to date anyone else. But he also knew she was wanting to take it slow, and he was willing to be patient. Flat out, he wanted her, badly. And the more he got to know her, the more he wanted.

Evan stripped from his constricting costume and took the time to hang it up in his trailer. He knew it wasn't necessary, but his mother always taught him to clean up after himself even if he had others to do it for him. He walked over to the shower and washed off the day's work.

He grabbed his sides and schedule left for him, ready to head home and relax. The gloomy weather did nothing to appease his grumpy mood and when his phone rang he groaned and debated whether to answer.

"Yeah?"

"Hey, Evan. Got a moment, buddy?"

"Sure." His voice didn't sound as enthusiastic as his agent's. Mike had worked with Evan since he'd first arrived in Hollywood over fifteen years ago. He'd helped him rise through the ranks. Mike's decisions weren't always the best, but Evan trusted him.

"I got this great script I'm sending. Tell Zach to print it out for you. It's going to be big."

Evan ran his hand through his wet hair as he put his Bluetooth on and walked toward his car. "For directing or acting?"

"Why do you even bother asking?"

Evan heaved a sigh as he turned on the ignition and made his way out of the studios where filming took place. "Mike, come on, man. I'm looking for a directing gig."

"You have to strike while you're hot, Evan. This is a John Whitford film. It could mean an Oscar win for you."

"You said that about *Meet Me in Moonlight.*"

"And you were nominated. You won a Golden Globe." Evan stayed quiet as his agent continued. "Come on, Evan. It's a solid script. They're willing to pay you fourteen mil."

"You know I don't care about the money." He had enough money to last him over three lifetimes.

"You will when you're mentioned on Forbes List of one of the highest paid actors in the world." Evan scoffed as Mike was insistent. "Evan, the *Ending Series* will be over. Don't you want to show your diversity in the roles you pick?"

"I thought I did already. I want to direct, Mike. And if I do take on a role I want something more independent."

Evan's mind went over what it would mean to win an Academy Award. Most actors dreamed of winning one. It was never something he aspired to like some actors he had met. Sure, an award would be nice, but with that gold statue came added pressures, expectations, and loss of privacy. The bigger he got, the smaller his world became.

"Evan, I got you Captain Drew Abrams, and you're glad you took it."

He thought that over and knew it was true. Without the push from his agent and the persistence of the studio heads wanting Evan, he'd still be fighting for the roles he wanted instead of having the luxury of choosing. "Where's this thing filming?"

"Atlanta."

Evan moaned. He hated the humidity and heat, but put up with it when having to be on location. "When's principle begin?"

"Principle photography starts in May."

He finished filming in Austin around March or April. That would be a quick transition, but maybe it would be for the best. Evan still hadn't found the script he wanted to direct, and having a project lined up meant he would have something on his plate instead of nothing. "Send the script. I'll read it and call you to set up a meeting with John if I like it."

"Great. I know you'll love it."

Evan threw his headset off and continued his commute in the Austin traffic—one of the small downsides to staying in the quirky city that was beginning to grow on him.

When Evan pulled up to his driveway, he saw Grace's garage open. He debated being around her at that moment. A shit day made for a shit attitude, and he didn't want her to see his cranky side. Besides, pictures played back in his head of the way she looked in that damn bathtub, and if any man had seen her the way he had, he'd win an award for restraining himself from taking that sweet mouth. Instead he gave her a chaste kiss on the forehead, knowing full well that wasn't the right time to make his move.

He walked over and peered inside, listening to her as she belted along to Van Morrison's "Into the Mystic." He crossed his arms and leaned against the wall, a smile sneaking on his face as he studied her hips swaying to the beat. Her hair was bunched at the nape of her neck and a red bandana was tied around the top of her head. She wore those old, paint-stained overalls that were two sizes too big with a long sleeved Henley underneath. Worn-in boots and yellow working gloves completed her look as she swung to the music and sanded the top of an old desk sitting in the middle of her garage.

The day from hell was instantly forgotten. All Evan could think about was how perfect the words to "Tupelo Honey" fit Grace as it started to play, and how he wanted to hold her in his arms and dance with her. Kissing that angel was something Evan had to make happen. And soon.

Grace turned and yelped as they caught each other's eye. "Evan, you can't creep up on me like that. How long have you been there?"

He smiled and approached. "Not long enough. You started working on the desk without me, Gracie Lynn. I'm hurt."

She put the sandpaper down and wiped her forehead with the back of her wrist. "Well, we haven't done much in the way of cashing in on that bet, so I figured we'd drop it."

"Hah, nice try, beautiful." He stood beside her and looked at the desk. "Okay, tell me where to start."

Grace began digging through a box sitting on some wire shelving. She tossed a pair of gloves toward him and then brought him an apron. He scrunched his nose. "You want me to wear that?"

"Unless you don't care about your clothes."

He removed his leather jacket and placed his keys and phone aside along with the apron. "I can always work naked for you, Grace."

"Although I would just *love* to see you sand my desk completely in the nude, the neighbors may not approve."

He chuckled at her sarcasm and put the gloves on. He then grabbed the sandpaper and put it over the completed desktop. She stopped him. "Whoa. Slow down, Hollywood. You'll work on the drawers. Most of it I already did with the power sander, but we're just catching the intricate areas I might've missed." She pulled a drawer toward him and motioned for him to sit. She followed and dragged another drawer towards her, settling it between her legs as he copied her position.

"You want to go against the grain. Not too hard, we don't want to get down to the wood completely. We're going to stain it."

Evan watched as her hands operated and he caught on quickly. He let himself get lost in the work and began to enjoy himself, listening to the sounds of ol' Louis Armstrong fill the air. It was nice to use his hands and feel creative, like he was doing something useful.

"When did you start doing this type of stuff, Grace?"

"Collecting antiques or fixing them?" She finished her drawer and grabbed another. She was much better at this than he was.

"Both."

"A little after college. I went to the City-Wide Garage Sale they hold at the Palmer Events Center, and just loved it. The first piece I refurbished was that hall tree at the entrance of my house. It's fun and keeps me busy."

"That chair I sat on in your room, did you fix that one too?"

"Yeah, I reupholstered that one. It was pretty old. The wood on it was in great condition. I stuffed the cushions and fixed the foot stool to match."

"It was a damn comfortable chair."

Grace paused her work and stared at him. "Did you stay there all night?"

He grinned, hoping his answer would give him some brownie points with her. "I did. I started nodding off a few times, but kept myself busy."

"What were you reading anyway?"

"*Jane Eyre.*"

Grace laughed. "You serious? You read *Jane Eyre?*"

"Yeah. What's wrong with that?"

Grace shrugged. "Just surprised. You don't seem like a Charlotte-Brontë-type reader to me."

Evan moved the drawer aside and grabbed another and continued his work. "I'm not. But it was there, and I saw you underlined all your favorite parts."

He saw the flush on her cheeks as she bowed her head, concentrating on the task at hand. Glancing around the garage, a few other things caught Evan's eye. An easel and canvases were set up against the wall. Most of them were blank, but one canvas had an unfinished landscape. "You paint, Grace?"

She hummed an answer as she followed his gaze to the supplies. "I haven't had much time to focus on it lately. I need to buy more paints and new brushes."

"That's my new favorite thing about you."

She chuckled, that rosy hue appearing on her skin again. "That I paint?"

"Yeah. Not everyone can do that. You're very creative." The sounds of Nat King Cole filled the garage space and Evan found himself in awe of this woman. She knew what her passions were and worked on them without apology or fear. "Do you sell your work?"

"When I actually complete a painting, yes. I'll go to the Blue Genie Art Bazaar or sell online."

Grace stood and began to reach for the can of wood stain in the corner. Evan followed and placed his palm on the desk. "And this desk? Where's this going to sit?"

"I'm going to sell it."

"What?" His voice dropped in disappointment as he took off his gloves. "Our first project together and you're selling it?"

"We can't all be paid millions for our work, Evan. Gotta pay those student loans off somehow."

He unexpectedly felt his profession was unfair and absurd. Here he was getting paid an obscene amount of money for memorizing lines while Grace put so much energy in working to make ends meet. Her eyes were on him in a flash. "Don't you dare, Evan Matthews."

His eyes crinkled in confusion. "What?"

"Don't feel bad. I was teasing you."

"I know, but it is outrageous what I get paid. I feel guilty sometimes."

He exhaled in frustration and saw the gleam of inspiration in Grace's chocolate eyes. She tugged her gloves off and moved near him. Her voice was firm. "Your work is just as important as anyone else's. People are happy when they see your movies. They get transported and escape their lives. It's just like reading a book. You deserve your success."

Evan shrugged unconvinced, but Grace grabbed his shoulders, turning him toward her. "Evan, you're a very gifted actor. There's no reason for you not to get paid well. If it wasn't you getting the money the studio heads would get it all. And why should they when you're the one selling the film? You give up your privacy, your vulnerability, and all of yourself on that movie screen. It's your art. Don't ever feel guilty for that."

This woman eased his concerns in a moment,

making him feel as though everything was right in the world. He could no longer hold back. He dropped his head to hers and let his lips descend, taking the sweetness of her mouth to his and demanding it without regret. His hands cradled her face gently, his thumbs caressing her cheeks. The kiss was passionate and slow. He took his time, pacing himself under the circumstances.

His tongue gently slipped between her lips and a moan escaped her under the sensual movements. His hands motivated, he pushed her bandana off and tangled his fingers in her soft brown hair. Their urgency grew and they savored and drank each other in as she fisted his shirt at his waist. He had her, but only for a flash of a moment until he felt her body tighten.

He let his lips withdraw, taking a tiny last taste before moving back. He studied her as she tried to get her bearings. Her forehead rested against his chest and he kissed her crown as their breathing steadied and his heart rate decelerated. "You alright?"

"No," she whispered and moved away. Her back was now to him as she grabbed and fixed her bandana and Evan wondered if shit was about to hit the fan.

Instead of saying anything, however, she disregarded what happened and moved toward the can of wood stain and began to pry it open. The heat between them had left and was replaced with uncertainty and hesitance. "Grace?"

She grabbed two large brushes and handed one to him. A tiny smile strained on her lips, but Evan knew a million thoughts were running through her brain as they were his. "Let's finish this desk, Captain."

He watched as she dipped the brush in and began to buff the top of the wood. Her eyes stayed down, but her breathing was labored and her cheeks flushed. He started on the other side of the desk following the same direction she went. He cleared his throat after some time passed and Nat King Cole transitioned into James Taylor.

"We're not going to talk about what just happened, cupcake?"

Grace looked up at him looking like a deer caught in headlights. The expression on her face changed from fright to a mock smile. "Like what a good kisser you are? I'm sure you've been told that by many girls already."

"Grace…"

"It was a kiss, Evan. It was sweet and I enjoyed it." She shifted to a kneeling position at the side of the desk, her arm swishing the brush quickly over the wood. "Guess that's one date down." She stopped and winked at Evan.

"Not a date."

"You said when you kissed me it was considered a date."

"Two parts of the bet can't be cashed in at the same time." He would find any and every excuse possible to extend spending time with her. He felt her trying to push away from him. Her defenses were up and she was trying to pretend that kiss meant nothing, when it certainly meant something. "This is the 'refurbishing the desk' bet. The date thing is separate."

"Now you're just making up silly rules that weren't even discussed."

"You seem hell-bent on getting my payment over with," Evan commented as he moved toward the back of the desk. "You wanna go to Boston with me for Thanksgiving?"

Grace chuckled. "I'm not going to Boston, Evan."

"Why not? You'd love it."

She peered over the desk to him and made a face of incredulity. "I don't need to go to Boston."

"Everyone needs to go to Boston."

"I think you've said that before. Maybe someday." She wanted the subject dropped, and he would oblige for the time being.

"I still want to read your memoir, Grace. How's it going with the writing?"

"Slow. Painstakingly slow."

Much like making you mine, he thought to himself. That kiss shook him to his core, but she wanted to discount whatever this thing was between them and he wasn't so sure he could. Grace Clark was changing something in him. He didn't know exactly what it was, but he knew he needed to find out.

They continued to chat until they had finished the staining process. Evan glanced out of the garage and twilight was setting into the night. Drizzle began to pick up to a heavy rain. Neither of them kept their eyes on each other for long, but he could sense her watching him when she thought he wasn't looking.

"Okay, now we wait to let the stain dry."

"For what, a day?"

Grace began to gather the brushes to wash. "Yeah, maybe more. Then I have to sand it again, then put the finish."

She put all the rags and gloves and masks into a plastic container for safety and shut it with the lid. He supposed she'd wash the paint brushes inside. "It's a lot of work."

"No shit. Why do you think I made that bet?" She yawned and stretched. "I'm ready for a hot shower."

"I can join you." He winked.

She squinted her eyes and punched his arm. "Nice try."

He caught her hand in his, the heat instantly climbing back between them as he hovered over her. His breath became weighty as he reached over and moved a stray lock of falling hair. "I really want to kiss you again, Gracie Lynn."

She gulped, her chest expanding and falling rapidly as her eyes widened. "I-I need to..." She took a step back and bumped into the shelving against the wall. She turned heading toward the door that led inside. "The brushes need to be washed before the stain dries. I should call it a night."

He tried to keep his laugh contained as she shucked her boots off on the doormat and set them aside. "Thanks for helping me with the desk, Evan."

He gathered his things. "I'll be seeing you, Grace."

Evan walked into the rain, letting the water stream down his body. What the hell was he going to do about this woman? How would he be able to leave Austin after that crazy kiss? Moreover, would he ever be able to kiss another woman without comparing it to the skittish neighbor who was beginning to hold his heart with a grip so tight it bordered on problematic? Evan knew he had to figure out a way to solve the issue once and for all.

Chapter Ten

Sunday morning began with Grace slogging out of bed and getting ready for the day with averseness. She slowly dressed in a black button-down blouse paired with matching jeans and kept her makeup subdued.

She made her way to the kitchen and sipped her coffee as she picked at a blueberry muffin she had made the night before. It usually wasn't this bad, but the guilt was present hardcore today, just like the recent nightmares. She snatched up her phone, double-checking it and seeing no messages. *Don't cry, Grace.* This was a normal occurrence; she should be used to it. It had already been long enough.

The doorbell chimed and startled Grace out of her desolate thoughts. Evan stood in her doorway wearing a black buttoned down shirt, similar to hers, and charcoal slacks. His face was free of stubble, his hair perfectly in place. Grace felt her heart speed up as she stood in front of him. He was so breathtakingly handsome. The last time she had seen him he knocked her back with that amazing kiss.

She had been kissed many times before, but she had never felt her heart beat to where she thought it was going to break through her chest. It shook her beyond anything, and she reminded herself a thousand times since then to be smart. *Lead with your head, not your heart,*

Grace.

"Hi, Gracie." His voice seemed rickety as he inhaled deeply. A bouquet of flowers were in his hands, and she looked at them questioningly. He followed her gaze down and handed them to her. "I came to see how you're doing today."

She wanted to smile, but couldn't muster up the frame of mind to do it. "Not that great, actually." Clasping the flowers, she raised them to her nose and inhaled the sweet scent. She thought it was nice that he was there to possibly ask her out, but the last thing she felt like doing was assembling the ability to say no to him.

"Jonquils," Evan murmured, caressing a yellow petal. "You'll have to look up the meaning for them."

Grace lowered the bouquet. "Or you could just tell me."

He stuffed his hands in his pockets and gave her a small smirk. "Where's the fun in that, Gracie Lynn?"

She finally broke a smile, and almost felt guilty for it. She was about to tell him she wasn't up for company when he began. "Hey listen, I know today is hard for you, cause it's your brother's birthday. I just came by to see if you needed anything."

"Wow, you remembered that?"

"Of course. It's important to you."

Grace's breath caught and pressure hit her chest like a freight train. Shock crossed her face as she understood. "The flowers? They're for Nathan?"

"Or for you. I'll go with you to see him, if you're up for company."

She stayed silent, looking at the bouquet in her hands. She tried to swallow the lump that stuck in her throat as she nodded. She pulled one flower out and placed it on the hall tree near the door. Turning, she looked at Evan. "Let's go see my brother."

~

Evan held Grace's hand as they walked toward Nathan's plot. The clouds had taken over the sun, making the day feel as gray and dreary as the emotions that simmered under the surface. He watched as the somber woman next to him stared at the headstone. Fake flowers sat in a small vase, and Grace kneeled on the ground, placing the real ones with the others. She rearranged them and dusted off debris around the memorial.

"Want some time alone?" he asked softly. She shook her head, but didn't turn to look at him. Evan lowered his body beside her. "Tell me something about him."

"He made me laugh all the time," she recollected old times and picked at the soft, rich, grass near her. Playing with a small blade in her hands, she gave a reminiscent smile. "He'd always take me to Kerbey Lane to eat on Thursday nights. We'd sit for hours and just talk about the dumbest things. His favorite band was Led Zeppelin. His favorite movie was *Ferris Bueller's Day Off*. He called me 'Stumpy' because he thought I was short."

Evan chuckled. "You're not that short."

"He just liked teasing me." After some time, she broke the long silence. "I haven't heard from my parents. Not that I would hear from them today anyway." Her voice trembled. "Sometimes I don't know what I miss more. Them or just the idea of them."

Evan watched as a tear spilled down the corner of her eye and his heart pitched. He wished he could take her pain away, make her feel better. He wiped the tear, but she tilted her head back. "I'm okay, it's been a long time."

"It doesn't matter how long it's been, Grace." He clasped her hand in his and gently caressed it as his eyes roamed her face. He could see she was determined to hold everything inside. "You don't always have to be strong. It's okay to miss what you had before you lost it." He reached into his pocket, handing her some tissues. "Here, wipe those boogers."

"Thanks," she breathed out a shaky laugh, pulling one apart to use over her eyes. "I don't know why I let it get to me. I'm sorry."

"Hey, don't apologize for having emotions, Gracie. It makes us remember we're alive." He moved her hair back over her ears. Cupping her face in his hands, he wiped away a few stray tears with his thumbs.

"You feel a bit better?"

She nodded as he stood and held his hand to help her up. They dusted the grass off their clothing, and she turned to stare at the gravestone once again. Grace whispered, "I miss you. And I'm trying to keep my promise. I love you."

Evan wouldn't pry, but he was curious as to the promise, and he hoped she would one day confide in him. It perplexed him how such a sweet woman would feel unloved, especially by her own parents. Grace had no idea how special she was, and with every moment Evan spent with her, her heart was opening his to the possibility of something deeper than he had ever experienced before.

~

Grace hadn't felt like doing much else and she was relieved when Evan drove her back home. He was so thoughtful to be there for her on the day she usually liked spending unaccompanied. Marla and Jaime called every year to check up on Grace, but this felt different. Evan was slowly getting her to open up, and that was something she rarely ever did. Being around him, she sensed generosity and a type of intimacy she hadn't felt with anyone before.

Evan going with her to the cemetery was as far as she could go with letting him in though. Grace couldn't forget what happened to Nathan. Grief was predominant, and she wasn't comfortable enough to confide in him completely. Not just yet.

How could she overlook that it all began by sleeping with her brother's friend? A guy who seemed just as nice as Evan. He turned out to be a wolf in sheep's clothes. Kyle spread vicious rumors about her and everyone in the school knew of her shame. All the girls hated her, thinking she was an easy whore. All the guys hit on her for the same reason. Words of hate were spray-painted on her locker; photo-shopped pictures were passed around the school. People she thought were her friends had deserted her. Waking up every day to go to that nasty place was torture. She was mercilessly teased and harassed to the point where she wanted to drop out.

Grace had begged her parents to take her out of school. She thought she couldn't take much more. Thomas Clark refused to let his daughter cower away. He forced her to deal with the repercussions of her actions. Her mother, Nancy Clark, was extremely humiliated by her daughter's behavior. Women began leaving Nancy out of volunteer functions and the ladies luncheons. Grace was an embarrassment to her. Luckily, her brother supported her. Nathan helped her pick up the pieces by teaching her that high school wouldn't last, and people would eventually forget. He made her realize that she was worthy of someone special. She deserved to be valued and loved, and she needed to wait for the right man to come along and see that in her.

If she had thought being dumped by Kyle Erikson and being shamed was the worst feeling in the world, it hadn't compared to the heartache she felt when Nathan died. She had tried to stop him. He was drinking though, and she was too small to hold him back. He had convinced her to go to that stupid party, saying she had a right to be there as anyone else. But she saw it all happen, as if in slow motion, and it was something that was seared in so deeply, it would never leave. The way the accident happened, the silence from everyone spoke volumes as she begged her brother to wake up, and yelled for someone to call an ambulance. They stood around staring, then most of them scattered like roaches when the police came to break up the party. The EMS fussed over Nathan's unconscious body and loaded him into the ambulance taking him away from her forever.

Grace wished for so long she could change things. Redo everything. But after years of therapy, she tried to comprehend that it was out of her control. The past needed to be left there, her brain had to hush the noise of the consuming guilt she had felt for so long. And she had finally come to peace, even without an apology from Kyle-fucking-Erikson, or the estrangement from her parents.

Her memoir went over all of it, and although she wanted to honor her brother's memory, she was terrified of letting anyone read it, let alone Evan Matthews. It made her vulnerable to him, voicing all the insecurities that ran through her head. There was a chance he'd reject her, and she was beginning to like him more than she wanted. Would he be willing to wait for her to be ready? Would he be patient enough for her to feel secure with him? Did she really *want* to be with him? These were all questions she didn't have answers to, and she wasn't sure she was willing to find out.

There was a knock on the door and Grace rose from her couch wiping her tears away. Too many emotions had given her a headache, and before she had known it, the evening had approached. She checked the peephole and gave a small smile.

"Zach? Hi."

He stood cradling several bags in his arms and made his way inside. "Delivery."

Grace walked with him to the kitchen as he placed

everything on the counter. A red cloth caught her eye as he unfolded it and walked to her dining table. He covered it nicely and placed out a candle and lit it up. He continued to dig in the bag, and took out a wine glass and nice dishes for one, including utensils.

"What is all this?"

He took out full Tupperware and began to serve the plates immediately. He gave a sweet smile. "Homemade dinner for the winner of the poker game. Compliments of Evan Jonathan Matthews."

She chuckled as he served soup into a bowl. "For starters, you have New England Clam Chowder. It's fresh, so you'll want to start eating now." It wasn't lost on her how his "r" words ended with an "h" in that Boston accent. She enjoyed listening to it until he paused and looked up at her. "You didn't eat already, did you?"

Covering her mouth, she tried to sustain her laugh. "No, I haven't."

"Good, come sit and get ready for a wicked feast." He placed a cloth napkin on her lap and then opened and served a glass of wine. "And then I'll set out the dinner course for you. You're having a Boston Lobster Roll. And for dessert you've got an awesome cannoli from Mike's Pastry, delivered all the way from Boston for you."

Grace was stunned at all the food as Zach took the time to take everything out of their containers and set them out. "Evan made all of this?"

"He did. I might've gone to buy the stuff, but he prepared it all on his own. Except for the cannoli, of course."

"I don't know what to say." She scooped up a spoonful of chowder and let it warm her throat. It was like Evan knew exactly what she needed to feel sane and happy. How could someone understand her with only having known her for such a short amount of time?

"Just let him know you liked it. But if you didn't, let him know that too so he doesn't cook again. He was a pain in the ass today."

She chuckled. "Aren't you guys going to eat too?"

Zach shook his head. "No, this is only for you. A bet is a bet. He said it hadn't included two people, just one."

"I really wish we had set up these rules all beforehand," Grace grumbled. "Why isn't he here?"

"He has a night shoot."

Her mouth opened in shock. "He's working all night?"

"Yeah," he stored the extra food in her refrigerator. He read her facial expression perfectly. "Don't worry, he'll be okay, Grace."

"I feel terrible. He was here so early today, and then he spent his time cooking?"

Zach smiled his cute, crooked smile, a small dimple on one side of his cheek, and began his trek out the door. He turned to face her, his mossy green eyes twinkling. "Maybe he thinks you're worth it."

Grace gulped as he made his way out the door. "Lock up, and don't wash the dishes. I'll come back for them in an hour."

She looked over to the single flower she had put in a vase when she'd come back from the grave. She grabbed her phone and searched the meaning of the yellow jonquil. She smiled as she read that it signified sympathy when life got overwhelming. More than that, it denoted the desire for returned affection.

Opening her text screen, she began to type.

Grace: I don't really know how to thank you for today, Evan.
Evan: I can think of some things…that involve lots of kissing.

Grace hesitated texting him back. How would banter ever be normal with this guy? Especially now that she was liking him more. Whatever she tried to text didn't seem sufficient enough. She kept erasing and re-writing as he awaited her response. Those three dots must've appeared and reappeared many times for him as she tried finding the words.

Grace: …
Evan: The ellipses drives me nuts, baby cakes. Are you writing me a novel for a response?
Grace: No.
Evan: That's the text I was waiting for? "No"?!
Grace: I'm loving the clam chowder.
Evan: Wait til you taste the lobster roll. But I will say everything is 20 times better in Boston...*ahem*… Thanksgiving?
Grace: I'm not going to Boston, Evan.
Evan: A bet is a bet. I need to make sure you go.
Grace: You didn't have to do this at all tonight. Are

you tired?
Evan: Yes, I did. You needed it. I'm fine.
Grace: Thanks again, Evan. And don't make Zach wash the dishes for you. A bet is a bet!
Evan: I now have proof that you just texted that. I'm holding you to it, Gracie Lynn.
Grace: Goodnight, Evan.
Evan: Night.

Grace tried the next dish and it melted in her mouth. She moaned and began to text again.

Grace: Holy crap! This lobster roll is seriously orgasmic.

Grace waited for a response and chuckled when she didn't get one right away. Now she knew what it felt like to be on the receiving end of those dots.

Evan: …
Grace: Ok, now who's the one with the ellipses? Where's your witty comeback, Matthews?
Evan: *Evan is unable to text back due to dying and going to heaven imagining Gracie Lynn Clark having an orgasm. Please leave naked picture after the text.*
Grace: DON'T BE DIRTY!
Evan: You started it, but I'm just saying, you want something orgasmic? I'm your man, babe.
Grace: Okay, egomaniac, calm down.
Evan: I'll be seeing you, Gracie.

Evan Matthews had made her a homemade meal. As she sat at her table and went over the events of the day, she wondered to herself how much better he could be, and if he was indeed a dream come true. She knew the time would come when she would have to eventually wake up, and recognize that the dream would be just that. How willing was she to live in a fantasy if it could break her heart all over again? This time gossip wouldn't be set in a high school, but the entire world would know her business. Was he worth it?

Chapter Eleven

"Moooooooom! Jake won't let me push the ball!" A young girl shrieked across the backyard to one of the many parents in attendance of Jake's Superman-themed birthday party.

"Jake, let Molly push it!" Jaime called as she plopped down with Marla and Grace at one of the foldout tables set up under a big patio. It was the first chance she had to sit with them during the chaos. "Dean, please watch them!"

The sun was out and the weather was a perfect combination of cool and crisp with a light breeze. Grace clasped her cardigan to her as Marla finished off a burger Dean had barbequed. The sound of children playing filled the air. The smell of food tempted nostrils of hungry party-goers.

"What did your agent say about a book tour? You scheduled for anything?" Marla was so great at asking questions about Grace's marketing strategies, she wished she could hire her.

"There's nothing planned. I could possibly set up another signing at Book People, but I'm not sure yet."

"You need to get in touch with blogs. Isn't there a way to contact a separate PR company?"

"Not unless I go out on my own, or until my contract is over."

"Well, you should think about doing something different. Word needs to get out about it. Are you going to hit up any book conventions?"

Jaime intervened, "My friend is going to that big one they hold every year."

"Yeah, I'm thinking of going." Grace grabbed a sugar cookie. She picked at the frosting and took some of it off before taking a bite.

"Why do you do that? The frosting's the best part." Marla reached over and dipped her finger in the excess, taking a small taste.

"Too much sugar."

"Says the girl who puts seven tablespoons of it in her coffee," Jaime teased. "So, how are things going with Cameron, Marla?"

Marla rolled her eyes as she stood and began to help Jaime pick up the used paper plates. "He's a little annoying and it's sometimes creepy."

"Marla, you really need to fix that. Tell him you've had enough." Grace started to grab clean plates and helped set up for the dessert.

"I can't just tell him off, he's my boss's son. I've worked too hard to get where I'm at, and I'm not going to let an ass like him ruin things for me." Marla then smiled. "I have been talking to Ryan Dane a lot though."

"Ryan Dane? Seriously?" Jaime almost squealed in delight. "He's pretty dreamy."

Marla nodded enthusiastically as she wiped down the table. "Yeah, I think we're getting together tonight. Just waiting for his text."

"And you, Grace? What's going on with hunky

Matthews?"

Grace bit her lower lip and felt her cheeks heat up. "Nothing."

"Ohmygod, you are such a little liar. Look at that sly grin." Marla laughed and playfully shook her friend's shoulder.

"Tell us what's going on, Grace. Did you thank him for rescuing you from your drunken stupor on Halloween?" Jaime made a kissing gesture as Grace tried to shush her.

"She probably did. With tongue." Marla winked.

"Shut up."

"She's not denying it," Jaime smiled as she positioned the cake in the center of the table. "Isn't he coming? Have you heard from him?"

Grace checked her phone but saw no messages. She wouldn't doubt he forgot or changed his mind. "I don't know, I haven't seen him since..." They were quiet when she blurted it out. "He went with me to see Nathan. On his birthday."

The women stood still and stared at Grace as she kept her eyes down. She tried not to make it a bigger deal than it was, but they all knew. It was a huge deal. She was opening up to someone, and he was slowly beginning to win her trust.

"Wow, that's really sweet of him, Grace." Jaime smiled.

"We could've gone with you too, you know," Marla asserted as she took a bite from a cookie.

She smiled and remembered how they had taken her in as if she was family. These girls were all she had, and they meant the world to her. "I know. I love you guys. It was just unexpected."

"Well, he seems like a great guy. I think you should give him the benefit of the doubt," Jaime said softly.

"Unless he doesn't show to the party, then he's just a douchebag," Marla partially joked.

"Have you heard from your parents at all?" Jaime asked Grace as she prepped the paper plates and plastic utensils.

"My mom texted last week."

"Hey! Look who's here, kids!" Dean yelled out as Evan walked through the sliding door and onto the patio.

"Looks like your Mr. Sexy made it, Grace," Jaime whispered under her breath.

"He's not *my* Mr. Sexy." Grace's heart sped up immediately and she smiled as she saw him in his costume. He was holding a wrapped present in one hand and his blaster prop gun in the other. The kids all turned and gasped as Jake ran toward him.

"Uncle Evan!" He jumped into his arms as Evan knelt in front of him.

Grace looked at Jaime with incredulity. *"Uncle* Evan?"

"I didn't tell him to call him that." Jaime got up and walked toward the kids who swarmed around him. "Okay, kids, give Captain Abrams room to breathe."

"He's kind of too good to be true, isn't he?" Marla asked as they watched him animatedly talk to the kids. The parents began to gather around in amazement at the fact that the real Captain Abrams was present at a kid's birthday party and started to snap photos and videos with their phones. The moms were particularly swooning over how handsome he looked in his space gear.

"Hey ladies." Josh approached with a brown, furry, four-legged friend following, and Grace greeted him warmly. Marla was more reserved.

"This handsome devil must be Hank?" Grace had recalled Evan's and Zach's conversation about the dog and she bent down as he excitedly began to play with her.

"Yes, this is Hank." Josh smiled coyly.

"How you doing boy?" Grace laughed as the dog spiritedly snuggled up to her.

Hank then went to Marla and jumped. She yelped and backed away. "Hi." She gently tried to pet his head and then warmed up to him after a bit.

"There's some hamburgers and hot dogs, chips and sodas, if you want, Josh," Grace offered.

"Thank you. I'm fine though."

Marla scoffed. "He doesn't eat that stuff, Grace. He drinks his protein." Hank tried to jump up on her again, and she pointed, her voice stern. "Hank, sit."

The dog obeyed dutifully and Josh shook his head with a smile playing on his face. "You think you have me all figured out, don't you?"

"It's not difficult," Marla smirked.

He crossed his large forearms, and Grace was sure she saw Marla swooning. "Well, keep trying, because you're wrong."

A chime on Marla's phone interrupted their intense

glares as she reached for it. "I gotta go, Grace. Ryan's wanting to meet up, but I'll see you Monday night."

She said her goodbyes to everyone and took off. Grace watched Josh stare at her as she left. "She's not always like that, you know." She was defending her friend, knowing there had to be something beneath the surface that bothered Marla about this burly and earnest man.

"She's going out with Ryan Dane?" His sky-blue eyes met hers with sincerity as she nodded. "He's not the greatest guy, Grace. Tell her to be careful."

"I will," she replied with gratitude.

Grace moved over to the grass and began to play fetch with Hank. She glanced to Evan who was surrounded by rambunctious children who were fighting for his attention. They asked him questions and he raptly answered. They asked to see his blaster and they took turns passing it around. He was so comfortable and at ease with them, as if they made his job seem completely worth it. She hadn't thought it of him, but Evan Matthews loved being around kids.

Jake opened his gift from Evan with permission from his mom and everyone was in admiration as he received his own replica blaster from the set. There was also an autographed photo of the entire cast included. Grace beamed and when their eyes locked, she felt her nerves shoot all through her body and straight to her core.

When Evan's attention was dragged away by Jake, Grace felt a whoosh of relief. His gazes on her were getting way too intense. They were the type of stare a girl dreamed of being on the receiving end of. The type of look that only happened in romantic novels adapted into films. The way Mr. Darcy looked at Elizabeth Bennet, Colonel Brandon's want of Marianne Dashwood, or Mr. Rochester's powerful need for Jane Eyre. It wasn't a good thing that she was comparing those gazes at all. It meant she was liking it way too much. She was beginning to like Evan too much.

She went inside to wash her hands before cake would be served. She observed herself in the mirror and saw her cheeks blushing just by thinking about the man outside who was making twenty kids extremely happy. He was great with kids. So what? Lots of guys were great with kids. So what that he was funny and romance novel handsome? Grace had met plenty of men who fit the criteria of perfection before. It didn't mean that they were the right guy for her. And she wasn't sure Evan was either. *Get yourself together, Grace.* She exited the restroom and yelped as two hands yanked her aside, enclosing her against the wall.

"Hi, Gracie." Evan grinned with a playful mischief that made her belly flutter.

"Hello, Captain." She placed her hands on his chest and played with the gear on his uniform. "You're looking like you're ready to save the world." She gazed at his full lips and licked hers out of reflex.

A small groan escaped from his throat as he roamed her face. "So you met Hank, I see. He really likes you, Grace." He cupped the back of her neck, staring at her with a need so passionate she couldn't breathe.

"I…" She gulped, feeling the electricity tingle in her stomach all the way down between her legs. "I like him too."

"Do you?" His eyebrow raised in a lively gesture. "Do you like me?"

"That's still under review."

Her breathing elevated as his thumb ran over her mouth. She felt her body responding to his as he pressed up against her. An uncontrollable whimper exited her and she couldn't stop what was already in motion. Even if she wanted to, the pull was too strong, his masculine hands touching her was earth-shattering. Every caress from him felt like she was an instrument he knew how to play with expertise.

"Let me help you decide then."

She tipped her chin up to stare into his eyes. The blue from them had disappeared with his dilated pupils taking over and drinking her in, as if he needed to be sated. His stunning face, and those lips, she remembered how soft and welcoming they had been. He confidently placed them on hers, his tongue slipping inside ever so slightly as she opened up to him. Instead of telling him to back away or stop, she let her hands wrap around his shoulders, feeling the hard structure of his costume under her fingers.

A moan broke from her mouth and she unexpectedly asked for more as she sped the kiss, relishing every soft thrust of his tongue. His fingers moved to the clip in her hair and pulled it open allowing the soft waves to fall over her shoulders. He took his time tangling his hands in the thick locks and pulled her head back demanding to taste more of her. She felt her knees weaken and was indebted to the wall behind her for holding her up as her mind tried to grasp exactly what was happening.

"Ew! Gross! Cooties!" Jake yelled pulling them both back to reality.

Grace gripped onto Evan's arms to steady her body as he began to laugh. "Jake, your Aunt Gracie needed a little CPR is all. I'm saving her."

"I'm telling!" Grace couldn't stop him as he ran out the door. "Mommy, Aunt Grace and Uncle Evan are kissing!"

"Tell them it's about time!" Jaime yelled.

"Shit," Grace whispered under her breath and looked down at her feet. She was trying to get herself together as Evan pulled away from her slowly. "So much for discretion."

"You're flushed." He smiled at her and cupped her cheek. "Let's go out on a date. A real date, Grace."

"I think we've met our quota for the bet, Evan."

"Monday after I get out of work."

"I have plans with Marla on Monday night."

"Wednesday then. I'll get out of filming at around six." He kept his eyes focused on hers as she nodded. "It's a date." He leaned toward her again and gave a small peck on her lips. "I plan on kissing you a hell of a lot more, Gracie Lynn. You'd better get used to it, sweetheart." He held out her clip and winked before sauntering away from her.

A shiver trailed through her body, the warmth she felt from Evan having vanished the moment he had walked outside. She let herself lean against the wall a moment longer, and needed to truly consider what was happening between her and this man. This beautiful man who could gloriously break her heart.

Chapter Twelve

"Watch out! Passing through."

Grace scrambled over as two burly men moved props on the outdoor lot of the studio where *The Ending Series* was filming. She had no idea when Evan had asked her out on a date that she would be meeting him there, but he had texted saying he'd be running behind. A car had picked her up and she met Zach at the entrance of the filming location. From there, he guided her to a trailer and told her to wait outside. So there she stood, shuffling her feet in uncertainty.

Watching movie stars walk back and forth was something Grace wasn't accustomed to, and though she tried to feel as though she belonged, everything in her body screamed that she didn't.

Evan hadn't given Grace any indication of where he was taking her, and when she asked if she needed to dress up, he told her to wear something comfortable. She opted for a pair of jeans and a pinstriped blazer with a shirt underneath that said, "TEXAS, HECK YEAH!" She wore her hair down because she sensed Evan liked it. He kept trying to tangle his hands in it when they kissed, and the thought of him possibly doing that again tonight gave her a slight thrill.

"Hi." A girl with caramel hair and sun-kissed skin approached her. With pixie-like features and a tall stature, she could have been a model.

"Hi."

"I'm Jenny. Can I help you find something?"

"Oh, I'm waiting for Evan Matthews." Grace smiled and stuffed her hands in her pocket after shaking the other girl's.

"Oh, okay. I'm one of the A.D.'s on set. Evan's just getting showered and finished for the day."

"Okay." She nodded and noticed the way the woman was surveying her with a glare. Grace tried to make conversation. "So, how are things going with the shoot?"

"Oh, it's great! Evan is... He's, well, you know how he is." Grace didn't reply and Jenny continued. "He had interviews today, and he's just such a flirt with all the reporters. Of course, the women eat that up. One of them practically offered him a blowjob." She laughed as Grace inwardly grimaced. As if without a filter, the girl relentlessly yapped. "I mean, I wouldn't be surprised if he took her to his trailer after. That sort of thing happens a lot with these actors."

Grace was beginning to get angry. Whether it was true or not, this girl had no right to be talking about Evan that way to anyone. He didn't deserve it. "Maybe you shouldn't be spreading rumors like that."

Jenny sneered and hovered over Grace. "Look, sweetie, from one woman to another, I'll warn you about Evan Matthews. He's a charmer. He'll say and do all the right things, and then he'll dump you and move on to the next conquest. You might see this all as a fairy tale, but don't get your hopes up for a happily-ever-after. I've been there and done that. Don't think you're the girl who can change his ways. You'd be deluding yourself."

"Thank you for your candor, Jenny. I'll keep it in mind," she responded dryly as the irritating female sauntered off.

"Hey, Gracie!" Evan stepped out of his trailer and Grace tried to forget everything that was just revealed to her by this girl, although that would be easier said than done. Jenny could have been talking out of the same pain that had affected Grace when Kyle Erikson had hurt her. Could Evan be capable of doing that to a woman?

Anyone was capable of anything, especially hurting those they loved. Grace had to keep that in mind as she neared the handsome man wearing a tight-ass maroon Henley, his brown leather jacket, and jeans. Was it possible for him to ever look ugly? Because his level of hotness was just ridiculous.

"Hey, Evan."

He gave her a side hug, his arm resting on her shoulders, and she could smell his masculine scent mixed with soap and shaving cream. Of course he was a womanizer, what could be expected when a man was as gorgeous as he was?

She tried not to let Jenny-the-bitch bother her, but Grace couldn't help but wonder how much all of this was just a silly game to him. Was he trying to win her over and drop her after he got what he wanted?

"You look scrumptious, Grace." He leaned toward her and let his nose smell her hair. "I love your hair down," he whispered in her ear giving her automatic goosebumps.

"Where are we going?"

"To the car." He led her toward a sleek Lexus convertible with the top down and opened the door for her. She felt shivers down her spine as his hand grazed her back. He leaned over her and reached into the glovebox. "Here's a cap."

They took off onto the freeway as the sun began to set over the horizon. Grace was sometimes grateful for the fickle Texas weather. Tonight was perfect for their outing… wherever they were headed.

"Where are we going, Matthews?"

"You'll see." He smiled wryly. "How was your day today, Gracie Lynn?"

"Good. I wrote a little bit. I had to check into fumigation for the houses, and I did some paperwork. Kept busy. You?"

"Well, I killed Dreydecon, my ultimate enemy, in a huge battle. Lost some soldiers, but I'm okay otherwise. Came out unscathed."

Grace chuckled. "Thanks for giving away the ending, loser. Now I don't have to see the movie."

"You know good always wins over evil."

"Not always," Grace sighed, a flash of her brother crossing her mind. She sensed Evan wanting to question so she changed the subject. "Where are we going on this date?"

"You'll see."

"Jaime posted the photos on Facebook from the party. Did you see them?"

He nodded as music played in the background. "I did. There are some good shots in there. I'm surprised they haven't come out in any tabloids yet."

"She has a good group of friends. I'm sure she told them to keep the photos private."

"Well, eventually they'll leak, but my people will take care of it."

Being part of a franchise that people adored meant a responsibility of having a proper reputation. Grace wondered how much his people had to work on covering scandals. "Lots of skeletons in your closet, Matthews?"

"Define 'lots,' Gracie." He winked in jest.

Laughing, she rolled her eyes as Evan led them into the downtown area. "We're going to see the bats, aren't we?"

"That we are." They found parking and walked to the bridge where people lined up along the area to see thousands of bats take flight at dusk.

"How the hell did so many bats get here?" he asked, leaning against the concrete structure.

"In 1980, they remodeled this bridge, and they just started hanging out here. The crevices made it an easy home for them."

"You said 'crevice,' Grace." He nudged her elbow.

"Why do you try to make everything sound dirty, Matthews?"

"Come on, you know it's endearing." They both laughed and watched as the black cloud emerged and thousands upon thousands of bats took flight over Lady Bird Lake. "Holy shit. That was one of the weirdest things I've seen in years."

"Cool, huh?" She smiled looking out over the sunset.

"Look, as much as I want to be as awesome as Christian Bale, I don't think I can handle the idea of getting bitten. Rabies doesn't suit me. Let's get out of here."

Evan clasped her hand and pulled her after him as Grace chuckled. "Chicken." They settled back in the car and he took off into traffic once more. "So where are we headed now, Matthews?"

"You'll see, Gracie Lynn. Stop being so impatient."

"Bowling?"

"No."

"Torchy's Tacos?"

"Nope, this is a little more private."

Private. She got uneasy at the idea of being completely alone with him for a long amount of time. There was always someone there or something to do to keep her busy whenever she was with him. There was an excuse to leave and rescue herself from him. But alone? That was risky.

Evan turned the car into an empty lot and Grace saw the sign and laughed. "The Blue Starlite Drive-In. We're watching movies?"

"Yeah, old movies. And hopefully making out." An attendant guided them in and let them park wherever they wanted.

"We're early?"

"I rented out the entire lot."

Her mouth gaped open in shock. "If this is what you do on a first date, I have no idea how you'll ever pull off the second."

"Don't underestimate me, Gracie Lynn."

~

She looked damn gorgeous. Sure, she was in plain jeans, a silly Texas t-shirt, and a blazer with black Converse on her feet, but that's what he liked. It was as if she knew he did. And her hair was down. God, she probably did that on purpose just to make him crazy. Hints of pink would rise on her cheeks when he'd joke with her, and Evan wondered how flushed they would get when he brought her to orgasm. He wanted so badly to find out.

But more than that, Evan wanted to find out why she seemed uncomfortable being alone with him. He wanted to show her he could put in an effort, be a great date. He longed to make her feel safe around him, but she seemed so adamant to keep him at a distance. He was determined to find out why.

Grace took the cap off her head and ran her hands through her hair, the rich brown waves tumbling down her back and shoulders. He stirred as his jeans tightened against him. Gazing at her face wasn't helping him calm down, especially when her lips parted. Those lips were desired on his body, he ached for them on his skin. He appreciatively studied her face, the way her hair fell, her expressive espresso-colored eyes focusing on his.

"What movies are we watching?"

"*The Philadelphia Story* and *Casablanca*," Evan replied, taking off his cap and setting it aside.

"Both great films. And from the 1940's, I noticed."

She smiled.

"Yeah, I told them I wanted it 40's themed. Your favorite era."

"You listened." The twilight had fallen into night and the cityscape could be seen behind the big screen in front of them. "This is so amazing, Evan. I can't believe you rented out the whole place."

"Well, I have a picnic basket here with some wine, cheese, crackers, and sandwiches. And then we have all the concessions we want—popcorn, soda, candy."

And all the NDAs in place. He made sure Zach had the employees fill out the proper paperwork as needed. He hated that part of his job, but he had to protect himself and the woman he was with. Privacy meant a huge deal to him, and he had a feeling Grace was on the same page.

The screen lit up and old sounds and photographs of the Glenn Miller Band played before the film began. Grace sighed, closing her eyes and taking in the music. "Wow, this must be heaven."

"You want to make a s'more?"

"We can make s'mores? I really am in heaven." They both exited the car and walked over near the concession stand where a small fire was set up. They were given a kit with everything needed and they both fixed their snack and ate.

Evan watched as chocolate dripped on her chin. He reached over and wiped it off of her, then licked his thumb. She laughed and cleaned herself with a napkin, then finished off her graham cracker. "That was awesomely delicious."

"Will you dance with me, Grace?" He saw the confusion that played on her mind as if she battled with her thoughts.

He held out his hand and led her back toward the car. He clutched her in his arms as she held on to his shoulders, her eyes reluctant to meet his. He hadn't seen it before, but a shyness crept over her, a naivety, as if she didn't know what she was doing. He let his index finger and thumb grasp her chin and pulled it up to look into his eyes.

"Hi, doll." He smiled at her as "Moonlight Serenade" filled their ears.

She gave a hint of a smile as they swayed, their bodies pressed close. The essence of strawberries on her skin mixed with a vanilla musk and chocolate called to him. "Hey," she whispered softly.

His heart leapt up at the gentle sound and he bent lower, letting his cheek rest on her head as she placed hers on his heart. The song took them to a heightened state of euphoria. He could feel her chest breathing against him, her heart synching with his, and he felt like it was two souls finding harmony in one another.

The song switched to Nat King Cole's "Stardust" and Grace tried to part from him, but he held onto her, cradling her face with both his hands and staring at her with the yearning of feeling her lips on his again. "You're so beautiful, Gracie."

His eyes shut and his mouth lowered, eager to taste the hint of chocolate and marshmallow on hers. In an instant, their lips melded and he leaned onto the side of the car, pulling her to him in between his open legs. His arms encapsulated her, his hand holding her head in place as his forearm drew her against him.

Grace ardently clasped the back of his neck, her hands roaming through his hair as she tugged at him deeper. When his tongue browsed her top lip slowly, she moaned, insistent and wanting more. However, Evan kept control over his reaction and stayed tender as his hands journeyed down her spine to her waist. Before it went further, she parted from him, looking down and shaking her head. "I'm…I'm sorry."

The color had vanished from her face, and lust had been replaced with doubt and fright. He wondered what had happened to make her change the momentum that had been gathering the past month-and-a-half. "What's wrong?"

"Look, Evan, I appreciate all of this…but…shit." Her back now faced him and he knew what was coming.

Hell, no, this wasn't happening. He wasn't ready to be rejected, and he'd to fight to win her over. "Talk to me, Gracie. What is it?"

She stayed quiet until he moved toward her, grasping her arm and pulling her around. "Grace, what?"

"Evan, I'm not up for whatever we're doing here."

"What do you think we're doing here?"

"Look, you seem great, but I'm just not your type."

His eyes flashed with anger, he tried controlling an urge to grab her and kiss her to her senses, but by the look on her face he'd scare her off even more. "So, you know what my type is, Grace? You think you know everything about me?"

"You want something I'm not ready to give."

He stopped, his brow furrowing as he put his hands on his hips. He wasn't looking forward to the next answer to his question. "And what's that?"

"Casual sex, friends with benefits, whatever you want to call it, Evan. It's just...you're a womanizer."

His scowl deepened. "That's what you think of me. Why?"

"Because, you're so charming. You say all the right things, do all the right things. Look at all this? How could I not think this was a way to end up seducing me?"

"Thanks for judging me, princess."

"I'm not your type."

"Stop fucking saying that, Grace!"

"I've seen the magazines talking about all the girls you date. Then, Jenny just reiterated what I already knew."

"Wait, what?" Azure eyes burned into hers, watching as she dragged in her breath. "What the hell did she say to you?"

"That I was basically the flavor of the month. That she'd been there and done that."

"I never slept with her, Grace!" he exclaimed, shoving his fingers through his hair in frustration. "She's been trying to hit on me since she started working on the movie. I don't want her. I want you. And why the fuck are you believing tabloids and a random woman instead of talking to me?"

They were both silent a moment, their breathing labored. Grace's shaky voice continued. "The whole point of this is that I don't give myself easily, Evan. Especially when it comes to sex. I've been hurt before, I don't want to end up-"

"Who hurt you?" He watched her body stiffen as he approached her.

"It doesn't matter."

"Gracie…" His face paled as he carefully spoke, "Please tell me you weren't raped. Tell me some asshole never hurt you like that."

"No, Evan, nothing like that. I just have to be cautious."

His body relaxed in relief, despite the fact that he wanted answers, and he wanted them all instantly, even if she wasn't ready to provide them. "When did this happen?"

"A while ago." She tried to keep her eyes off of his, but he was getting a sense of her uncertainties. She was fearful of making herself vulnerable. It wasn't about him; it was about her choosing the wrong guy.

He moved toward her and cupped her face in his hands. "How long since you've been in a relationship?" She tried to keep her eyes off of him, as if she wanted to run and hide.

"Long," she whispered it so softly he barely heard.

Realization dawned on him. "I get it now. This is all scaring you."

"I'm not scared." She gave a defiant tip of her chin, finally meeting his gaze, but giving herself away with subtext.

"Look, Grace, you already know this, but I'm not one for bullshit. And I wouldn't have done this for you if I just wanted to get you into bed. Sex is easy."

"But…isn't that what you want?"

"Any straight, red-blooded man would want that with you, but that's not my first goal with you." He leaned toward her and kissed the side of her jaw where her pulse raced, thrumming hard as her breathing picked up. "Come to Boston with me, Grace. For Thanksgiving. Let's spend time getting to know each other."

She shivered as he trailed his lips down to her collarbone. "The sex will get in the way, Evan. Even not having it will get in the way. It'll get too complicated."

"We won't let it."

She backed away and looked at him with a skeptical glare. "You're saying you're okay getting to know me, even if it means we don't have sex right away?"

"How long we talking?" He laughed, and then grunted as she punched him in the stomach playfully. "I was only joking, Gracie." His hand clasped around the base of her neck, his fingers digging into her hair. "I'll wait on you. We'll court like in your books." He bent low and kissed the tip of her nose. A look of fear crossed her eyes and he lifted his head. "What is it?"

"It's okay if you don't want to. We can chalk it up to a few months of friendship, and you can cut out now."

"What? Like all the others?" She was used to being left when the guys found out she wouldn't give them what they wanted. He saw it play over her face. There was so much more to this than she was telling him, and he wanted to break through that barrier she had around her heart. "I'll tell you what's going to happen, Gracie

Lynn. You're going with me to Boston. You're going to meet my family and friends, and find out that I'm a good man. We'll take it at whatever pace you decide, and we'll see where it goes from there." He gave her a final small kiss. "We got a deal?"

He could still see the hesitance in her demeanor. "I promise I'll behave myself around you, Gracie. I won't pressure you into anything you're not ready for." He let his hands brush through the soft waves of her hair. "Although I will continue to kiss you if that's alright with you. And maybe try to cop a feel."

A timid laugh finally broke from her lips, and he leaned forward to take them to his. He had no idea when he had met this woman what he was in for, but now that he was jumping in, there was no way he could jump out.

He wanted her, desperately, and with a hunger that ran far beyond anything he'd ever felt. Sex was off the table, but just how long would they be able to keep up that charade? She wanted him just as badly as he wanted her, and it was only a matter of time before they both fell in together. He was determined to find out everything about her past, who had broken her heart and how he could get her to trust him. Boston would be the time to do that.

Chapter Thirteen

Grace followed Evan into the lobby of the building off of the Atlantic Wharf district. She was instantly grateful for the warmth inside, as the city of Boston was getting ready for snowfall that evening. Grace looked forward to experiencing it even though she wasn't used to such cold weather.

Evan had been great to her the days leading up to this little trip she had agreed to. So many times she fought with herself on going at all. She even texted him late the night before leaving.

Grace: "Hi."
Evan: "You're not backing out. You better be packed and ready to go bright and early, cupcake."

He knew her too well. So, there they were. The last time Grace had travelled anywhere had been in college on a class trip to England. Since then, she didn't have the funds to really go to all the places she dreamed of experiencing. Just the sensation of getting on a flight, the cab drive over, and the idea of being in a different location was enough to have her excited.

A concierge with deep-set tawny eyes and salt-and-pepper hair greeted Evan by his last name and shook his hand. Grace smiled as he offered to take their bags to the penthouse for them, but Evan insisted they were fine and thanked him as they made their way to the elevators.

The quiet ding of each floor that passed made her more anxious at the thought of being alone with Evan in his home. Her furtive glance caught his electric eyes anchored on hers. A coy smile played on his lips as her mind raced with all types of situations she might find herself in with him over the weekend. *Mind out of the gutter, Grace.*

The lobby was beautiful but it was nothing compared to the loft itself. She gasped at the luxurious ambiance of his home. High ceilings with tall arched windows instantly caught her eye. Gray ash hardwood floors, oversized doors, sleek furniture, and a glorious kitchen made Grace feel like she had stepped into a lavish lifestyle that she was in no way accustomed to.

"This is extremely fancy," Grace breathlessly stated as she walked over to a window and gazed over the water.

"This is where I spend some time, but not all of it."

"Where do you spend your time then, other than on location?"

"At home."

Grace gave him a puzzled look as she followed him toward a bedroom with colors of white and cream. Everything screamed clean, large and modern. "How many homes you got, Matthews?"

"Well, I have this and a place in L.A., but my childhood home is my real home. The one my mom lives in. I stay there a lot more than I stay here." To say that answer filled her heart was an understatement. She loved the idea of him being close with his family.

Evan moved her suitcase to the top of the bed. Grace shuffled to it, wanting to quickly empty the contents of her luggage. Not because she was hasty to accomplish the task, but because she didn't want the bedspread to get dirty.

"Don't worry about unpacking now, Grace." He turned her around to face him and clasped the collar of her wool coat. In one swoop, he brushed it off her shoulders and scooped it into his arms. She had to stop herself from thinking how sexy it would be to have him strip off her clothes. Her daydreamer's mind had to stop from getting out of hand with those tempting thoughts.

"I'll give you the tour." Evan clasped her hand in his. It was warm, strong, and rough, and by now she could recall by memory how it felt. But she never got used to it when he touched her. It sent shockwaves through her body.

He showed her each room, but when he took her to his office, she gaped at the books lined against the walls. "I may have to examine your book stash later." Grace smiled.

"Examine away. I'm sure they'd love it."

"This seems so…" She didn't want to say unlike him, but it really was. "Is this your bachelor pad? You bring your women here?"

A rumble released from his chest as they traveled to the kitchen. He opened the fridge and took out two bottled waters, handing one over to her. "I guess you could say that. I definitely don't take girls to my mom's house."

She gulped her water and tried to remain unruffled about the honesty of his response. She wondered how many women he had screwed in his bed, and how she would stack up to the ones that had much more experience than she did. That was if she ever decided she wanted to sleep with Evan. Which she didn't. No, she didn't. *You don't want to, Grace.*

"I'm sure those women loved this place. If I were you, I'd show off the books. It'll make them fall that much harder."

"I only show those to special girls. Which means nobody has seen them but you." He winked at her and she tried to repress the fluttering in her stomach.

"You're smooth, Matthews. How many women fell for that line?"

"Honestly, Grace? Most girls I had flings with didn't give a shit about books."

Of course. Grace tried not to let that whole *not-his-type* impression get to her again. He quickly changed the subject. "You hungry?" Once again, he strolled to the fridge and looked inside it. "I had Zach stock up for us, but we can go out. Then some of my friends want to meet tonight at Stoddard's. It's a bar nearby."

"We can eat something here for now," Grace answered, wanting to relax after their flight. The evening was spent fixing sandwiches, talking and unwinding, before heading out into the stinging wind.

Grace had been nervous to meet all of Evan's friends, but the fun manner of all of them put her at ease. Zach jumped on the chance to introduce her before

Evan could. A group of what Evan endearingly called "misfits" all made Grace feel like a part of the crowd, accepted as one of them. They were a humble, gregarious, and smart bunch. Hours of socializing had passed, and Evan had led her to an intimate corner to steal a small kiss. He let his nose rub against hers softly. "They like you."

"I like them, Evan." His face showed relief, as though he were aiming to please her. His hand cupped her cheek and he kissed her forehead gently.

"You okay? Ready to leave soon?" he whispered, his lips hovering closer to her as he sported a beer in his hand.

She nodded and finished off the local lager he had suggested. "Yeah, but I could always use one more of these."

"You got it, sweets. Stay here." She smiled as he went to order her another drink. His Bostonian accent was definitely coming through. It might be that he was relaxed after so many beers, or just the atmosphere. He was comfortable. It was a different vibe he exuded compared to being on high-alert, always worried about being recognized. His friends brought out the best in him. They were lively and kind. Much like him.

Grace was nervous to head back to Evan's loft. That alone thing played on her mind again. Overnight. In bedrooms near one another. She wasn't so sure she was ready to either deny or accept him. Part of her wanted him so badly that she could barely breathe, the other part told her to be guarded, not fall for the guy who could bring her pain. A lot of pain.

"Hey, babe." An arm swung around her shoulders. At first she thought it was one of Evan's friends, but upon further inspection, she noticed he wasn't part of their group. His business suit had a few wrinkles and his tie was slack around his neck. He was good-looking and he knew it. A douchebag to the extreme. She was used to guys like this trying to pick her up and loathed these entitled men who thought women were so lucky to even be talking to them. "I'm Colin. What are you drinking? I'll get you something."

"No thanks, Colin. I'm fine." Grace tried to shrug him off of her, and he clasped her tighter to him. He reeked of alcohol. "My date's coming back."

"Date? Who, that Captain Abrams kid?" Colin snorted and leaned in closer, his mouth touching her ear. "I could please you more than that fucking twat ever could."

"Watch the way you're talking about my boyfriend."

"Boyfriend? That jerk-off? Honey, I could go more rounds. Longer, faster, harder."

Grace laughed. "Well, his dick is bigger than an elephant's, so just take your tick-tac, Mike and Ike, teeny weenie and get the fuck away from me. Got it, Colin?"

She glanced over and saw Evan standing with a shocked expression. "Evan."

He gathered his wits and placed the drinks on a table nearby as Colin got closer to her, putting his nose near her temple and taking a whiff. His fingers tangled in her hair and she tried shrugging him off again. "Your boyfriend won't mind me taking you for a spin, right,

Captain Abrams?"

"You heard the lady. She wants you to get the fuck away from her, and that's exactly what you're going to do, asshole." He gathered Colin by the collar and extracted him from Grace, backing him up into the jukebox.

"Okay, fuck. I didn't think you were such an uptight prick." The inebriated jerk shifted and pushed Evan's hands away. When he turned back toward Grace, Colin muttered, "Who'd want that slut anyway?"

Evan turned and swung at Colin, landing a hard uppercut under his jaw. Colin groaned in pain, but before Evan had a chance to block himself, he caught a return fist to his nose. Grace yelped as they lunged, both of them pushing at each other and propelling blows. She began to panic, the scene before her bringing up vile memories she would have rather forgotten as the crowd around them began to grow. "Evan, stop! Stop!"

Evan's and Colin's friends both gathered around, backing the two men off of each other as they called out every single vulgar name imaginable. Grace moved in front of Evan and fastened her hands on his jaw as he struggled to remain still. "Evan, look at me. Let's go." Panic played over her face as she moved forward and kissed him. It stopped him in his tracks as he looked down at her. "I'm begging you. Let's just go. Please."

He breathed in and clasped her in his arms tightly. He took several deep breaths trying to steady himself, to control the outrage she could feel coursing throughout his body. He was much stronger than the other guy, so she knew he had restrained himself, but it had still petrified her.

Zach grabbed Evan's shoulders and tugged him around whispering to them. "Get out of here before they call the cops, man. Last thing you need is to get bagged. I'll try to talk to the bar manager and calm this sauced fucker down."

He nodded, pulling Grace in his arm and taking her outside. "Let's go."

She could barely feel the cold wind hitting her face as she wrapped her scarf around her neck. Loosening Evan's grip when he grasped her hand, she paced and wrapped her arms around her shoulders as they waited for a cab.

"Are you pissed off at me?" he asked in surprise as he saw her expression.

"Yes. Yes, I am."

"Grace, I was just protecting you."

"I don't need protection. I can take care of myself," she barked in anger.

He huffed, looking down and shaking his head. "I get punched, and you get angry? Un-fucking-believable."

"My brother died getting in a fight, Evan."

Evan stood immobilized after her outburst. Her breath caught, but she dared not look at him too long. She didn't need his pity. "You said he fell and broke his neck."

"He did," she responded quietly as she dug a tissue out of her bag. She approached him and dabbed at his nose with it, then handed it over for him to keep. The cab rolled up and Grace hurried toward the door, glad for the shelter from the wind that was beginning to prickle her skin. Evan sat beside her and said nothing. He knew she didn't want to be bothered.

After a quiet cab ride, they made it back to the loft and removed their coats. Grace wrapped pieces of ice in paper towels as Evan sat on the arm of his couch, pulling out tissues from his bleeding nostrils.

She stood in between his open legs and cradled his jaw in one hand, resting the ice against his nose with the other. He closed his eyes and sighed as he placed both hands on her hips, pulling her in closer to him. His grip was firm as she sifted her fingers through the locks of brown-sugar-colored hair that fell over his forehead. She tried to ignore how hard he was against her, and how much she desired him. "You scared the shit out of me, Matthews."

He nodded, those sapphire eyes staring right into her. "I'm sorry, Gracie Lynn."

Water threatened to leak out of her eyes, but she stopped it and kept her voice steady. "Don't do that to me ever again. Please, Evan. It's not worth it."

He squeezed her hips hard, his gaze sweeping over her, his expression hungered as he studied every curve of her face. "You're always worth it, Grace."

Her face softened and her throat tightened as she scooted back from his grip. "You feeling okay now, buster?"

The tension between them was thick as she handed him the cold wrap she made. She needed to keep her distance. He was dangerous for her control. "Yeah." He grabbed it from her as she backed away. "What happened with your brother?"

She shook her head. "We'll talk about it later. It's late, and I'm ready to call it a night."

Grace walked toward her bedroom when Evan called her name. She turned to look at him, a gleam in his eyes. "I'll wake you tomorrow. And sweetheart?" He stood and ambled toward her. He placed his lips on hers, and she could taste a hint of sweet caramel malt on his tongue. "My dick isn't the size of an elephant's. But it's close." He winked and tramped off, leaving her in a state of shock.

~

Grace cried out as punches were thrown at Nathan. He and Kyle were both big guys, but her brother was faster and more agile as he began to fight back. "The whole school knows she's a slut, Clark."

The scene switched and she was in her room, crying, as her brother sat beside her. "Don't listen to those people, Grace. It won't matter years from now. Nobody will ever care, you hear me? Let's go to that party. You should be there."

Nathan pushed Kyle onto the grass and knocked him in the face. "Leave her alone, Kyle! She's gone through enough!" They tumbled toward the swimming pool, the crowd surrounding them as they cheered on opposing teams.

They were back in her room. "Gracie, promise me."

She gasped for air, flailing her arms as she attempted to call for help, but the water took over again, and she fell underneath holding onto Nathan. He was too heavy, and nobody was offering help. She grabbed a hold of his shoulder and pulled him to the surface.

"Nathan!" She dragged his body to the shallow end of the pool and shook his lifeless body. "Wake up, Nathan." They left. They all left her. "Help me! Please, call 911! Nathan, wake up! Please, I promise, I'll do what you said, just open your eyes."

Perspiration dripped from her body, despite the cold temperature. She tried to steady her heart as she got her bearings. This wasn't Austin; it wasn't her bed, her room, her house. Her phone showed it was quarter-to-three in the morning, and she had no desire to fall asleep again. All those awful images were conjured and she couldn't get them out of her head. Grace quietly made her way toward the kitchen and grabbed a bottle of water from the fridge.

She moved toward Evan's office and turned on the lamp that sat in the corner. Different shapes of frames surrounded the room and she took her time studying what she figured were photos of family members. Her eyes then roved the shelves of books. Even if she stayed in that room all night, she doubted she could browse over every single title, but he owned classic literature, poetry, religion, science, and finance. Books on acting, filmmaking, directing, screenwriting, and producing sat grouped together on a different shelf.

An old leather-bound copy of Shakespeare's sonnets caught Grace's eye and she grabbed it. A faint street light filtered in through the sheer curtains covering the large arched window. A cushioned bench sat under it, so she took her spot and peeked outside. Large snowflakes fell over everything like a blanket, and she enjoyed watching it unfold. She leafed through the book in her hands, reading through some of her favorite sonnets.

"Gracie? What's wrong?"

His voice was gravelly and his hair spiked up. Black sweatpants hung low on his hips and he sported a white thermal that stretched across his broad swimmer's shoulders. He moved toward her, and she never craved him more. There was sexy actor Evan Matthews. He came to her defense at the bar, brought her to this magical white-covered winter wonderland, was well-read, and looked like a god even all rumpled from sleep.

Was it possible for this guy to be *it* for her? Grace got that thought out of her head as swiftly as it has entered. Last thing she needed was to want something she knew was beyond impossible. Even if they both desired each other, she knew it couldn't last. He lived in Boston, never stayed in the same place. He was a movie star. She was a normal girl trying to be a fulltime author. They were from different worlds and wouldn't fit.

"Can't sleep."

He sat near her on the bench, his tired eyes still sharply blue. "Nightmares?" She nodded as he glanced over his shoulder. "Snowfall finally started."

She hummed resting her head back against the wall and appreciated the view. "I've never seen it like that. It's so beautiful."

"Is this your first time seeing snow, Grace?"

"Well, it snowed once in Austin, but it was about an inch and disappeared as rapidly as it fell."

His voice sounded more alert. "Wow, really? We

gotta make a snowman. Now."

"What? Now? It's crazy freezing out there!"

"Come on." He got up and grabbed her hand, leading her to his room where he began to open and search his dresser. She scanned his bedroom and saw his unkempt bed. On the nightstand sat about seven scripts along with a familiar paperback. "Is that one of my books?"

He glanced to where it sat open faced down. "Yeah, I couldn't sleep well either. And I'm anxious to see if Lady Ella ends up with Duke Seymour." He threw a thick thermal at her along with some long johns. "Put those on and then put these over." He handed her warm-ups and a sweatshirt with Mickey Mouse on it. "I have an extra pair of snow boots you can use."

She stood with the clothes in her arms. "Do you even know what time it is?"

"It's the best time to go out. Nobody's around, Gracie. Get dressed. I'll meet you at the door. Unless you want to change in front of me. I don't mind."

"Going."

They stood near the entrance and she stuck her feet in the giant snow boots Evan had placed in front of her. "I look like that kid from *A Christmas Story* when his mom puts him in those layers of clothes." She tried to move around in her wool coat as he laughed.

"Don't trip over your big feet, Grace."

"You're the one with the big feet, Sasquatch." Everything fit her twelve times too big, but part of her felt good in his clothes, like she was closer to him somehow.

He put a woolen beanie cap over her head and pinched her cheek. "You look adorable, pumpkin."

"Shut up, Matthews."

He took her hand and they were greeted by a different concierge as they walked out. The cold air hit Grace with a strong force and she shuddered, her breath coming out in swirls of smoke. "Shit, this is freezing."

"This is nothing, Grace. Last year it was piled up like crazy." The snowball came flying faster than she expected and hit her on her shoulder.

"I can't believe you just did that." She gathered snow in her gloved hands and they began to fight each other, but she soon tripped over the big shoes she wore and he tried to catch her only to be taken down with her.

They laughed as he rested on top of her, and he leaned to brush his lips on hers. "It's romantic, isn't it, Grace?"

She nodded. "Except for the fact that I can't feel my nose."

His husky chuckle coated her with heat as he let his lips touch the tip of her nose. He then lay flat next to her. "Snow angels?"

"Snow angels," she responded as they both moved their arms and legs back and forth. He then told her to stay there as he took out his phone and snapped photos. He helped her up and they took selfies. He leaned in on one of them and kissed her cheek as she smiled into the camera.

After attempting to build a snowman, and singing along to *Frozen,* in which she teased him for knowing all the songs, they went back inside to warm up.

"I never thought a grown man of thirty-four years loved Disney so much."

"I have a nephew. He loves Disney."

"*He* loves Disney? Then why am I wearing a Mickey Mouse sweater that's your size, slick?"

"I…I may have taken him to Disneyland last year, and Disney World. And I may or may not go with my family a few times a year."

Grace laughed as they took off all of the now wet shoes, hats, coats and gloves near the doorway. "I want to go someday."

"You've never been to Disney, Gracie? You'd love it."

"Busted. You're such a fan, Matthews!"

"I can't help it! I love cartoons! And I have an annual pass. You should go with me." They moved to the kitchen where Evan took out two mugs. She leaned against the counter, her eyes fixed on him as he took out milk and began to make them hot chocolate.

He carried both drinks to his room where they sat on his bed. He turned on the television, but the sound barely came through as they sipped on their cocoa.

"You got more marshmallows," Grace pouted, as she looked over to his cup.

"I didn't. I gave us each the same amount, crybaby."

"I didn't see you count," she defied.

"Have a little faith in me, babe. We each got eight marshmallows."

"That was so much fun, Evan."

"Wasn't it?" They stared at each other for too long

until he broke the silence. "Wanna talk to me about those dreams now, doll?"

She gnawed on her lip and played with the mug in her hands. "I keep having these nightmares about Nathan."

A coldness snuck over her, but she tried to stay on track, to open up to him, to let him in her disturbing thoughts. "They stopped years ago, and when I began working on the memoir, they started resurfacing."

He placed his mug on the table and reached for hers, doing the same. He then grabbed her hands. "What happens in them?"

"Sometimes they're of me drowning or unable to wake up. I'm alive, but I can't move, can't talk, and I'm left for dead." Her eyes stayed focused on her hands inside his. She had no idea where she got the strength to continue to talk, but she did. "Usually I'm holding Nathan in my arms, begging him not to leave me, and sometimes he opens his eyes and he's okay. When I wake up and realize that's not true? That's the worst feeling in the world, and all I can do to make it a tiny bit better is to remember to hold onto that promise I made him."

"What promise?"

"I can't..." She shook her head, not ready to share. The lump in her throat was too large to ignore, and when she looked up at Evan and saw the sadness he held for her, a few tears trickled down her cheeks. "The fight started because of Kyle Erikson. He was a friend of Nathan's, although they weren't close. I started seeing him, despite my brother's misgivings. He sensed something wrong about him that I didn't pay attention to. I slept with Kyle and he turned. He spread rumors about me at school. I got bullied pretty badly for it. Lost all my friends." She shrugged, but continued. "At this party, as Nathan and I passed by Kyle, he was telling a group of people how I was a dirty slut. My brother instantly began to defend me. It didn't end well."

Realization hit him as he exhaled. "That's why you were so scared tonight at the bar." She nodded. "I saw that look on your face and it just stopped me, Grace. God, sweetheart, I'm so sorry."

He hugged her to him and she found comfort in his arms. A piece of her wall was slowly crumbling, and as vulnerable as it was, it felt necessary to tell him.

"The similarities freaked me out," she confessed.

"What happened when they fought?"

"They were near this swimming pool. They both slipped in, but Nathan hit his head on the edge. Kyle and I pulled him out of the water. EMS came and I thought he'd be okay. They'd revive him by giving him CPR or that maybe he was just unconscious."

"He was already gone."

Tears welled as she tried to keep her voice steady. "My parents sat with me in the waiting room. They told me how disappointed they were with the way things were being handled with my drama. I don't think they realized how serious it was. Then the doctor told us Nathan had broken his neck. I had to watch my parents take in the news. And I had to soak in the fact that it was because of me that their golden child was dead."

"That wasn't your fault, Grace. It was a horrible

accident." His hand reached forward, removing tears from her cheeks. "Look at me. I'm sure they don't blame you."

"Years of therapy helped me to think that. Sometimes it's a little hard to believe it though."

His hand ran through her hair and stopped at the base of her neck, squeezing and kneading it for her comfort. "And your parents just left?"

"They moved as soon as I graduated. We were all so…empty. I stopped caring about impressing them. They had wanted me to be like Nathan. He had a full scholarship to Columbia, and he wanted to go into law like my dad."

"You're an artistic soul, Gracie. You're not like he was."

She smiled and nodded. "I was always different, and by that point, I just don't think they cared anymore about anything. I was always into the arts, writing, drawing, daydreaming. They didn't think I could be an author or make a decent living at it." She laughed away the stirring of more tears. "I guess they were partially right, but I got a good side job and I can take care of myself. I don't need their help."

"And the memoir? What's going on with that?"

"I don't even know. I thought it was a therapeutic thing, but it might be causing more damage. I'm not even sure I want it published."

"Sure you do."

"I just want to write what I love. It might not make me much money, but at least I'm happy doing it."

He gave a gentle kiss over her lips and caressed her

face. "You're living the dream, Grace. That takes courage. Keep doing that because it's beautiful."

"Thank you, Evan."

"Thanks for confiding in me, Gracie."

They both moved back over the pillows and fell asleep in each other's arms, Grace never feeling closer to anyone until then.

Chapter Fourteen

Evan woke up and gazed at the woman sleeping in his arms. He shifted slowly in an effort not to disturb her slumber. The rosy color on her cheeks, her dark lashes and the way they fluttered—she looked like a porcelain doll—and the last thing he wanted to do was wake her from the valuable sleep she never seemed to get.

Those nightmares were intense. He hadn't thought they would still haunt her the way they did, but he wasn't so sure anyone could get over something that harrowing. He had wanted to ask about that promise she mentioned, but he didn't want to pry, and if his instincts were correct, which they usually were, he already knew what that promise was.

The asshole—this Kyle guy—seemed to be behind a huge part of Grace's issues. He put the thoughts aside and watched her for a moment longer. She whimpered in her sleep as she stirred, and he inwardly groaned at the discomfort he felt near his groin. She was too beautiful, and he was horny as hell. But he would be patient with her because he figured the guys she dated weren't willing to tolerate her standards, and they had let her down. Their loss was his gain.

Her phone chimed on the dresser next to him and he quickly reached for it so she wouldn't wake. He glanced at the screen and saw a text from her mother.

"I hope you have a happy Thanksgiving."

It was good that her mother made contact. There must have been a way to salvage this relationship somehow. Perhaps Grace was being harder on herself than they were. He moved to the kitchen, letting her sleep. Evan took his time fixing his coffee and worked his way through emails and eventually began reading the John Whitford script Mike had sent him.

When Evan closed it, he exhaled from the mental exhaustion and ran a hand through his hair. It was a fantastic story, and it was a character he could play well. It wasn't a typical role, nor a typical movie, and he never wanted more than to take the part. He reflected over what this meant for him and the woman sleeping in his bed that he craved terribly. Long distance was a bitch. He wasn't so sure he could deal with her absence from his life, nor was he sure that she would be willing to commit to someone who never stayed put.

He reached for his phone and began to text Mike.

Evan: "I read the script. Set up the meeting with John."

His finger hovered over the send button as his mind battled with his heart. He had never put a woman over his career, but if he was going to commit to Grace—which he was very much considering—he'd have to make some type of compromise. Hesitating, he finally hit send.

The response from Mike was instantaneous.

Mike: "I told you it was an amazing script."
Evan: "I didn't say I was taking the part. I need to meet with John first."
Mike: "I'll set it up."

"Morning. Happy Thanksgiving." The lilt of Grace's croaky voice pulled Evan away from the phone. Watching her stumble to the kitchen made him instantly regret sending that text message to Mike, and his feeling of compromise didn't actually seem like he would be. Not when he was spending time with her. She was swimming in his sweatshirt and her hair was piled up on her head with tufts sticking out all over the place, but she looked perfect.

She served herself a cup of coffee and took out the creamer Evan had instructed Zach to buy. She yawned as she sleepily poured what must have been half a cup of it into her coffee. He laughed as she took a sip and gave a small sigh of content. "Happy Thanksgiving, snow angel. How'd you sleep?"

"The best I've slept in a long time."

"And we didn't even have sex," he joked as he made his way to serve himself another cup of coffee. Before he did that, he swooped over and wrapped his arms around her center, pressing his chest to her back. Lowering his head, he nibbled her neck and trailed his lips to her ear.

Grace wrapped her arm around the back of his neck and gave him better access to her skin that smelled like strawberry and honey. Her moan made him tighten his grip on her waist as he showered her with slow and light kisses. His body responded, but he set to control himself as she breathlessly spoke. "Why didn't you wake me earlier?"

"You looked so peaceful. I didn't have the heart to do it."

Her hand in his hair spurred him on and he cupped her jaw, guiding her body to face his. Circling his arms around her back, he pressed her to him as he took her mouth with eagerness. Grace let her arms cloak his neck as she stood on her toes, trying to get better access as he bent low and encased her body.

Their mouths fused with heat and lust, their tongues dancing against each other in a perfect waltz that made him feel like he was floating. Her hips bucked against him in a move that surprised and aroused him to an ache almost unbearable.

Her taste was an intoxicating blend of mint and coffee, and he was ready to go caveman, hoist her over his shoulders, drop her on his bed, and see how great she tasted on the rest of her body, specifically between her thighs. She coveted him just as much. He knew she did. Impatient fingers stroked his shoulders, and the way her lips trailed his jaw to his neck told him she did. And he was sure if he stuck his hand down her panties, he'd feel just how turned on she was by him.

Grace enraptured him, made him lose his senses—made him want every single bit of her with a ferocity he couldn't understand. How was this girl knocking him off his feet and creating sensations in him that were beyond unexpected? He forced himself to gain control, recollecting how vital it was for her to feel full confidence with him. And as much as he thought that perhaps she might feel ready, he guaranteed she wasn't. And he promised he wouldn't pressure her.

With heavy reluctance, he pulled his mouth away from hers as they both caught their breath. Her rose petal lips were puffed and she sulked as she reached forward trying to take his mouth again. He chuckled and embraced her jaw with his hands holding her back. "Gracie, we gotta slow it, babe. My body might not be able to take too much of this right now without wanting more."

"Oh." She looked down, her eyes widening as she saw his evident erection through his sweatpants. Her cheeks and neck flushed a deep crimson as she spluttered her regret. "I'm…I'm sorry. I'm so sorry, Evan."

"Don't be sorry for turning me on, doll." He laughed and kissed the tip of her nose, letting his hands caress her cheeks.

"No, I mean, I should've stopped. I knew better, and I didn't mean to tease…I'll just get ready." She maneuvered her way around him as she continued to uncomfortably fumble through her words. "I'm sure you need to get ready too, and I need to…you know, um, get-get r-ready."

"Yeah, I'm gonna need one hell of a cold shower, Gracie Lynn."

He watched as she shuffled toward him and picked up her coffee mug. "I'm going to take this with me. Because, well, because, I want to drink it. And, um, yeah. We'll get ready."

He laughed as he watched her walk away. This woman was driving him mad, and he was enjoying every single minute of this whole foreplay thing that would eventually lead to some amazing sex. But for now…*Patience. Keep your promise, Matthews. You asshat.*

~

The drive to his hometown of Cohasset was almost an hour commute, and it was one Evan was accustomed to making. Grace was enjoying the scenery, but he could sense the anxiety that ran through her. Her leg bounced as she stared at the snow covered trees that surrounded the highways. He reached his hand out and clasped hers. "Don't be nervous, Grace. My family will adore you."

She nodded, a crinkle in her forehead showcasing that what he said didn't make a bit of difference. "Jonah hates *Star Trek*," she recalled.

"Oh, yeah, he *hates* it. Says I'm way cooler than Captain Kirk. Don't ever mention you dressed up as him for Halloween. He'll hold it against you forever."

Grace became apprehensive. "Okay, then. Um, Hilary runs her own blog. Katie is a drama teacher. Her husband, James, is a dentist."

"Yeah, he'll probably ask you when you had your last dental appointment." He heard her groan and he laughed. "No dental insurance?"

"I'm a writer. What do you think?"

"Honey, as long as you floss and brush, I'm not judging."

"I do take very good care of my teeth, thank you very much."

"You do have a gorgeous smile, Grace Lynn."

She picked his hand up and kissed his knuckles. "And you have the straightest teeth I've ever seen. Spill it, Matthews. Are they caps?"

He busted out laughing, but kept his eyes on the road. "No, pumpkin, they're all mine, but I did have braces. They pulled into a grocery store and Evan unbuckled his seatbelt after parking. "My mom needed a few things. It's cold, so I can just run in and out."

"I wanna go inside."

"You want to see the inside of a grocery store?"

"Yeah. I like grocery stores. I like any stores, actually."

He grasped her hand in his as they walked the length of the parking lot. It was crazy that an act as simple as holding her hand to guide her into the store felt so natural and comfortable. They entered and Grace looked around. "It's pretty in here!"

"You're so weird."

"You like it," she retorted sassily.

He did. There was no denying that. They walked to the bakery department where he searched for the typical dinner rolls they ate during the holidays. He threw the bag at her and she caught them. "My reflexes are fast, Matthews."

"Oh, really?" He began to poke her sides and tickle her as they walked toward the dairy section. "You don't seem that quick to me, baby cakes."

"I'm letting you have your way for now,

Hollywood," she yelped as they tussled.

"Give me bedroom time, and then I'll have my way in there, Gracie Lynn." He clasped her close to him and gave her a kiss on her temple as she wrapped her arms around his waist.

"Evan?" He saw a woman from his past standing with a cart full of food. Sitting on the seat was a little girl of about two years old with mousy brown hair that matched hers. "Oh my god, Evan. How are you?"

"Christy, hi." He moved forward and embraced her, the familiarity was still there, but different, and he gave a genuine smile her way. "I'm good. How are you?"

Memories flooded through him as she answered. She looked the same, just older. Much more mature and serious. Then again, she'd always been serious. Her green eyes focused on Grace, and Evan knew her curiosity had been piqued.

"This is Grace Clark. My girlfriend. Gracie, this is Christy Shaw."

"It's Nelson now," she corrected with a grin and shook Grace's hand. "Hello, Grace. This is my daughter, Clara." He waved to the little girl, pinching her soft cheek as Christy spoke. "You look wonderful, Evan. Congratulations on all your success. You seem happy."

"Thanks. I am. You?"

"Yes. My boys love *The Ending Series*." She handed the squirming toddler a bag of yogurt bites to sustain her.

Evan asked their ages, names, and how everything was going with her family. It was a pleasant exchange of catching up as Christy spoke with animation. "Please give your sisters and mom my love."

He nodded as she and Grace exchanged pleasantries and she walked away. They finished their grocery shopping and walked to the car, Evan contemplating how different his life would have been if he had stayed with Christy.

"So, you going to tell me about her, Matthews? Or will I have to dig for dirt?" He glanced at Grace's expectant eyes, and he knew he had to explain to her. He couldn't make her open up to him if he didn't offer the same consideration.

"That was my ex-fiancé, Grace."

"You were engaged?" He started the car and let the heater warm them up, but he didn't drive. Not when she looked at him with her mouth gaping open. "To her? But you guys were so…cordial."

He chuckled as he rubbed his hand together for warmth. "No need not to be."

"What happened?"

"We knew each other in high school, but I ran into her a few years after graduating when she was attending college in New York. I was working at a casting office and auditioning for plays and films. We started dating and eventually moved in together."

He sniffed a moment and shook his head. "I was just over-the-moon for her. I proposed, she said yes, but things were tough. I was a struggling actor."

"Then what?"

"I was getting more roles, started making a name for myself in the industry. I needed to move to L.A. sooner or later, and I expected her to go with me." He sighed, giving a small laugh.

"She didn't want to."

"No. She hated the idea of the fame I was gaining. She wanted to come back to Cohasset. She broke it off with me. I begged her not to, but she knew better."

"When did all that happen?"

"I was young, Grace. I focused on my career, she's built a family and found stability. But rejection from someone you love always hurts, even if it was the right thing to happen."

"Do you miss her?"

"I did for a long time, but not now. We weren't right for each other." The silence was thick as she stared at him with those mocha eyes. And he knew why he wasn't affected by seeing Christy. It hit him so strong, a force unlike any he'd felt before. He wanted Grace. "It wasn't meant to be, Gracie."

Her lips parted and she held her breath as she grabbed his hand and kissed his palm. "I'm still sorry that happened to you, Evan."

"I became numb to the idea of an intimate relationship for so long because it's easier that way. And you know all about that, babe. You do it too."

"No, I don't." She became flustered as she released his hand.

"Yeah, Gracie, you do, sweetheart. Just in a different style."

"When did this become a therapy session about me? We were talking about your issues, not mine."

He closed his eyes, resting his hands on the wheel in front of him. "Gracie, you're always shutting yourself off." He looked at her as she stared straight ahead. He wanted all of her, not just the small part she was giving, and he was trying to maintain his impatience. "Sooner or later, you'll have to let me in."

"We better hit the road. I'm sure your mom is waiting for this stuff." Her phone chimed and she reached in her pocket. She took one look at the screen and rolled her eyes. He had a feeling he knew who it was.

"You can take the call if you want."

"No, it's fine. It's a text."

"Your mom?" He glanced as he began to drive. She nodded. "Isn't it good that she keeps in touch? Let her know you're okay at least."

She shook her head. "I'll text her later. I don't need her making me feel bad about myself right now. I'm edgy enough as it is."

He grabbed her hand and kissed it. "Gracie, don't be worried. My family's awesome."

Their day had just started and they had already run into his ex and had a large discussion over a part of his past. What a hell of a revelation to have on Thanksgiving Day, but now that Evan knew what he wanted for his future, he had to make sure Grace craved it just as much as he did. If she wasn't on the same page as he was, they would fail epically, and he wasn't ready to let that happen.

Chapter Fifteen

He had been engaged. He wanted to get married to that woman. Grace never took Evan to be the settling-down type. She had a new perception of him that hadn't been expected. He was once a normal guy, who dated and fell in love with a normal girl, and in the process, had gotten his heart broken. It was a very common story with uncommon circumstances. Evan had become famous, and Christy couldn't handle it. He kept meaningful relationships at a distance to protect himself, just like Grace did.

The road led to a gorgeous colonial house that looked out of a fairy tale. Grace gripped her hands tight trying to calm the nerves she felt. Regret panged through her and she wished she hadn't agreed to this trip. It was bad enough she found Evan generous, funny, and handsome as hell, but now he was introducing her to his family. Letting her enter his world was something Grace had never imagined happening, and the more she was stepping in, the more she was getting caught and never wanting to leave.

"This looks like a Thomas Kinkade painting."

"This is home," Evan announced with a serene expression as they exited the car.

He opened the front door and let Grace enter first. The two-story home was expansive, with high ceilings and wood floors. Smells of turkey and spices filled her nostrils. The brick fireplace was burning in the large, open living room, and she felt an instant balminess that gave her comfort. It was lavish but cozy and welcoming. She loved it.

"Mom, we're here!" Evan called out.

A woman with short, blonde hair and sparkling blue eyes emerged from the kitchen. As she approached them, Grace saw where he had gotten his attractiveness from, especially the perfect nose and sharp jawline.

"Finally. Did you bring the dinner rolls?" The attractive older woman wiped her hands on a towel that wrapped around her waist and embraced Evan tightly as he then gave her a kiss on her cheek. "I missed you, honey."

"Missed you too, Mah." She was the exemplification of what home meant. Her warm character showed a beautiful, open, and strong lady. Grace often wondered how things would have been if her mother had been the type to be loving and encouraging. That was a resentment she had left behind long ago, but once in a blue moon, she had pondered how different her life would be.

Before Evan had a chance to introduce her, a tall, sporty-looking blonde rammed her shoulder into Evan. "Oh, it's *you*." The girl's tone was mocking as he grabbed her and put her in a headlock, mussing her hair. "Ouch, stop. You know I missed you, dork."

The two of them hugged before all sets of eyes landed on Grace. He placed an arm around his mother's shoulders. "Gracie, this is my mother, Rebecca, and my baby sister, Hilary—the adopted one." He grunted when she punched him in the stomach.

Grace's cheeks heated as she smiled. Rebecca brushed off Evan's arm and engulfed Grace in hers. "Hello, sweetheart, I've heard great things about you. Welcome to our home. If you need anything at all just let us know."

"Thank you, Ms. Matthews."

"Oh, no, honey. Call me Rebecca." She reached out and placed both hands on Grace's cheeks, examining her with flourishing affection. "You've been making Evan so happy. I'm just so thrilled you came with him on this trip."

Grace gave a nervous chuckle and amiably replied, "I'm thrilled to be here and it's lovely to meet you."

Evan's mother's eyes shined as she nodded, taking the bag of groceries that hung from Evan's wrist. "I gotta check the stuffing, but Evan, give Grace a tour of the house, be a good host and offer her a drink. Use your manners," Rebecca stated as she walked back.

Hilary was standing with her arms crossed over her chest. She wore a heavy knit beige sweater and skinny jeans with tall brown leather boots that made her look like a gazelle. Her appearance was different from her brother's, but she was just as gorgeous. Grace became quite curious to see what their father looked like and how it was possible for a whole family to be so beautiful. Hilary cocked her head toward Evan and said curtly, "This idiot hasn't shut up about you for over a month. He's got a huge crush on you."

Hilary playfully punched her brother in the bicep. In

turn, he put his arm around her neck drawing her closer to him. "Thanks for throwing me under the bus, Hil."

"Well, I have a crush on him too, so I think it all works out okay," Grace admitted with a lighthearted smile. She saw Evan glance down at his feet, his grin playing wide across his lips. *He was shy?* That surprised her, given she thought he was the most self-assured man she had ever met.

"Where is everyone?" Evan asked as he took his and Grace's coats and hung them up on a hall tree much like the one she owned.

"They're on their way. I'm shocked Zach isn't with you," Hilary stated in an unusual tone as they made their way to the step-down living room. "Did he go to L.A.?"

"He's here. Just had a late night out, but he'll be over soon."

Hilary rolled her eyes pushing her straight honey-blonde hair over her shoulder as she plopped down on a large, plush couch. "That moron needs to calm the hell down. All he ever does is drink and get laid."

"He's sewing his oats."

"Yeah, and if I said I was sewing mine, you'd kick my ass."

"I'd lock you up in a fucking tower, Rapunzel."

"See how he treats me, Grace? Ask me how I put up with this shit."

"You don't," Evan answered.

"That's right, I don't. How's your face doing, anyway, you loser?"

"It's fine. A little sore," Evan said as he pressed his

fingers against where that asshole had punched him.

"You could've totally blocked that punch, but I'm glad you got yours in first. That ass deserved it."

Grace looked at Evan questionably as Hilary explained. "The bar fight was on the TMZ website. There was a video. Grainy, of course, but there were some pictures too. The story leaked out of what happened. I'm bummed they beat me to it. I could've posted it on my blog," she joked, but then turned serious. "I get you defending Grace, but you gotta be careful, big brother."

"I did what I had to do. I'm sure Zach got it under control," Evan attempted to dismiss it. "Grace, you want a glass of wine?" he offered as she tried to wrap her head around what was happening, then nodded.

"I'll get you guys some. We have white or red." Hilary observed both of them knowing they needed a moment. "Which would you like, Grace?"

"Red, please."

"Me too," Evan winked at Hilary as she ran off toward the kitchen.

"Were you going to tell me about this mess, Evan?" Grace asked as she stuffed her hands in the pockets of her jeans. "I was included in it?"

He closed his eyes. "I didn't want to ruin your Thanksgiving, Gracie. I hate that tabloid shit."

"So, I *am* in it."

"They don't know your name yet." He looked down and rocked on the heels of his boots. He shrugged his shoulders. "I'm really sorry, Grace. But they won't bother you. I won't let them."

"How's that even possible? If they find out who I am…" She had wondered when this was going to take place and how it was going to affect her life. She didn't want to be seen as one of Evan's flings. Blasted in the media as one of the many girls he was seen with and being speculated about wasn't something she had wanted.

He sauntered toward her and cupped her face in his hands. "I'll be sure you're just as protected as I am when it comes to privacy, babe. If not, more."

"There's no guarantee though, Evan."

He sighed and shook his head in defeat. "No, there isn't. I'll do what I can though, Grace. I want you feeling secure when you're with me. I'll talk to my publicists after this weekend, alright? See what they suggest. I have a great team. It's a lot more controlled than you think."

Grace knew there wasn't much she could do. Worrying about it wouldn't help stop what would and wouldn't be thought and said. She nodded and tiptoed to meet his kiss halfway. She let her fingers run over his nose and then swept her hand over the two days of stubble that grew in on his face and was sexy as hell. "I like your sister, Evan. She's really sweet." She smiled, missing her brother beyond words could ever express.

"Yeah, I tend to feel protective of her, too. I know she can take care of herself, but that girl sure likes to pick the stupidest guys to date."

"Sounds like Marla."

Evan chuckled, shaking his head as he led her to the banquet sized dining area. "She still seeing Ryan?"

"Yeah," Grace sighed with a disapproving nod. "She's been having some issues with him."

"He's an idiot. Josh hates him." Grace wondered if Evan and Josh had discussed that whole scenario. Grace had a suspicion that Josh was interested in Marla, but she wasn't going to meddle. "He reminds me of the douche Hilary was dating last year. I had to catch a flight home during filming of one of my movies because this guy crushed her. It took all my willpower to stop from beating him down."

"You're a great older brother. I'm sure she really appreciated it." They walked toward large glass doors that led to a huge patio overlooking dense brush and trees. Grace gazed outside as small snowflakes began to float down, bringing even more of a cozy feeling to the holiday.

"I'd do anything for my family." He looked at her with a sincere smile and clasped her hand. She believed it. She also wondered what it would be like to be a part of that. Accepted and loved in a family unit was something she lacked and was missing.

"So, is there something up with her and Zach?"

"What do you mean?" Evan looked baffled by the question which amused Grace. He scoffed at the idea as they walked slowly across the room. "Hilary and Zach? Hell, no. I'd know about it. And then I'd kill him."

She pressed her lips together and kept quiet. She had a slight suspicion Hilary liked Zach, but there was no need to bring that to Evan's attention. At least not now.

"This is my favorite room, Gracie."

He opened a set of wooden doors, and her eyes

widened as her body tingled with exhilaration. The library was huge, with an oak desk in the center. Shelves lined along the entire backside of the room, and an antique winged leather armchair sat near a window that overlooked the trees. "Can I live in this room?" She gasped as she searched the shelves and found an aged copy of *Little Women*. "Are you even kidding me?" She grasped it carefully and thumbed through the pages. "This house is a dream-come-true."

"My mom is a bit of an antique collector herself. Sort of like you."

He gazed at her as she began to look upon the walls that held family photos. "Oh, this is you, isn't it?" She pointed to a photo of a young boy.

"That's me," Evan confirmed, and for the first time Grace caught him blushing.

"Look at you! You're so cute with your bowl haircut."

"I was rockin' it, what can I say? And check out how I buttoned my shirt all the way up to the top."

She looked amused as she pointed to the photograph. "And what in the world? Is that a bolo tie necklace you're sporting?"

A laugh ripped through him as he placed his hand on his chest. "God, I had no sense of fashion. I'm lucky I survived my formative years, Gracie. It was only because of my older sister, who was much cooler, that I didn't get picked on."

Grace was wiping away tears as he continued to be self-deprecating. He led her to another school photo. "Here were the braces years. And I was so cool in my

Hypercolor shirt and Girbaud jeans. I also wanted to be like Kris Kross."

"Stop it, I can't stop laughing." She clutched her stomach and finally got a hold of her reactions.

"Oh man, you're showing her the school photos? He was such a dork!" Hilary laughed as she joined them, handing wine glasses to the both of them. "Everyone sees him as this big time action-hero movie star, when really he was just a drama nerd who sang to musicals in our cellar."

"What's your favorite musical?" Grace asked with a glowing in her eyes.

"You'd think it's like *An American in Paris* or something renowned. It's *Newsies,"* Hilary teased.

"I can always count on my kid-sister to razz me out."

"I'm wicked good at it too."

"Hey, *Newsies* is fabulous. Christian Bale nailed that *Santa Fe* number," Grace defended Evan.

"Thank you, Gracie." He pulled her against him and placed a delicate kiss on her brow. "At least someone is on my side."

"When it comes to you liking Christian Bale, I'll always be on your side."

Hilary laughed in agreement. "Hey, Evan, Mom needs your help with the turkey."

Evan excused himself and Grace took an anxious sip on her wine. She tried to avoid the gaze from his sister's piercing hazel eyes, nervous of what she'd see. Finally, Hilary spoke. "He doesn't bring girls home. Ever. Especially someone he's just met."

"I'm really grateful to all of you for allowing me-"

"Except that Christy chick, who I told him off the bat, would break his heart." Grace opened her mouth to intervene, but Hilary continued on her rant. "I warned him about her. He didn't believe me, and then all that happened."

"Well, it was for the best, perhaps."

"Of course, Grace. I can tell you're not like her, and I love my big brother very much. God, I couldn't imagine ever losing him." Grace froze as she realized what Hilary was saying, and in turn Hilary's eyes widened. "I'm so sorry, Grace. He mentioned you lost your brother. I didn't mean to...shit, I'm such an idiot."

Grace gave her a reassuring smile knowing the young woman meant no harm. "It's okay."

"It's just, he told me how resilient you are, and how you're this brilliant writer and artist, and you've gone through all this stuff and have come out of it still shining. He really likes that about you. And meeting you in person, I get it. You sort of…fit with him."

"Well, we just..." Grace shifted awkwardly. How would she explain his lost bet? "Started dating." She didn't want the family thinking they were serious. There were still so many steps to work towards. And sure, Evan had introduced her to Christy as his girlfriend, but it didn't mean anything. He was trying to save face like she had when that jerk had hit on her at the bar.

"I'm just saying I like you for him. Zach told me he likes you too, and Zach's part of this family. When Evan allows someone into his home, it means something." There was a pause before she continued. "Don't break his heart, Grace."

"I wouldn't want to."

Grace was more afraid Evan would break hers.

~

The rest of the family had arrived and before long, everyone was having fun, chatting. Jonah asked Grace a lot of questions about Texas and whether she was a big *Ending* fan like he was. Katie was genial and kind, and James definitely asked about her oral hygiene, which Grace thought was hilarious and a bit embarrassing. Zach came over slightly sleepy, but also chastised Evan for the bar fight, telling him that cleaning up the mess was underway. They all watched the football game and relaxed, catching up on life events and including Grace in the conversation. Her nerves had disappeared and she found herself getting along well with everyone.

The late lunch was ready and everyone congregated around the table. They all held hands before settling to eat, Evan leading them in a prayer of gratitude. Grace hadn't remembered the last time she sat down for a real Thanksgiving Day meal. She usually picked up Chinese food and called it a day.

The snow had started falling in abundance, and evening was beginning to creep up. Grace stood by the window in the library to watch the beauty of it. Evan peeked in and walked toward her. "Hey, pumpkin. We're getting ready for dessert soon, then we wanted to play charades. You feeling okay?"

She nodded, but an ache in her heart had grabbed a

hold and squeezed. "Yeah. I really like your family, Evan."

He placed his warm hand on her cheek. "I'm glad you came to Boston with me, Grace." He brushed his lips on hers softly and nibbled her lower lip for only a moment before parting. His sharp eyes focused on hers and gave her a feeling of comfort. Something she hadn't felt in so long that it seemed foreign to her, as if she didn't recognize it or the meaning. "Now tell me what's wrong."

"It's so silly." How could she begin to express the love she sensed from this family dynamic? It was something that had been underprovided in her life, and something she was terrified she'd never have. She couldn't let herself get too attached. It would only hurt more if it didn't work out. This was the fulfillment of a bet, nothing more.

"So what? You saw my school pictures. Those were silly."

She chuckled through her pain and released a breath trying to hold in her sadness. "Seeing what you have here. I wonder what Nathan would've been like. Married with kids like Katie and James with someone like Jonah."

"That little punk? Nah, Nathan would've had girls." The comment caused her to laugh, but it broke as water filled her eyes. His arms enveloped and rocked her. "I'm sorry, Grace." He kissed her hair and held him to her. "What if we could go to California and visit your folks? When's the last time you saw them?"

Grace parted from his embrace and shook her head

violently. "No, I couldn't see them, Evan."

"Why not? Look, just talk to them. I'm sure they'd understand."

"Understand? They left Austin. If they really wanted to see me they would've made an effort. They don't care about me."

"They care. Listen, I think if you talked to them about how you feel –"

"No. Please, just drop it." She felt the onslaught of a panic attack, her defenses starting to build. "I couldn't take the way they'd look at me. I used to hear it when I talked to them over the phone. The resentment. I know it's still there."

"Okay." He hugged her to him once again, wiping small tears that had escaped onto her cheeks. "I'm sorry. Gracie, it's okay."

Evan would never comprehend the way her parents treated her, how she was reminded that she was a constant letdown. The last thing she needed was to try and fail to heal a wound that would remain forever gaping. "Let's go relax. We'll sing and play songs on the piano."

She looked up to him as she sniffled. "You play the piano?"

"A little."

"Is there anything you can't do, Mr. Perfect?"

He looked up in thought and hummed. "I can't caulk a crack or wrap a pipe like you can, Grace Lynn. And I can't draw or paint to save my life."

She pushed away from him and laughed as she dabbed her tears away with the sleeve of her sweater.

He reached out and helped. "You got some mascara smeared." Her heartbeat quickened as he wiped her cheeks. Then leaning over, holding her face so gently, he kissed each eyelid. "Your tears gut me. Every time, babe." He kissed her lips making her feel consoled. "Let's go make you laugh. That's my favorite sound in the world."

The rest of the evening was spent having fun. Grace loved seeing the relationship between Evan and his sisters, but she especially enjoyed watching him with Jonah. His nephew was the cutest thing, and Evan loved him beyond reason. He promised another trip to Disney soon, even saying that he hoped Grace would tag along.

She watched as Evan gave Jonah a piggy back ride throughout the living room, and she felt a stirring in her heart. She yearned for a family of her own, even though she had never longed for a child before. The fact that watching Evan could change her mind alarmed her. Whatever brought on that predilection, she brushed it aside as quickly as possible.

It had turned late, and Evan's mother convinced most of them to stay overnight. Grace whispered in Evan's ear. "I didn't bring anything with me."

"Sleep naked," he deadpanned.

"You wish."

"I'll lend you some pjs. Come on, Grace." He pulled her upstairs to his room. It was spacious with a big bed. Shelves were lined with books. Photos of Evan with family and friends riddled corkboards near a small desk. The rest of the walls were stripped bare. "I used to have stupid posters up in this room."

"What kind of posters?"

"Old movie posters and other crap."

"Naked girls?"

"No, Mom would've ripped those down." He laughed as she remembered that he was raised in a household full of strong females. "She was a big advocate of respecting women, Gracie. She taught me well."

Her gaze shifted to the monster in the room as Evan rummaged through his dresser drawers. "So, we're sharing a bed?"

"We shared a bed the night before."

"Yeah, but we sort of just fell asleep." Grace peered at him with apprehension as he approached. "Your mom, she's gonna think…"

"What? That we're having sex?" She nodded as he chuckled. "Most couples do have sex, baby. I think we're the exception. She'd be more shocked that we aren't having it yet."

"I didn't really think we were a couple, Evan."

He paused in reflection before he handed her a Henley and flannel bottoms. "Hilary has some makeup remover stuff you can use. And when we introduce each other as boyfriend and girlfriend that usually means we're a couple. I heard you tell that moron at the bar that I was your man." He smiled mischievously as he shuffled to the bed.

"We haven't even had our second date."

"We've kissed a lot more than twice though, Gracie Lynn."

Those dubious poker non-rules were causing havoc

on her ability to argue with him. "Yeah, but it hasn't counted. Well, the first kiss counted when we worked on the desk, which should've been considered a date. Actually, I think this whole poker bet has been completed because kiss number two was at the drive-in."

He laughed, "Well, that desk kiss wasn't our first, princess. And now you're just trying to confuse me."

"Uh, yeah, it was," she argued. "And the bet's pretty much completed."

"No, it wasn't." His face was alight and his eyes twinkled as he began to fix the bed, pulling the duvet down. "And let's just get over this bet thing."

"Do you date that many women you don't even remember our first kiss, Casanova?"

He approached her again and slid his hands over her shoulders and down her arms. Grabbing her hands in his, he guided them up to prop them on his shoulders then glided his to her waist. Her breath caught as his gaze and voice grew heartfelt. "You're the only girl I've dated exclusively since Christy, Gracie Lynn. And the only one I've thought about since the day I met you." His lips hovered over hers as his voice sounded rugged. "The first time we kissed was when you were dressed as a very drunk Captain Kirk."

She gasped as she thought over the revelation. Her cheeks felt hot as she squeezed her eyes closed. "Oh, God, what the hell did I do?"

Evan's amused expression helped lift her embarrassment. "Not much. You passed out soon after. But I was glad you kissed me, Gracie. You were so closed off, I wasn't quite sure if you liked me or not."

"I told you I liked you?"

"Well, you said you were really annoyed at how sexy I looked in my SWAT costume."

"Yeah, that sounds like something I'd say." They both laughed as she shifted in his arms. "But, Evan…all this, it all just seems a little too fast, and I'm not sure if-"

"Stop overthinking it, Grace. We'll let it progress naturally, okay?" He stood in front of her, his eyes lingering, as if he was unable to look away for fear of the moment ending—as if he wanted so much more from her than just a normal evolvement of things. She couldn't speak. "Get ready for bed. I'm going to say goodnight to my mom."

She watched him leave the room and looked at the bed in trepidation. That piece of furniture was giving her a hell of a time. Temptation to give in to her rampant hormones was vast, and she was getting worried that her promise would soon be broken.

~

"I really like this girl, Mom."

Rebecca wiped down the table with a cloth as her son gathered the placemats and put them away. Everyone was asleep, and Thanksgiving dinner had been a success. Plus his favorite football team had won, and Grace was upstairs in his bed, so that called for a great day. "I like her too, Evan. I like her a lot."

"I feel like she's holding herself back from me though." He served himself a slice of pumpkin pie then rummaged through the fridge and took out the whipped topping.

"Well, maybe she's just nervous. You two haven't been dating long."

He grabbed two forks and handed one to his mother who stood beside him and shared. "I saw Christy today at the grocery store. She sends her love."

His mom's mouth warped into a sneer. "That girl's something else." She took another bite of the pumpkin pie then reached into the tub of whipped cream, slathering it on. "Did she see Grace with you?" Evan nodded and his mom chuckled. "Good. I hope she saw you stepped up and found better."

He laughed. "Mah, that's a horrible thing to say."

"You know it's true, hon. She did a number on my boy, and for that, I heavily dislike her."

Evan played with the whipped cream on the pie and smiled at his mother's attempt to defend him. "Heavily dislike?" He took his last bite and scooted the plate to his mom so she could have the rest. "That's hilarious."

"Well, she was your last serious relationship. I know she hurt you. I don't care how long ago it was." She ate the last of the dessert and threw the plate away. "How did you feel about the whole thing, Evan?"

He contemplated for a moment how to put it into words, then remembered Grace's expression, her comforting look, her warm kiss on his palm. "I was relieved. So grateful that I didn't end up with her. But I also realized what I'm missing and what I want for my future."

"Grace?"

"Yeah. Is that crazy?"

She put a hand on his cheek and kissed the other. "Of course not. When you know, you just know. But enjoy your time with her. Take it slow. Listen to her. Be the gentleman I know I raised."

"Thanks, Mom."

"And no more bar fights, got it?"

They laughed as he made his way upstairs to the woman he wanted for the long haul.

Chapter Sixteen

Grace moaned as Evan braced the back of her head with his strong hand and kissed her deeply, raw heat building between their bodies. A frustrated growl of sexual tension ripped through him, turning her on and making her weep. She throbbed for relief, begged him to touch her. And when his hand scanned down her body and reached the apex of her thighs, she trembled as her body roared to life.

She could feel the arousal grow between them as his greedy kisses ruined her for any other man's. His teeth nibbled her lip and his fingers dove deep inside her as warmth pulsated between her legs. She wanted the relief of him fully entering and claiming her body, putting her out of her aching misery. He took his time licking and biting her skin as he moved lower and sunk his head between her legs. She cried out as his hot breath hovered over the sensitive, swollen part of her.

"Grace…"

"Don't stop, Evan."

"Gracie…"

~

Her eyes popped open and she sat up, panting in panic. Looking over, Evan sat beside her in bed and snickered with a knowing grin on his face. "Hey, doll, you were dreaming."

Heat flooded her cheeks as she caught the scene before her. She was in his childhood bedroom. And she…*shit.* Glancing over at him, she saw his shoulders bobbing as he pressed his lips together in an attempt to contain his laughter.

"I-I h-h-had a nightmare."

"Mmmhmm. Sure you did." His lightening blue eyes studied her and scanned her breasts. She glanced down and saw her nipples hardened through the material of his Henley. His tongue licked over his bottom lip, and she knew she was busted. "So, how good was I, princess?"

"Shut up!" She fell back into her pillows and covered her face with the bedspread as Evan bellowed in laughter. "Shut up, Matthews! Leave me alone."

"Grace, baby, nothing to be ashamed of." He leaned back and tugged on the covers, lowering them to see her expression. She huffed out in an attempt to move stray locks of hair fallen over her face. His hands brushed the tendrils aside. "Those moans were fucking sexy. They woke me up and turned me on. Especially the way you said my name. I was debating whether I should've let you finish."

Grace slapped her hands over her eyes and shook her head. "You're driving me crazy, Matthews."

"And you're driving my restraint crazy, Clark." He clasped her wrists and pulled them away. "Don't cover your face, beautiful."

"You're like a damn saint for putting up with me,

Evan." She pouted, knowing that she was asking a lot from him. It was only a matter of time before he bailed. "No other guy would wait this out. Why are you?"

He stayed silent as they studied each other, his eyes turning heavy and dark. "There's something about you, Gracie Lynn." He gave her a tender kiss and her body thrummed in desire. "And I promised to be good, so I'm trying my best not to take you over." As he parted, she looked at the opening of his shirt. It had a scooped collar with a three-button placket, and under the left side of his collarbone peeked words from a tattoo.

Grace reached forward and grazed her fingers across it. "You have a tattoo?"

Smiling, he let his fingertips trail her jawline. "I do."

She pondered how she'd gone so long without knowing that, and she wanted to take time discovering all of him. "What's it say?" She reached out with her hands to move his shirt aside, but he caught her wrists, his body pinning her down as he pushed her arms back above her head.

"You'll have to get me naked to find out, Gracie."

"I thought you said you were trying to be good."

"I'm still just a man."

She wriggled under him trying to unlock his grip. "Show me the tat! You're such a tease."

"Really, cupcake? Don't even." She tried to fight him, but he was too strong, and when she felt his erection against her thigh, she stopped squirming and whimpered in want. "Hi, Gracie Lynn." His voice was heady and dripping with lust.

"Hey, Matthews." They gazed at each other with

wide eyes, both of their chests pumping in and out with a fervent blaze.

He let her wrists go and he grasped the collar of his shirt with one hand, moving it aside. Her fingertips skimmed across the words inked on his light skin. She inhaled faintly as she read his tattoo, the cursive lettering small –

Boldness has genius, power and magic in it.

His eyes remained on her as her lashes swept up and she blinked. "How long have you had this tattoo, Evan?"

"Since I was twenty-six. I told you Goethe was my favorite poet."

She traced the lettering gently, then placed her palm over his heart. "It's beautiful, Evan."

"Thanks, Gracie," he said in a quiet whisper as he leaned down and kissed her forehead.

"Why that quote?"

"Dreams will always stay dreams until you become bold enough to act on them." Grace stared at him, her mouth agape as he moved to his side of the bed, his back turned towards her. "Try to get some sleep, babe. Our flight leaves tomorrow evening."

Grace would never get sleep. Not when her body yearned for the man next to her. Not when he desired her just as much. Not when she was falling for him so damn hard and fast she was losing her balance. Being practical and being in deep infatuation at the same time was highly improbable, but not impossible…was it?

~

The daylight streamed through the window leaving Grace the opportunity to study the handsome glow of Evan Matthews. She listened to his steady breathing, watching his chest rise and fall under his hand and the way his long lashes fluttered with closed eyes. Her body curled beside his and she contemplated how far her feelings were bourgeoning for this man and his family.

Men never wanted to work for her trust, yet here was this gorgeous creature striving to earn hers. Of course, there had been a few men who swore they'd wait for her, but when it came down to it, they weren't serious. She saw the red flags, expected them, and she instantly backed away as soon as she spotted them. Evan's red flags weren't popping up, and the closer she got, the less she noticed them, no matter how much she kept her heart at bay.

She squiggled out of the bed as quietly as possible and took her clothes with her to the bathroom to change. The smell of something freshly-baked wafted up throughout the second floor and Grace made her way downstairs.

Evan's mother sat at the kitchen table reading a magazine and sipping on a steamy cup of coffee. Her crystal blue eyes peered over half-mooned spectacles and she smiled. "Good morning, Grace."

"Good morning." The younger woman greeted as she made her way over to the coffeemaker and pointed. "May I?"

"Of course, sweetie. Come join me. I have some fresh biscuits here you can munch on. Cream for the coffee's in the fridge."

Grace fixed her cup and sat beside the woman Evan so loved. It wasn't difficult to see it radiate from him when he was around her. Rebecca reached over and handed her a plate then opened the basket with recently baked goods. "Thank you."

"I hope you've had a great Thanksgiving with us, Grace. Evan was so excited when he told me you had agreed to join him."

"I'm thankful. You have such a fun family."

"Oh, honey, you just saw a small bit of them. You haven't met the aunts, uncles, and cousins. We're a large bunch, so we can get rowdy. Christmas is insane."

Grace smiled at the notion of a full house. "That's amazing. Did Evan always know he wanted to be an actor?"

"Oh, yes. Every summer he went to acting camps. He was in every single school play since he was five years old. That boy basically popped out of the womb performing."

Grace laughed as she drank her coffee. "He's very talented."

"Yeah, he's always had a knack for it. And he was always putting on productions here at the house with his sisters. He was the director, of course, and they had to follow the script he'd write for them. Then when he got the cousins involved it became a huge deal. He was always putting on shows."

Grace could see younger Evan running around, bossing people into stage positions. "And how did Zach come into the picture?"

"Middle school was tough for Evan. He's always

been my sensitive boy. His father and I divorced and it wasn't easy on us by any means, even if Evan makes it out to be so. He was affected by it, but he stepped up in the family and took care of us girls. Zach became like his brother, and we took him in when his parents moved away."

"And Mama Matthews became the number one woman in my life that nobody will ever live up to." Zach approached and bent to give Rebecca a kiss on the cheek. She reveled in the affection, loving her children more than anything. Including Zach.

"Morning, Zachary. Coffee's on, and I hope you made up the bed."

"Since when has Zach ever cleaned after himself?" Hilary entered yawning and pushed Zach away from the coffee machine, grabbing the carafe before he could.

"I'm not a total slob anymore, Hilary."

"Just a part-time one." She leaned against the counter and sipped on her black coffee, her eyes closed as she rejoiced the taste. Her straight hair was ratted up on the back of her head and she was still in her oversized pajamas. "Coffee is my life."

"Thanks for taking the last of it." Zach grimaced as he began to make more. "Scoot over, walking dead."

"What's for breakfast?" Evan strolled in and moved toward the table. He gave his mother a kiss and then leaned over toward Grace, his lips taking hers swiftly. "Mmm, you taste like very sweet coffee, Gracie Lynn."

"And you taste minty fresh," Grace said as she ran a hand over Evan's stubbly jaw.

He sat beside her and served himself a biscuit,

slathering butter and strawberry preserves over it. "How'd you sleep, Grace? Anymore nice dreams?"

She gave him a warning look, but nobody seemed to catch on to the intent of his question. "I slept fine, despite your snoring."

"I may snore, but I definitely don't talk in my sleep."

"Evan, stop," she whispered under her breath.

"That's not what you said last night, baby doll," he rumbled near her ear. She reached under the table and pinched his thigh. "Ouch," he laughed and clasped her hand away from his leg. "Okay. Stopping."

"I'm guessing there's some inside joke or sexual overtone type thing going on there, but I'm too tired to inquire or tease at this point. Pass me a biscuit, please." Hilary sat across from Evan and began to fix her own biscuit as Zach sat beside her.

"You leaving today too, Zach?" Hilary asked as she fixed another biscuit and handed it to him. Rebecca took out eggs and bacon from the fridge and got prepared to cook.

"No. Tomorrow. Gotta catch up on some stuff at my place." He ate, looking to Evan who had his eyes anchored on Grace. Zach snapped his fingers at him. "Loverboy, Mike told me to set up that meeting for next week, so I'll get with your schedule and see when you can fly out to L.A. for that."

Evan's eyes latched to Zach's with caution, then looked away and nodded slightly. "Fine."

"What meeting, honey? You finally found a movie you want to direct?" His mom cracked the eggs into a bowl, poured milk and started whisking them.

Grace watched as he closed his eyes in frustration and shook his head. "No, I haven't found one yet. John Whitford wants me to be in his next project."

"Holy shit!" Hilary's eyes popped open and her coffee cup banged on the table. Evan might have been an actor, but Hilary was a huge movie buff. "John Whitford? That's huge!"

"You taking it, sweetie?"

"I don't know yet, Mom." He glanced at Grace, letting his knuckles brush her cheek as he went to the stove, taking over the eggs and helping his mother cook.

"He will if he knows what's good for him," Zach asserted.

"Well, ultimately, it's what Evan thinks is best," Rebecca stressed as she turned the bacon.

"He thought *The Ending Series* wasn't best, and look how that turned out," Zach reminded them. "Thank Christ they kept on offering it to him."

"Yeah, he'd be kicking himself in the ass," Hilary laughed. "And be making genital herpes commercials."

"Thank you, Hil, but I don't think it would've come to that."

The sound of bacon sizzling filled the room as everyone sipped on their coffee. Grace tried to settle her stomach as she grasped she had been ignoring a huge red flag. Evan was already thinking about his next project. She had to remember his address wasn't permanent, and he would soon be leaving Austin and her behind.

Chapter Seventeen

Grace had come off her vacation high, and over a week without seeing Evan was giving her major withdrawals. With the combination of his hectic filming schedule and her dealing with maintenance issues from tenants, catching up with her small fan following, and finishing her memoir, time with each other had been limited. They texted and called when they could, but Grace couldn't help but feel herself pulling back on purpose.

Evan was in Los Angeles over the weekend, agreeing to one of the biggest film directors in the world, and Grace needed to make sure she was in the right headspace when she realized he was going to leave her. To take her mind off of everything, she worked on finishing the desk in her garage.

The sounds of Chris Stapleton drifted from her radio as she sanded through the stain. Memories of Evan and his family flashed through her mind, and she began to miss the idea of being in Boston. She had checked the weather app and saw it was snowing there. Texas in December was in the high 70s, and she wasn't yet in the Christmas spirit. Perhaps it was because she would spend her Christmas the way she spent every one before that. Alone.

Grace scrubbed at the desk frantically, her mind and heart at war with one another as she fought emotions that were bubbling to the surface. The memoir, Boston, Evan and his stupidly perfect tattoo, and his wonderful family, and his beautiful hands and the way he touched and kissed her was too much. He was making her want so much more with him and she wasn't sure it was possible. He was all too much.

"Gracie." Breathless, she glanced up to see Evan standing in her garage. "I called out your name several times." Had it really been almost eleven days since seeing him? It felt like ages. He moved toward her, tall and clean and so handsome her heart twisted. "Are you okay?"

"Yeah." She panted and dropped the sandpaper down on the floor. She turned away and reached for the can of gloss and a paintbrush. Looking at him was painful. She had missed him so much and was longing for his touch. "I thought you were coming in tomorrow."

"Caught an early flight."

"How'd it go?" She took her gloves off and uncapped the varnish setting it on the desk.

"It was fine."

He moved toward her to give her a kiss but she backed away. "I'm sweaty, Evan."

Grace began to dip the brush and she studied the task at hand, ungluing her eyes from him. Her arm swooshed over the wood in a hurry as she tried to bottle her emotions inside. "Gracie, what's going on?"

"Nothing."

"Stop it. You've been weird since we left Boston."

"We haven't seen each other since Boston, Evan."

She chuckled forcefully, trying to keep things light. He wasn't buying it, but she continued. "Tell me about the meeting. Did you take the role?"

"What if I told you I didn't?"

Grace froze and shot him a glance, his eyes feeling cold. She tried to catch her breath as she set down the paint brush. "You have to, Evan. You'll regret it if you don't."

"You think?"

"I know. It's an amazing opportunity. Please…tell me you took it." Although it hurt, she meant what she said to him. He wanted the part, and she wanted that for him. The last thing he needed was a woman who would keep him from what he was born to do, and she loved that he was passionate about his job.

"Things are being discussed."

She gave a half-hearted smile, looking down at her hands. "Good. You don't just turn down an opportunity with John Whitford." Looking back at him, she saw his lips pressed in a flat line and a crinkle between his eyebrows. He was definitely deep in thought. "Don't give up that role. I know you want it."

"How do you know?"

She shrugged. "You don't think I can tell? Besides, his movies are always amazing, and you still haven't found your directing project. It'll be good for you to take it on. Fight for the role if you need to, but don't give it up."

He breathed in deeply, and she felt consumed by him, like the space he took was overwhelming her. "I should finish this up," she said reaching for the brush.

Before she could finish the attempt, he grabbed her wrist and pulled her against him.

Her arms flung around him as he kissed her with potency. His tongue swept over her, dipping inside with a needy motion that begged for more. "I don't care if you're sweaty, Grace. I don't care about the fucking desk. I don't give a shit about that movie, princess. Not when I need to feel you."

"Evan…"

His hands grasped the sides of her face and she felt the heat of his breath over her as he spoke with a ruggedness that vibrated through her. "Tell me what's going on inside your head, Gracie." Her body was tense, but her effort to move away from him failed as he grasped her shoulders. "Don't run from me. Talk."

"I just have a lot on my mind right now."

"Is this about the tabloid?"

Grace parted from him, confusion written on her expression. "Tabloid?"

"Guessing you haven't seen it then?"

"Another tabloid?" Here was something else she needed to worry about. What was being said now? Criticism and scrutiny was not her idea of fun. And what if her parents found out? How would they react to her dating a Hollywood star? Maybe they wouldn't care at all. It wouldn't surprise her.

"Look, why don't you get showered, and then we'll get some dinner and talk?" He tried to lean down to kiss her again, but she backed away from him.

"Or you could talk now."

"Like you're talking to me?" They were silent, the

electric sizzle growing between them. She didn't want to talk because the truth was scary. The truth that this might not last, that she would lose him sooner than she wanted. "Take a shower, Grace. I'll come over with some food and we'll discuss things, okay?"

She nodded knowing this was it. She was going to have to stop it all before she got in too deep, but everything hurt when she thought of how much she was going to miss everything about him.

"They found out, Evan." She held out her phone as he took out the cartons of Chinese food he had gotten delivered. "They know my name. Who I am and what I do."

He glanced at the screen and nodded. "Yeah, my people have been asking me about it."

"People?"

"Publicists."

She put down the phone that showcased an article of the two of them sharing a kiss at the bar they went to in Boston as well as a photo of them holding hands at the airport. "And?"

"I haven't given a statement yet." They sat at the table with food and silverware before them. Evan speared a piece of broccoli from her chicken with vegetables and chomped on it as he moved his Lo Mein toward her to share.

"Do you need to?"

"I want to," he answered seriously.

"But why? I mean, maybe it's better to keep it quiet." She picked at her food, but had no appetite. Fear, mixed with confusion were taking over her thoughts. He wanted to tell the whole world she was his, yet if it didn't last, that failure would forever be out for everyone to see. He didn't seem to care, yet she did.

"The more we keep quiet, the more they'll want to find out. It's better to announce it, Grace."

"Look, Evan," her stomach fluttered as she cleared her throat, "I've been putting off talking to you because I admit I've been a bit selfish."

He stopped chewing his food, his eyebrows raised in interest. "What do you mean?"

"I like spending time with you, and part of me doesn't want to do this. The fact that this should end-"

"Whoa, wait a second. What are you talking about?"

"Well, I mean, it has to end. This can't really go anywhere."

Annoyance flashed over his manner, and he instantly straightened in his chair. "It's been going great, Grace. I took you to Boston. I introduced you to my family and my friends."

"It was just a poker bet."

"Screw the fucking bet. Do you seriously still think I'm playing around with you? Or do you just not want me? What's the real problem here?"

He was intimidating when he looked angry, and Grace was losing ground. "We come from different worlds, Evan. I don't belong in yours. You need to follow your passions, and I don't want to hold you back. I don't want to be held back either, and I have work to do. I just don't know how this can happen between us."

He huffed and put his fork down. "Grace, you can't be thinking this is going to fail. I need you to open up and trust me." His all-consuming eyes pierced hers and it shook her to her core. "I'm not going to give up on you, but you need to let me know you're in it with me, okay? I can't do it on my own." He waited for her to answer, but her breath caught in her throat and she was unable to form a coherent thought. "I see a future with you, babe, but if you can't see me in yours then I need to know now, because I'm putting my heart on the fucking line, and I can't stay in limbo anymore."

"But, you'll leave and long-distance…" He was always so rational. It made her whole argument seem ridiculous, and she was no longer able to find excuses to keep him away.

"I don't care. I want you with me, Gracie. Do you want me?" She could hear the flow of blood rushing through her ears. He was putting himself out there, and she needed to take the risk. Who cares if they were from different worlds? Truth was, they weren't that different. They'd both been wounded, they both needed someone to trust, and that was enough for them to understand each other. "Do you want me, Grace?"

His expression showed just as much vulnerability as she felt. She found it in her to walk toward him and sit in his lap, cupping his face in her palms as she stared into his azure eyes. Their breathing picked up as she took her time studying him, letting her hands run through the sides of his hair. She had never felt more secure than with him. He was open, honest, and guarding her in the way she had always wanted from a man, and in that second, she saw herself reflected back in his eyes. It was unreasonable to be at war with her own desires. *Follow your heart, Grace.* "I'm falling for you, Evan Matthews. My mind is telling me to stop it from happening, but my heart won't allow it, and it's terrifying."

He swathed his arms around her and let his head rest on her heart. "Surrender to it, baby. Live it with me, please. I'm scared too, but I want you so much." He looked up at her and clenched the back of her head, bringing her down for her mouth to merge onto his.

Her arms pulled him closer, her lips took his in, and her heart felt like bursting. She let herself fully open to feel every emotion she had been holding back. She wanted him with everything she had, and she was finally willing to do what it took to trust him, have faith in him, and believe in what had been missing from her life for far too long.

His heart almost stopped when she said she didn't think things could work between them, so he put his foot down, unable to take it slow any further. He needed to know she was committed to him, wanting to build something stronger with him. Girls had come and gone in his life, but nobody ever made him feel what Grace made him feel.

Now he was holding her in his arms, and he wanted her there forever. Her body heat was overtaking him, making him want her with such raw ferocity, he wished the clothes between them were gone. His lips parted from hers and his gaze caressed her pink cheeks. He pushed a strand of fallen hair back with gentle strokes, but covetousness blazed within him, and his body ached with desire. His jaw ticked as he shifted her and he knew she could feel him hard and wanting.

"I'm sorry. I know you're uncomfortable," she panted.

Grace tried to get up, but he clasped her body to his. "No, you're uncomfortable, angel, but you better get used to me being this turned on around you, because it's constant."

She held her breath and then sputtered out laughing as she leaned against his shoulder. "I am driving you crazy, huh?"

"You're just now realizing it?"

She shot her head up and leaned forward, letting her nose trail up his jaw to his ear. Her warm breath brushed against it as she whispered in a throaty voice. "Maybe I'll make it up to you." She nibbled his earlobe and flicked it with her tongue and he felt himself strained against the zipper of his jeans.

"Don't tease me, doll," he growled into her hair and drowned in her strawberry scent. He pulled back again and looked into her dark eyes. "Gracie, tell me when the last time you had sex was."

Her body fell rigid against him as she looked away. He caught her chin with his fingers and guided her to look at him. "Does it matter?"

"Yes."

"When was the last time you had sex, Evan?"

He gave a small grin. "Three months ago. With an ex-fling. We see each other from time to time to time just to catch up." She caught his meaning and tried to get off of his lap. He fastened his arms tighter around her. "Don't get upset."

"I'm not upset, Evan."

"You are upset, Gracie Lynn. Don't worry, there hasn't been anyone since I met you." He looked at her scowling face and chuckled. "You're so cute when you do that."

"What?"

"Pout like that."

"I'm not pouting."

"Yes, you are. Grace, I've never gone into something with a woman without letting her know what the intentions were." His eyes focused on hers. "I want you long-term, and I want to know all I can about you. It can't happen if you don't tell me. When's the last time you slept with someone?"

"I was sixteen…" Grace mumbled quietly as she picked on a loose string on the collar of his Henley.

"Wait…when you lost your virginity, right?" he asked for clarification.

She nodded. "And when I last had sex."

"What?" He looked at her in shock. What the hell was he supposed to say to that? He knew she had been cautious with who she gave her heart to, but this went deeper. "One guy? Just one guy, ever?"

"One guy. One time."

Evan exhaled from the astonishment. How had she

not slept with anyone else? How could a man not want to take her, love her, and want to give her the world? "That fucker. He hurt you."

"It was a long time ago." He watched her in fascination as she struggled to find words. "I've dated, tried, but nobody ever stuck around long enough to get to the point-"

"Where you felt comfortable?" Evan finished. She nodded and he felt angrily protective of her. "There's more to it though, isn't there?" He kept his hands roaming her back, soothing her and coaxing her to spill more secrets.

She shrugged as he kissed her lips, letting her know her revelation was okay. Despite the pressure he'd feel being the only other guy she'd sleep with since the douchebag, he actually looked forward to the idea that he'd be the one to make her sexual experience something to enjoy.

Melting into him, she let her mouth become wild as she licked and nibbled and stroked. She arched against him for more, a simple kiss beginning to fan a flame that was growing. "I think I'm ready," she breathed between kisses as she devoured him, tugging her fingers through his short hair.

He broke their kiss, and drew for breath, his eyes taking in her puffy lips and making him want more of her. "You feel so good, Grace, you don't know how much I want you. But sweetheart, I want you to know, not to *think* you know." He was so hard, so frantic to feel her body under his, but tonight wasn't the night. Not until she felt unquestionably relaxed with him, and she was almost there. He smiled at her and gave her one last peck before slapping her butt cheek. "Food's gotten cold. Let's reheat and watch a Christmas movie."

Grace's grin grew wide. "On Hallmark? Please?"

"Sure, why not?"

"Seriously?"

"They make me feel all fluffy inside with their cheesy endings," he joked.

"I think I met the man of my dreams."

"Oh, honey, I know you did. Your moaning in my childhood bed proved it."

She jumped off of him as she punched his arm playfully. "Shut it."

"Oh, Evan, don't stop…" he mimicked her voice and watched as her cheeks reddened. "It's been haunting me since. I can't wait until I get to hear that for real, babe."

He started taking the containers of food toward the microwave. Grace followed. "You keep this up and you won't ever hear it for real."

"At least tell me what position we were in. Missionary? Cowgirl? Doggie style?"

She ignored him as he heated the food and watched her as she swung her hips toward the fridge taking out a bottle of white wine. She served two glasses and set them on the table. "You'll never know, Matthews."

He could still imagine her perky nipples under his Henley, her long brown hair flowing over her shoulders, and her lips expelling those erotic teasing sounds of what was in store for him when he pleased her soon. He couldn't wait for the day he could taste her, take her, and make her scream and beg for more.

"Come on, Gracie, give me just a little…"

She turned and smirked at him. "You'll have to get me naked to find out, Evan."

"That's the line I used for the tattoo. You can't use my line."

"It is, and I did."

"But then I showed it to you. I showed you mine, you show me yours, doll."

"You already played your card. Sorry, bud."

"Dammit."

They sat down to reheated Chinese food and talked about their week. By the time he knew it, Evan needed to head back to his place since his call time to the studio was set for six in the morning. Grace followed him to the door and grabbed his hand. "Evan?"

"Yeah?"

She lifted his knuckles to her lips and kissed them gently. "Thank you for being patient. I know it's not easy."

He leaned in and kissed her brow. "Anything for you." He winked at her and then added for good measure. "But yeah, it's fucking hard…literally."

She rolled her eyes and laughed. "You had to ruin the moment, Matthews."

"Goodnight, beautiful."

"Wait." She moved toward her laptop sitting on her desk in the corner of the living room and walked back to him. "Here." She handed him a USB drive.

"What's this?"

"My memoir."

He grasped onto it tightly, and looked into her

concerned eyes, feeling as if his heart were going to burst. He wanted to know all about her, and it would be there for him to discover. She was giving him the key to her world, and he was ready to open it and find out all he could. "Thank you, Gracie Lynn."

"You're welcome." He began to walk away when he heard her voice turn throaty. "Evan? Your face was buried between my legs, your tongue was licking me, and you were amazing at it."

His mouth dropped open as she winked and shut the door. He groaned at the imagery that played on his mind. Evan had a strong feeling his little angel was actually a vixen in disguise.

Chapter Eighteen

He was in love. At least that's what Evan realized the moment he closed the document that held the words Grace wrote. He knew more or less what she was about, but this book, it was an insight into her soul that went beyond what he could. It was her heart, her thoughts, her fears, her hurts, her wants, her needs, her vulnerabilities all put before him. And he treasured every single word.

He glanced at the alarm clock on his nightstand and cursed. It was probably too late to see her. After a long day on set, he had plopped on his bed and read through the entire memoir. Only stopping for a restroom break and Zach's annoying demand to eat a fucking sandwich, Evan had devoured what Grace had written.

His body was full of frenetic energy that he couldn't contain. He had to see her. Light streamed from her bedroom, so he adamantly made his way over, and rang the bell, his heart and mind in overdrive. What would he say to her? What could he say? How could he put into words what he felt when the words would never be enough? She took ages to answer and he began to worry. He knocked on the door with urgency.

Grace finally stood before him, her hair flowing down in long waves. Her skin glowed under the porch light and her expression showed concern as she wrapped her robe around her small body. He found her so sexy it was hard for him to breathe. "Evan? I just got out of the bath. What's wrong?"

He studied her, taking a step inside and closed the door behind him. He hadn't said those three words, and watching her now, he wasn't sure he should. But God, he wanted to. With every fiber of his being, he wanted to shout it out and tell her. Instead, he embraced her with his warmth and strength.

Her soft arms wrapped around his waist as his chest inhaled and exhaled against her cheek. "Evan? What happened?" Her head tilted up, her coffee brown eyes puzzled.

"Gracie..." Holding her in his arms felt so natural. She belonged in them. There was no way he could ever be without her. "I understand, Grace. I understand you now."

Her breathing faltered. "You read it?"

"All of it." He could feel the tension rising through her as she attempted to pull away, but he kept her against him. She said nothing as she stared into his chest. He lifted her chin so her eyes could meet his. "I really see you, Gracie. And I love it all."

He caressed her face in his hands and dropped his head, taking her mouth against his, wanting to prove to her he loved her, needed her, and wouldn't leave her. A whimpering sound emitted from the back of her throat as he let his tongue tangle with hers. Her body twisted against him as his hands gripped her hips over the robe he wished to discard from her body that needed to be kissed, licked, and possessed by only him.

Her fingers tangled in his hair as she greedily responded. He growled as his erection pressed against her belly. He never fit with a woman so entirely, but she owned him, and he would do what he could to own her right back.

They began stumbling their way across the room as they kissed. "Bedroom," Grace mumbled through their lips. It felt like forever, but they finally reached the bed and tumbled down. Grace yelped as she fell on top of him. He grasped her body to his as they laughed, looking into each other's eyes and smiling. Their panting breaths slowed and their gazes grew with passion.

"Hi, Gracie Lynn." He touched her cheek gently with gliding fingertips.

"Hey, Matthews," she whispered, kissing his lips tenderly. Her hips instinctively rubbed against him, and she let out the smallest moan. His hands moved lower and grabbed her waist, pushing her harder against him, the seam of his zipper hitting between her legs just right. She gasped. "Evan…I want you. Now."

"You sure?"

"Positive."

His mouth trailed down her neck to the opening of her robe. "You naked under here, beautiful?"

She nodded as he lagged his mouth lower, kissing the soft mounds of her breasts. His hands reached up and squeezed them as he took a nipple between his lips. He loved the way she panted at the sensations of his teeth, his lips, and his stubble against her delicate flesh. She then seized his hand in hers and moved it lower between their bodies.

His mind raced as she guided him, and he inhaled as he became drunk with the smell of her desire. He found the opening of her robe and dipped his finger between her legs. She was dripping wet and ready. She groaned out in pleasure, shuddering as she stirred her hips against him. Fabric was still in their way, but Evan took control as Grace's body writhed on his hand. He licked and kissed her neck steadily, her stomach clenching as his fingers worked with cadence.

He watched when those mysterious chocolate eyes opened and gazed into his with a dreamy expression. "God, that feels amazing," she moaned low as her lips hovered over his. The feeling of her slick folds over his fingers was beyond what he could imagine. The ache in his body was simply moved aside as he studied her facial expression, her reactions, completely mesmerized. Every time she bit her bottom lip, or sighed out in want, or squeezed her eyes closed, it made him thirsty for more. But when she opened them and gazed into his soul, she was breathtaking.

And she was his.

"Gracie, you're so beautiful…" His fingers continued to pump as they grazed the most sensitive part of her. He could feel the way she was beginning to clench around him as he dipped in and caressed back out.

"I can't take it…" She breathed in as she stilled and her expression tightened.

"Let go. Don't think." He brushed his fingers against her with the slightest stroke, and the ripples began as her hands dug into his shoulders. She broke and shook with an uncontrollable rhythm as her orgasm ripped through her body.

The pace of his fingers slowed as Grace rode out the spasms against him. He took his time covering her with kisses, elation running through him as he watched her fall from her high. He wanted to keep his hand where it was, but instead shifted his body to get a better look at her.

"Gracie? You okay, doll?"

"I think I died."

He chuckled as he lifted her hand and released it. It slapped him in the face as it fell lifelessly against him. "Ow!"

Grace lifted her head lazily and hummed as she kissed the cheek her hand hit. "I'm sorry. But we have to do that again. Like all the time."

He kissed her forehead and ran his hands up and down her back. "Mm…I could think of some other things we could do besides that."

"Let's get started, then." She stood in front of him and removed her robe slowly, letting it pool to the ground near her feet. His eyes devoured her beauty, the smoothness of her light, lush skin, round breasts, hips, and thighs meant only for him.

"God, you're stunning."

Evan stood and reached behind him pulling off his shirt. Her eyes roamed his chest, reviewing him with a longing to touch. She hadn't needed to say anything to let him know how much she anticipated him. He saw it in every breath she rapidly released and in every inch of her pebbled flesh. He reached for her hands and flattened her palms over his fast paced heart. "I'm nervous too, Grace."

And he was, for this was the first woman who ever held his heart so tightly, he would never find anyone who would compare.

Grace inhaled, wondering if Evan was in fact as anxious as she felt. After sensing his heart race, she began to trace over his body, drinking in the pleasurable pain that radiated through him. She let herself explore the strength of his shoulders and torso, moving to his tattoo and placing a soft kiss over it.

She took time appreciating his form. It was the first time she would be with a man and not a boy who fumbled his way through sex. Evan would be a generous lover, and the affection radiating from him was overwhelmingly beautiful. Her reticent fingertips scraped his rippled stomach as she headed toward the top of his jeans. He groaned. "Baby, you're driving me crazy."

She snapped her hands away. "I'm sorry."

"No, I like it," he chuckled breathlessly and waited for her to continue. She fumbled with the button and zipper, and lowered his jeans and boxer briefs in one swift motion. Stepping out of them, he stood before her.

Her eyes widened in apprehension. She wasn't quite sure she could accommodate him. He knowingly touched her cheek. "It won't be like it was for you before, Grace. I'll make sure I don't hurt you."

He had definitely read her memoir. She wrote of the uncomfortably awkward and painful night she slept with the *unnamed friend*. The backseat of a car, no anticipation, no care was how her only time went. Afterwards she had felt used, and Kyle hadn't given the slightest concern, calling her lousy and boring. The other times she thought she would try with the men she dated the memories always shot forward. The feelings weren't deep enough for her to give herself over to someone, and she couldn't break that promise. Being with Evan now felt completely different, and she knew why it hadn't worked with anyone else. She had been waiting for him.

"Lay back on the bed." His voice was raspy and firm as she followed his order. Anxious and anticipating brown eyes followed his movements as he reached for the wallet in his castoff jeans and procured several foil packets. Holding them between his fingers, he plopped them on the nightstand.

"Hurry." She reached for one of the packets and offered it to him with an unsteady hand.

"Don't rush, babe," he stated gruffly as he covered her hand with his, setting the condom aside.

"I'm ready. I want you inside me."

"We'll get there." He nodded softly, tension in his jaw as he tried to control his need to take her quickly. Grace lay back as he took a moment to let his eyes roam her body. She chewed on her lip bashfully, squeezing her lids shut. As if he could read her mind, he whispered, "You're so damn perfect, Grace."

His mouth took hers passionately as he moved over

her, taking his time until she let her searching hands enclose his neck. The feel of his bare chest rubbing against hers caused a friction she had never experienced. He trailed his tongue to her breasts, palming one in his hand as he took the other between his lips. He tugged and sucked leisurely until her nipples hardened and she moaned audibly. The pleasure was so strong, her hips rocked up trying to take his body against hers.

Trailing his mouth down, he squeezed her hip. "You're trembling."

"I-nobody, I've never done –"

"Open up, doll," he pleaded, his lips moving over the most intimate part of her body. His hands held the back of her thighs as he attempted pulling her legs apart. She clutched them together apprehensively. "Look at me, babe. Don't be embarrassed with me. I'll take care of you." His eyebrows drew together as he let his hands glide back over her thighs. "You have no idea how fucking sexy it is that I'm the first man who gets to taste you, Gracie Lynn. Sweetheart, spread your legs," he directed, his sincere eyes meeting hers, awaiting her compliance.

She slowly released to him, gasping when he lightly touched over her center with his finger. He urged her legs wider, advancing so his mouth was near. Tickling sensations from his warm breath feathered over her.

Evan descended, his mouth tugging on her with a tight suction that made her groan. His fingers pushed inside her, insistent against that soft spot that would make her lose control. Over and over, with changing motions, his fingers plunged as his mouth played. She felt the pressure building and her mind began to go numb as her mouth released unfamiliar sounds. Her eyes squeezed shut as her muscles tightened and her body let go. Her insides pulsed around his fingers and she loudly cried out, coming into his mouth and quivering. Her legs tried to close from the intensity, and he finally began to decelerate his touch as her body continued to ripple beneath him.

He trailed kisses up to her neck, then took her mouth gently as she tried catching her breath. Her lids were heavy as she gave a languid smile. "How was that, sweetheart?"

"That was incredible." She kissed him affectionately as he moved his hand back down between her legs and gently stroked her. She quaked from the sensitivity.

He reached for the condom and rolled it over him. He let his body rest over her, his erection brushing against her as he awaited her body to respond. She closed her eyes as he positioned his elbows against each side of her shoulders. His hands brushed her hair back from her face and he placed indulgent kisses on her mouth.

She panted with tension, her figure squirming up against him. "Grace, steady your breathing. Take a deep breath," he whispered delicately. He positioned himself, pressing inside her and feeling her shake. He composed himself, as she tried to push her hips up keenly.

"Slowly, baby," he whispered unevenly, dropping his head in her neck. He distributed his weight and nudged consciously in again, stopping after she whimpered. He could feel her stretching as he entered little by little. "Look at me."

When her eyes flickered open, he pushed inside and filled her. Grace assumed it would hurt like before, but the small moment of discomfort disappeared and was replaced by an all-consuming pleasure. "Move, Evan. Please."

His eyes never leaving hers, he responded, billowing in and out of her gradually. "You feel so good, Grace." His motions increased as she moaned. Her hips began to prod harder into him as he helped guide her, finding their rhythm. The sounds emanating from his throat were arousing her in ways she never thought possible. She gripped him tighter as their speed amplified.

Grace tightened up again quickly, then fell over the edge, crying out as her fingers dug into his slick skin. She pulsated around him while he nuzzled her neck and drove deeply inside her. He groaned through a wave of emotions that hit him like a flood. He called her name as he stilled over her, his hips jerking as he reached his climax.

Evan stayed inside Grace whispering sweet words she couldn't comprehend as he continued caressing her face with languid kisses. They both caught their breath, basking in the after-effects of orgasm. She had never felt anything that could compare.

His lips touched the shell of her ear as he whispered, "How you feeling, Grace?"

She hummed as he feathered kisses by her pulse. "Relaxed," she sighed as he then reviewed her.

"That's it?" She smiled at his questioning glare. "I

thought as a writer you'd have more words to execute your emotions," he teased.

"My brain's too lazy to think."

"Stroke my ego here a bit, Grace. I was hoping you'd say it was earth-shattering, mind-blowing, amazing." He winked as she giggled.

"How about beautiful?"

He kissed her lips genially, nodding. "That works."

"It was also my first orgasm from someone other than myself." She stated peppering kisses over his jaw as he laughed.

"Well, you're definitely stroking my ego now."

"I'll stroke some other things later."

"Woman of my dreams," he sighed and lifted himself off of her. She winced as Evan exited her body and made his way to her bathroom to dispose of his condom. She watched as he walked back to her with a washcloth, and he reached her thighs signaling for her to open them. Hesitation played on her features. "Too late to be shy, babe."

After wiping her with gentle strokes, he tossed the cloth to the bathroom, then helped her get under the covers. They found tranquility as both of them snuggled beside each other. Her head rested on his chest and their breathing steadied. "I didn't hurt you, did I, Gracie?"

"No, it was perfect." She smiled at him as her hand roamed his chest.

"You were perfect."

"Thanks. I'm going to need lots of practice since I've been out of commission for a while."

He chuckled as she straddled him. "I'll be all too

happy to help, sunshine. I'll never get enough of you." His bright eyes roamed over her naked chest.

"I'm sure you say that to all the ladies," she joked.

"Not once." His gaze set earnestly on her. He sat up and braced the back of her neck with his hands. "Gracie, I'm so in love with you, and I've never felt this way with anyone before. You're it for me."

Her fingertips trailed his cheeks as she regarded him. There was no hiding, no games, nothing but their exposed selves. He was taking her as is, and she believed him. With all her heart. "Good. I saw the little statement that was made, you know."

Evan smiled wide as his hands trailed up and down her spine. "What statement?"

"*What statement*?" Grace mocked. "Jaime called me up, gushing about how happy she was that it was official. I didn't think it would be blasted over every single media outlet so quickly though."

"Oh. That statement. Well, as someone who stubbornly avoids letting the public know anything about my personal life, it's a big deal."

She felt her nerves tingle at that thought. "What'd it say again?"

"Shit if I remember." He put a finger to his chin and gazed up in thought. *"I saw Grace Lynn Clark in her wet shirt and perky nipples, and I knew…that's the girl."*

They both laughed as she hit his shoulder. "You're such a goofball."

"You tell me what it said, Grace. I didn't read it."

"Let me see if I can remember. *A rep for the actor stated that Evan Matthews is dating Austin-born author*

Grace Clark." She let her hands run through his hair as he continued to hold her in his arms trailing kisses on her chest.

He stopped what he was doing to gaze up at her. "That's it? Just that?"

Grace chuckled. "Something about a source confirming that you were *head-over-heels,* that you *took her to meet his family,* and that it was *very serious*."

"Fucking Zach was the source. Tool."

"Oh, so he got it wrong, did he?" She gave him a warning glare and he laughed.

"He got it right. That's the problem. It's nobody's business but ours." He stared at her with concentration. "Whatever happens outside of us, just please talk to me first, Gracie. Trust in me. Not them, okay?"

A smile played on her lips as she let her hips glide against his. She felt him stir and groan as her body rubbed over him. "I will, Evan. Besides, none of it will matter if we never leave this room. And I never want to leave."

"Deal," he grunted as his hands bound around her waist.

"We never even went on our second date," she joked as he splayed kisses over her.

"I think our screwing tonight counts, don't you?" he asked as Grace laughed heartily against him. "You ready for another go, doll?"

She bit her bottom lip and nodded. "You're definitely ready. And quickly."

"You don't understand how desperately I've wanted you. I was getting irrational." Her laugh morphed into a moan as he pressed harder against her. He grabbed a condom and rolled it on, then lifted her body, guiding it to sink down onto him.

The declaration of love in her ear twisted her heart. Grace had no idea it could feel this wonderful being connected to someone in such an intimate way. Their bodies moved together, his words hitting deep within her soul. *He loved her. He was in love with her.* The mix of her moans along with the deep rumblings from his chest spurred her to move faster and harder over him.

Evan was unrelenting, and she felt a swell of emotions beginning to unfold as he pushed inside her, his hands gripping her waist. "Open your eyes, Grace." She wasn't sure if she could tolerate looking into those eyes—those exquisite eyes that told her these passions were taking her over the brink. "Look at me, Gracie," he demanded as she scraped his shoulders, unable to contain her feelings. "Please, baby."

Grace's eyes flickered open, looking deeply into those blue irises radiating a cherished feeling she had never known before. "Oh, God…" A sound ripped from the back of her throat, and harsh breaths filled the room. "Evan—"

"Keep your eyes on me," his voice dripped with anguish, their foreheads touching as he held back his ecstasy, awaiting the acceptance of hers.

Grace attempted to focus on him, say something, but there was no room for breath. She panted for air as a strong wave ripped through her. She cried out his name, convulsing around him. He helped lift and move her body, every motion in perfect tempo as her gasp stuck in her throat. He drifted his hand to the point where their bodies linked and stirred his fingers over her, rapidly rubbing the swollen and sensitive nerves. She began to jolt as another orgasm consumed her, and this time his voice came with hers.

From that moment, she didn't know whose moans belonged to whom. Her heartbeat was his, his flesh was hers, and their bodies belonged to one another. As they caught their breaths and she felt his kisses on her neck, a tear fell down her cheek, and he tenderly wiped it away.

"You alright, sweetheart?" Grace nodded and kissed him. Evan took a deep breath and braced her jaw with both hands. "That was amazing."

She gave a lethargic laugh. "I had no idea it could feel this way."

He lifted her off of him and set her on the bed as he removed his condom for the second time that night and moved toward her bathroom. She closed her eyes, felt his warm, naked body pressing against hers and the sound of him saying, "I love you, Gracie Lynn," as he fell into a peaceful slumber.

After his breath steadied, she turned in his arms, staring at the way his eyelashes fluttered and his mouth let out little puffs of air. She grinned as her fingertips traced his perfect nose and sharp jaw. Her heartbeat raced again as his heated skin rested against hers. The dream of finding a true companion finally felt real. She whispered gently, "I feel so safe with you. How's that possible?"

She looked up and wondered if her brother had something to do with it. Evan stirred, a small mumble exiting his lips. She waited as he stilled again. "I love you, Evan Matthews. I'm so in love with you," she said with delicate breath.

Her eyes closed and she gave a gratified sigh as she fell asleep, never knowing at that moment that he opened his eyes and smiled back.

Chapter Nineteen

Sex. Hot, unbridled passion. Now Grace knew what romance novels captured. It was no longer a fantasy, but she was living it. Her aching muscles reminded her it was real as she clenched her thighs together, recalling the feel of Evan inside her. Her thoughts played over every stage the night before, and she couldn't wait to have him all over again, explore his body in ways she had never experienced.

She was beaming as she flipped a pancake over in the skillet. She moved to the fridge and took out strawberries and orange juice. The coffee was brewing and the bacon was set in the oven. Grace could cook when she wanted to, and she was happy enough this morning to go full-out for the man that she woke up to just a half an hour earlier. The nightmares had stopped, and for the first time in years, she felt at peace.

Her hips swayed to the Stevie Wonder record playing on her hi-fi as she began to whisk eggs in a bowl. She sang along to "Signed, Sealed, Delivered" as she took out the finished bacon from the oven and set it down on the cooling rack. When she turned back, her eye caught Evan leaning on the opposite counter watching her. His eyes danced over her lithe frame as he approached with a grin on his face.

His hair was sticking up everywhere and day old

scruff covered his strong jaw. His tight long-sleeved shirt stretched over his chest and his jeans sat low. Was it only a few hours before that she slept naked next to this gorgeous specimen? She remembered it was true as he wrapped his arms around her and she attempted to pay attention to the eggs cooking. He nuzzled his nose into her neck, breathing her in deep.

"Hey, Gracie Lynn."

"Hey, Matthews." She turned her face toward him and their lips met. "Hope you're hungry."

"Ravenous," he growled, letting his hands travel to her hips and squeezing through her robe. "But I guess we could raincheck and eat food first."

She bumped him with her behind and he groaned. "Well, I'm starving—for food first. But I won't mind going another round with you after."

"Good. Hopefully I can get that in before Josh summons me to the gym."

Grace grumbled. "It's Saturday. You have to work out today too?"

"Every day except Sunday. I hate missing the Bugs Bunny cartoons in the morning." He picked on a piece of bacon and began to serve two glasses of orange juice.

"Do they even show Bugs Bunny cartoons anymore?"

"Don't think so. Sad, huh?"

"Daffy's my favorite," Grace said as she served two plates with scrambled eggs, pancakes with strawberries on the side, and some bacon.

They easily moved around the kitchen, as if it was an everyday occurrence, and sat beside each other to eat.

"This is delicious, Gracie. Homemade pancakes?"

"Well, if you call adding water to the ready mix, then sure."

She watched him move. The way his lips chewed on his meal, the way his hands gripped the fork—everything about him screamed sexy. The air between them was thick with electricity and sexual tension. She wanted him again, and she couldn't believe it had gone as well as it had. Everything they had shared the night before, it was wonderful, and he was everything she could hope for. He was affectionate, but in control of the situation and of her.

"Gracie, you keep looking at me like that, and I'll have to make love to you here and now."

She felt her cheeks flush as she smiled and took a bite of her pancake. "So, what's the plan after your workout, Mr. Hollywood?"

"Making love to you, *my cherie amour*." Grace's stomach rolled in anticipation of what he could do to her, teach her, and make her feel. "But I also want to talk to you about that memoir."

Grace stopped eating and looked at him curiously. "What about it?"

"Did your publishers get back to you? What did they think?" He continued to chew on his food and took a sip of his orange juice.

Grace shrugged, wishing to change the subject. "Alan, my agent, said he's pretty sure publishers won't be picking it up."

He finished off his plate and set it aside. "Well, don't give up hope, Grace. It's a great read. You could always self-publish, too." She chewed her bottom lip out of nerves and he cupped her face. "What's up, buttercup?"

"I don't think I want people reading it. It's too personal. I'm going to work on a contemporary romance."

"Personal is what makes it captivating. Listen, this book wouldn't be just about honoring your brother. It shows how strong you were in overcoming what you went through, and it might help others cope with whatever issues they could have."

Grace hesitated, and shook her head. "I need to write a contemporary. Get my sales up. Otherwise they'll cut me from my contract." She took a sip of her coffee, then smiled. "Although, my group of loyal readers have been bugging me about you quite a bit. They want to know all about the romance author dating the hot actor. That might stop my publishers from letting me go. Especially if my sales are growing because of this little tabloid I'm in."

"Let's get those sales up, Grace. Our story can be written as one of the greatest romances ever told." He chuckled, leaning back.

"Yeah, I'll keep that in mind. It'll go right up there with *Pride and Prejudice,*" she joked.

"I'll be your Mr. Darcy, baby cakes." Grace laughed as he roamed her neck with kisses. "Grace, I want you with me when I film in Atlanta. You can write from anywhere, right?"

She smiled at him hesitantly. "You doing the John Whitford film after all?"

"I'm still thinking about it, but if I do go, I want you

with me."

"Evan, you should take it. Zach says it's perfect for you."

He reached over and kissed below her ear, making her forget anything being discussed. "I'll figure it out." The music had stopped and silence was prominent other than his soft lips running over her skin, which trembled in anticipation. His hands grasped the sides of her hips and he easily lifted her to sit on top of him.

"On the chair?" Her eyebrow raised as she gazed down at him. His body was ready against her. It was a good thing she was naked under that robe. Easier access.

"Want on the table? I'll move the plates over, Gracie Lynn."

She rubbed her hands over his stubbled jaw and chuckled as she placed kisses on his luscious lips. "I'll let you take me anywhere."

"God, I'm a lucky bastard." He began to kiss her fervently, his lips and hands claiming her.

She was on fire, wanting him, throbbing in beautiful ache. It was as if she was outside of her body, experiencing something beyond the natural. The interruption of the doorbell brought her back to the world around her. Evan groaned. "Who the fuck is that?" He continued kissing her neck, sucking on her pulse. If he kissed her any harder she'd have a love mark.

"I should answer," Grace declared breathlessly.

He moaned a 'no' as she continued kissing him, her tongue licking over his top lip. "No, don't do this to me,

Grace. Don't stop."

The doorbell kept ringing and a pounding knock couldn't be ignored. "I'd better answer." She moved off of him as he growled in frustration.

"I have a hard-on the size of Texas. I'm about to kill whoever's at the door."

"Get yourself together, Matthews," she said as she straightened her robe and smoothed her hair.

"I don't know how that's possible." They both looked down at his tented jeans and laughed.

"Down boy. We'll continue later." She winked, letting her hand rub over his evident erection and he grumbled as she moved away.

"Marla!" Grace was shocked to see her friend there unannounced. "What are you doing here?"

"Hey, sorry about coming over like this. I tried calling but you weren't answering your phone." Marla sauntered in, handing Grace a latte from their favorite coffee shop as she held onto her own. "I was on my way to yoga and—"

She spotted Evan sitting behind the table, his face looking perturbed. "Evan. Well, no wonder you weren't answering your phone." Marla smirked at Grace, then looked over Evan's rumpled state. His bare feet under the table caught her eye and she slyly grinned and whispered, "Nice work, Grace. It's about damn time."

Grace blushed as she and Marla sat on the couch. "What's going on? You look upset."

"I've had it with Ryan. He's a disgusting pig."

Grace looked closer and saw Marla's eyes were puffy. She'd definitely stayed up late crying, though her friend would never admit it. "What happened?"

"We'd made plans earlier this week to go downtown. I wanted to go to the Continental Club. He kept saying he'd take me."

Marla was more for the posh places. A nice bar, or cool place where music was played by a live band. Grace had a feeling Ryan wasn't into that. "Okay, and what happened?"

"I went over to his place like we'd agreed. He had a girl there. He invited me in and then asked if…" She lowered her voice as she leaned closer to Grace. "If I wanted to join in on a threesome."

"Didn't Josh warn you about him?" Evan chimed in as he grabbed a piece of bacon left on Grace's plate and chewed on it. "I definitely told Grace he was an idiot."

"Josh didn't warn me of anything," Marla refuted.

"I'm pretty sure he did," Grace corrected as Marla rolled her eyes.

"Whatever. I can't believe I let myself be duped by him." She stood and walked toward the kitchen. "Why are all men such jerks?"

"We're not all like that," Evan contended.

"Skip your yoga class and have some breakfast, Marla."

Grace followed, but was tugged back when Evan grabbed her wrist, pulling her close. "You serious? She's staying for breakfast?" His whisper was harsh as he tried to get himself under control.

Grace looked down at his bulge and smirked. "Guess naughty time will have to wait."

"I don't like your friend right now," Evan grumbled.

"Well, your friend isn't high on my list either," Grace stated severely. "He screwed over my best friend."

"Ryan isn't my friend."

"I'm angry at all men right now. For Marla." Grace was being playful, but was enjoying Evan squirm.

"Get her out of here. I want to make you come until you're screaming my name, princess. And I want you now."

His mouth was near hers, but Grace only grinned as she drew near him and pecked his cheek. "Sorry, babe. Chicks before dicks."

The night before was nothing short of spectacular. Evan had made love to a woman so passionate he wasn't sure how long he'd last the moment his body had entered hers. Other than every thought of how amazing she felt against him, he was constantly having to make sure he wouldn't blow his load before she got off. She was a fucking gorgeous challenge that he'd never tire from, and he looked forward to experiencing more with her. The way she had whispered her love for him while she thought he was sleeping had melted his heart.

Evan grumbled as the ladies chatted in the kitchen. He tried to subdue the ache in his crotch and his grumpy attitude. So what that Grace had put her friend first? He'd do the same for Zach or Josh. Then why did he feel like shit? He was being a selfish asshole and wanted his way with her. That was why.

The knock at the door only brought his irritation level up a notch as Grace moved passed the table looking delectable in that robe—mainly because he knew she was naked underneath it and now had the pleasure of knowing exactly what she looked like without it.

"Who's that?" Her curious voice carried over as she moved toward the entrance of her home.

"I don't know, but I don't like them either," Evan pouted.

"Oh, get over it, crybaby." Grace made a kissing gesture in the air toward him. "I'll make it up to you tonight."

"Bet your ass on that."

She shook her head. "Careful, Matthews. You're getting into deep waters there." She opened the door and smiled. "Hey, Josh."

Evan groaned once again, knowing what he was in for. "Hello, Grace. Sorry to bother, but Zach told me Evan would be here."

"You are bothering. Go away!" Evan called out.

Grace rolled her eyes. "Ignore him."

Josh made his way in looking the same as he always did—dressed in workout clothes and ready to exert the shit out of him. He approached with his serious expression as his eyes took in the scene before him. A sly sneer ran over his mouth. "Mate. Sorry to interrupt this little intimate setting, but we need to head out."

Evan nodded. "Fine."

"Make sure you work him out extra hard today, Josh. He ate pancakes."

"Thanks for dropping the dime on me, princess." Evan indicated her betrayal as he slapped Grace's bottom playfully.

"I'm going to take a quick shower and change," Grace excused herself, which Evan was grateful for. He didn't need her prancing around half-naked in front of him and his friend.

"Hey, Grace, where's the syrup?" Marla entered the dining room and spotted the big guy. Her body stopped and she straightened up as she cleared her throat. "Hello." Her voice turned pert as she moved her plate toward the table and set it down.

Josh gave a slight nod but stayed quiet, his eyes ogling over her form. Evan grinned as he pushed the bottle toward her. "Right there, Marla."

It took her a moment to gather herself as she looked down. "Oh, right." She turned back to the kitchen to retrieve her latte.

"Guess not as intimate as I assumed," Josh muttered.

"Grace and I were having a moment until we were rudely interrupted. Why don't you take Red and get the hell out of here so Grace and I can get to it in the shower?"

"Did you just call me Red?" Marla sat down and began to put syrup on her pancakes. "I'm not going anywhere with him, by the way. He'd probably just take me to the gym." Marla smiled wryly.

"I'll try not to take offense to that."

"I'm sure this food's the bigger offense to you." Marla smiled mockingly as she took a bite of bacon. "Want some?" She stuck her fork of pancake out in front of his lips and he backed off.

"No, thank you."

"I think you have a food complex," Marla announced as she ate.

As they continued their banter, Evan stood, making no qualms about his frustration at their arrival by scooting his chair back harshly. "I'll get my things," he groused as he moved to the bedroom, knowing Josh needed to get to the gym soon. He had other clients in line, and Evan needed to do his job. He still was upset missing out on his quickie with the woman who was constant on his mind.

Evan sat on the edge of the bed and began putting on his shoes. The pillows were strewn everywhere, the sheets tangled, and just remembering Grace's whimpers under and on top of him was making him hard all over again. It didn't help when she exited her bathroom wearing a pair of yoga pants and a sweatshirt. How the hell could he be so turned on by her?

She walked toward him and stood in between his legs as he wrapped his arms around her and squeezed her scrumptious ass. His head rested on her stomach and she ran her hands through his hair. "I've never experienced cranky Evan."

"You don't write many of those types of men in your historical romance books."

"You're simply cantankerous, Lord Matthews," Grace chimed in an English accent. He finally cracked a smile at her as she dipped her head and gave him a kiss. "You need not worry, my Lord, I shall suck your cock in the most delicious and proper way later in the evening."

"Holy shit, Grace, you sound like those swanky British people in *Downton Abbey* and it's completely turning me on. Plus, of course, the idea of your mouth on me is fucking sexy."

"Behave. And I can't believe you watch *Downton.*"

"I don't. I watch the recap."

They both chuckled as they let their kiss deepen. She stopped and moved away as they heard Marla's laugh ring out by something Josh said. "Sounds like they're getting along out there."

"Yeah, maybe we should let them wait for us." He pushed up to standing and pulled her back flush against his chest. He nuzzled the nape of her neck as his hands reached down and touched between her legs.

Grace groaned as she moved away from his arms toward the bathroom counter. "Evan, we have tonight. I'm going to spend the day with Marla. I gotta get some Christmas shopping done." He leaned on the doorframe watching her movements as she put a cream on her face. "Go and get your workout done. Let all that pissy aggression come out in the bedroom later."

She walked by him and brushed his crotch with her hip. He caught her and tugged her close, his lips kissing her jaw and moving toward her ear. He grumbled low and long. "God, I want you so badly right now, Grace. You're just egging me on, princess."

She sighed as he jerked his hips up, letting her feel how hard he was for her. The phone on the nightstand chimed and she pushed away from him. "I should see who texted."

"Wait." He dragged his nose alongside her cheek.

"That's what it is."

"What?"

"Your strawberry scent." That scent that drove him crazy was her moisturizer. "I fucking love it." He sucked on her lips and then moved his nose under her chin tilting it up so he got better access to her neck. "I can't wait to taste you again, Gracie Lynn. Break you down with my fingers and mouth and watch you shatter."

"I'm looking forward to it." She smiled and moved toward the table, grabbing the phone, staring for a moment. Her eyebrows crinkled as she tucked the device in her sweater pocket. Evan noticed her reticence.

"Your mom?"

She nodded and began to fix the bed. "Yeah. She's been texting a lot lately. I don't know why."

"Why don't you try calling her? Maybe just to talk." He went over and began to help her arrange the bedspread. "What if there's a way—"

"No, Evan. There's not." She exhaled and plopped herself down on the edge of the bed. He knew whatever excuse she gave wouldn't be enough reason, but he listened as she began with an irritated expression. "Look, I know you mean well, but she doesn't get it. My dad doesn't get it. Do you know what I overheard my mom saying before they left Austin? *I'm glad to get out of here. Away from all of this.*"

"That might not have meant you, Grace." He sat beside her and grabbed her hand in his.

"I was staying in Austin. Of course she meant me."

"What if there was a way you guys could fix this?"

"Why bother? There's no point."

"Grace, you're clearly unhappy. You miss your family."

"My family isn't like your family, Evan." She moved away from him, busying herself with fixing the pillows on the bed. "Not everyone's that lucky."

"We've had our hardships, sweetheart, but we worked on it. Families stick with each other."

"I can't get myself to…" She shook her head and grabbed her purse. "I just don't want to deal with it."

He was well aware, and learning more about her the more time they spent together, that she most definitely was avoiding confrontation. "Brushing it aside isn't going to help."

"Josh is waiting for you. Go work out, and bring that sexy body back to me." It was clear she wasn't up for salvaging the rift with her parents. She sauntered that wonderful ass out the door and left him there, wanting her beyond reason, and wishing there was a way to fix her world.

Chapter Twenty

"I don't know what you buy someone who has everything." Christmas shopping was posing a bit of a problem for Grace when it came to getting something for Evan. The two friends wandered outside The Domain, an outdoor plaza in North Austin, as they sipped on warm tea they had acquired from The Steeping Room. December was a warm one this year, and they enjoyed the feel of the pleasant weather.

"Just give him more sex. He'll be fine with that." Marla smiled as they headed toward Anthropologie. Grace wasn't one to shop regularly, but she was definitely up for girl-time after having experienced one of the most amazing nights of her life.

"I'm sure he'd get that regardless. I can't stop thinking about how much I want him. It's almost every second, and he's worse than me. We might be trapped inside forever if he'd have his way."

"Oh, trust me, men can get irrational when it comes to sex. I mean, not in a bad way, just in a hot, caveman sort of way."

"Don't mention that, I might not be able to handle the thought of Evan going caveman. He's too sexy as it is." They laughed as they wandered throughout the beautiful store with the gorgeous, vintage aesthetic. Grace wished she could purchase every single piece of clothing, but was pleased with her true vintage finds when it came to home decor. When she bought an item at a garage sale that really was from 1858 it gave her a sense of satisfaction. As if she was giving refuge to something that had been abandoned. She took it, breathed new life into it, and helped it find a new home. Almost in the way she had felt when her folks left her. She had been broken, but was in the process of getting fixed.

She focused back on Marla as she continued to speak about Evan. "I'm sure that man has a lot of stamina. I'm glad you found someone who's good to you in the bedroom, Grace. You deserve that. You've waited long enough."

Grace nodded. "And you? You need someone good to you in the bedroom."

Her red-headed friend waved her hand in dismissal. "Any sex is better than no sex, I guess."

"Even when it's bad?" Grace scrunched her face remembering some horrible make-out sessions, not to mention her first time. "Trust me, I'd love to forget Kyle ever happened."

"Sometimes it can be good, bad, or mediocre. I've just dealt with more mediocre than anything else."

"I'll bet Josh has some endurance. He's sexy."

"He's okay." Marla didn't look at Grace and that was an instant giveaway.

"Oh, come on, Marla. Give it up. You like him."

Marla made a face. "No, I don't. He's not my type. Besides, I'm pissed off at Ryan and hate all men, remember?"

"Which you'll change your mind about eventually." Grace took time picking up jewelry and after glancing at the prices, immediately put the items back. "You had to have known about Ryan being a douche, Marla. We all said to be careful with him."

Marla picked up a necklace and decided on the purchase. "I saw warning signs, but ignored them, as I always do. Perhaps I'm hoping they'll prove me wrong. Or I'm just a fucking nutcase who's a hopeless romantic."

"Neither. You just haven't met the right guy."

"Well, look who's the optimist with love now." Marla lifted her brow at Grace. "And the memoir? You let him read it?" Grace nodded. "That's a huge deal. And the publishers?"

"I haven't heard anything. I don't think I want it published anyway. It's just so..."

"Revealing?"

"Yeah." Grace waited for Marla to finish her purchase and they wandered outside again. The sun was beginning to fade and the temperature was dropping. Seemed a cold front was on the way and Grace hoped it would get chilly for Christmas.

"I say let people read it, Grace. Your story's a complicated one, but it's unique. I'd tell your folks about it though."

"My mom keeps texting me. I think she found out who I'm dating. I wouldn't doubt she disapproves." Grace shook her head and finished her tea, throwing the cup into a recycle bin.

"He's Evan Matthews. I don't see how she would."

They made their way into another store and began to roam through the clutter of clothing. "She'd find a way."

"So, what else did the publishers say? Seriously, Grace, you might need to get another marketing strategy for your books. They don't seem to be doing shit for you."

Grace sighed knowing Marla was right. Years ago she had been so desperate for any type of acceptance from a publisher that she took what she could get. That had been a mistake. Her books weren't getting promoted, she was constantly being pushed aside for bigger names, and the industry had gone through so many changes within the past few years, it was difficult for her to keep up.

"I have one more contracted book in my *Scandals of a Duke* series, and then after that, they either decide to drop me or give me a new contract. The deal was shit from the start, and I'm not really sure what they'll propose, but I guess we'll find out. I'm sort of interested in doing contemporary. Maybe even self-publishing. I have a good following. I love them, and they keep me going."

"Well, that's good. You'll become a world-renowned author and marry Evan and have five babies." Marla smiled as she took out a blouse and studied it.

"Right, because it's always been my dream to have five babies." Grace rolled her eyes.

"Well, you do want to get married someday, right Grace? Evan's a good one to do that with. If you like that hunky, handsome, millionaire type."

Grace laughed as she ran through the clothing rack looking at t-shirts. "I'm just trying to get through this whole dating stage first. Everyone likes pushing us way ahead of where we are. I could've sworn his sister was already thinking we were meant to be."

"Well, aren't you?" Marla smirked at her and put the blouse back. "His source said he was *head-over-heels*."

"So you saw that," Grace laughed. "He does want me to go where he films next. It's weird to be thinking that far ahead." Gallivanting to God-knew-where while Evan filmed his movies was not how Grace imagined spending her time, not that she was complaining.

"Well, you could write wherever you are."

Grace tried to focus on the present instead of worrying about the future, including what she would do with her property manager job. "I love this shirt." Grace picked it up and Marla laughed. "What? I do."

"Of course you do. How many shirts do you need with Texas on them anyway? You have three others like that."

"This one says, '*Born and Raised*.'" Grace was getting it. Every now and then she let herself have the small luxury of something. She also found a present for Jaime and would work on Marla's gift later. As for Evan, she had no clue what she would give the man who had it all.

Grace's breath shuddered along with Evan's as he lifted her ankles up on his shoulders and surged inside her, unrelenting and fast. "I need you, give me everything, Gracie."

He drove deep into her, his body hot and damp as he hovered over, moving her legs aside and turning her onto her belly, continuing to claim her fully from behind. Grace could half hear her sobs escape her lips as she submitted. The feel of being so intimate, so vulnerable and surrendering to him, was overwhelming.

It was all new, fresh, and extremely liberating. He rocked his hips against her in a glorious bliss that thrived all over her body. His pace increased as he leaned his chest against her back, one hand squeezing her breast as the other trailed down over the sensitive center of pleasure that begged to be touched.

Grace's hands fisted the sheets below her as she bit her trembling lip. The tension was climbing to the point of agonizing as her third orgasm of the night was on the brink. "Please, Evan, please…"

He rolled his hips and took her higher until his body hit her just right and she screamed out as the wave took hold and then crashed. He persisted until her convulsions finished and then let himself go until he was spent. They melded into each other, sweat glistening as their limp bodies rested.

"Fuck-wow," Grace muttered breathlessly.

Evan grinned and faced her, his hand running over her tangled locks. "Fuck-wow?"

"Yeah, shit that was…fuck..."

"I love that dirty mouth, sunshine."

"Mmm." Grace closed her eyes, sated and glowing.

She then watched him crawl back to her after he disposed of his condom. His muscular body snuggled beside her and she felt it was too good to be true. She'd wake up and he'd be gone. She set that aside and remembered the way he stormed into the house when she had texted him that Marla had left. He had walked in, demanded her to kiss him, then whispered how he wanted to take her, and he wouldn't be as gentle as he was before. She was up to that challenge, and she'd just been served.

"So that was the pissy aggression? I think you need to get pissed off more often."

"Don't make me spank you, Gracie."

"I might like that," Grace gasped as Evan rubbed his body against her. She arched back into him, feeling herself still pulsing from her last orgasm.

"Already wanting more, doll?"

"Always."

"Now you know how I feel. Sorry, but I gotta go. Zach and I need to spend boy-time together talking about our feelings all damn day long." He moved away from her as she swung her hand out, slapping his chest.

"Go have your boy-time then, Evan. I've got a vibrator to keep me company." He grabbed her wrist as she sat up and attempted to leave the bed.

He laughed as he tugged her to him. "I'm teasing, Gracie Lynn. And throw that thing away. Nobody gets to please you but me."

"You saying you're jealous of a piece of equipment, Matthews?"

"No, sugar, but I want every orgasm to be mine. I'm

a selfish asshole that way."

"No, you're not, Evan."

He let his body lean over hers and she was once again drowning in a gaze of deep blue. They turned silent, reviewing each other, his nose gliding over hers. "Hi," he whispered softly.

"Hey." She let out a breathy giggle as he rubbed against her, his lush lips curving up into a smile. Grace thought about his account of all her orgasms belonging to him and her mind began to wander. She had such limited practice, everything was so intense.

"What's going on, Gracie?"

Grace shook her head. "Nothing."

"Nice try, baby cakes. Let's do that again. What's wrong?"

"How do you know when something's wrong?"

A rough chuckle released from his throat. His fingertip ran over the space between her eyes. "You crinkle up right here when you're worried or deep in thought." His lips gently kissed the spot. "So, talk to me."

Her hands ran through his hair as he waited for her to speak. "I'm just curious, if you…if this feels as amazing for you as it does for me. I know you've had a lot of women, and I'm not sure if…" She could feel him shift, his expression turning concerned. Her eyes focused on his chest that pressed against hers. "If I'm pleasing you enough sexually. I know I'm not as skilled, and if you get bored you'll tell me, right?"

"Gracie," his breath escaped his lungs and his eyes softened. "I've never felt this incredible in my life, sweetheart. I promise you, you're perfect." His hand caressed her cheek as he gave her a sweet kiss. "And we're going to have fun experiencing new things together." She gave a small smile. "I love you, Grace. Don't doubt that. Please."

Her heart skipped a beat and she knew that even if she was accustomed to thinking the worst, she had to have faith in this man. She had already given all of herself over to him, and she couldn't go back.

Chapter Twenty-One

"It's almost midnight." Evan glanced at the clock and shifted. The holiday season had approached, and he had decided to stay in Texas. He practically moved in with Grace in the weeks prior, so he bought a small tree and set it up near the large windows in her living room. She had a box of decorations in her garage that she brought up, and old Christmas records played as they decorated together.

She looked at him and smiled. "Evan, thanks for a great Christmas."

"Presents?" He clapped his hands together, rubbing them as excitement beamed from his expression.

She nodded as they sat near the lit tree. Evan grabbed a large rectangle-shaped box wrapped in shiny red paper and passed it to her. Grace let it rest on her legs as she handed him a Christmas-decorated bag with tissue paper.

"You first." He studied her hands as they gently tried to peel through the edges of the wrapping. He chuckled as he reached over and ripped part of it clear off. "Just go for it, doll."

"Hey! I liked the wrapping. I could've saved it." She smirked as she then flew through the paper and ran her hands over a wooden chest. She unhinged the lid, opening the box, which revealed different compartments that housed oil paints, brushes, palette cups, painting knives and other tools. Grace felt prickling of tears begin, but composed herself. "Evan, this is so wonderful."

"I also bought you some more canvases and an easel, but those are in the spare room. You said you needed to replace some things, so I thought this was a good pick for you."

"It's perfect." She knew how pricey all the supplies were, and he had bought something for her that meant so much. "I feel like my gift isn't as cool as this."

She watched as he tore through the tissue paper in the bag and saw his name engraved on a walnut desk wedge. He viewed Grace with a puzzled expression. "A name plaque?"

Grace smiled. "For your new desk. In the garage."

His face broke into a grin so bright and big that Grace swore she saw the sun. "*The* desk? The desk we worked on together? Where we had our second kiss? *That* desk."

She nodded. "That desk. And it was our first kiss. The drunk one doesn't count. Anyway, it's yours, Evan."

He reached over, taking her mouth into his and holding her tightly to him. "That's the most thoughtful thing I've ever gotten, Grace."

"You can't mean that," she giggled as he trailed his kisses down her neck.

"Well, I say we go christen said desk, which will just enhance the thoughtfulness of the gift."

She laughed heartily as he continued the trek of his

lips over her. "Desk sex will be new for me."

"For me too, sunshine," he whispered in her ear.

The thought of that made her blush and she shuddered in his arms. The phone chime interrupted their moment and Grace groaned. "It's late." She dug in her jeans pocket as Evan moved away from her. She looked at the screen and rolled her eyes. "It's my mother."

"Maybe it's an emergency."

She held out the phone for him to peer at the screen.

Nancy: "Have a Merry Christmas, Grace."

She rolled her eyes and didn't text back. "Never an emergency. Just letting me know she's alive." When she looked back at him, he gave her a disapproving countenance. "What, Evan?"

"You could try a little harder with her."

"Why should I?"

"Maybe she wants to know you better and you're not letting her. She's texted you several times and I've never seen you respond."

Grace sighed as she boosted herself from the floor with her wooden box of paints. She set it on the dining table and moved toward the kitchen to clean up. "I don't know why it matters to you."

"Because what affects you affects me too, sweetheart." He got up and followed her. She stood in front of the sink to wash the dishes, but he approached behind her and shut the water off, grabbed her hips and turned her around to face him. His voice lowered as he raised her chin. "Gracie, you gotta let this resentment go. It's eating at you, baby."

She stared into his smoky blue eyes and gave a weak smile. "I have my friends. I have you. I have Nathan's memory. That's more than enough for me."

A temperate look crossed his face, and his voice conveyed care. "It would have been nice to know him. To know your family."

"You and Nathan would've gotten along really well."

He paused in contemplation before asking. "Why don't you have any family photos up?"

Grace shook her head, unable to fully explain the depth of her pain. "It's too hard, Evan. It just reminds me of all I lost."

He wrapped his arms around her tightly, letting her body crush against his. The feel of being with him made her feel comforted and safe. She wished she could bottle the sensation and keep it forever. She might've lost her family, but she was gaining so much with Evan. More than she ever imagined.

"Merry Christmas, sweetheart," he whispered quietly against her.

~

The beginning of the year proved to be a busy one. With Evan's full filming schedule for the month and award season approaching, he knew time with Grace would be limited. She had been so overwhelmed with trying to meet her deadline for her next book, working with the

Home Owners Association, and other paperwork that the little time they had together was filled with quick lovemaking that Evan wished would last all day.

Tonight he made it a point to have time set aside. He needed to talk with her, and she had promised she'd meet her word count for the day. He had Zach order from a local pasta place and Evan set the food on the dining table as Grace sat on the couch typing up the last of the pages she needed to hit.

"You almost done, babe?" He served wine as her fingers flew over the keyboard.

"Shh. Just give me a few." Minutes passed and she sighed as she closed her laptop. "Okay, done for the night."

"Is Lady Emilia gonna ask Duke Ellington about the affair with Lady Mary?" He handed her a glass of red.

She pushed off the couch and stretched. "You'll have to wait and see. Sometimes I think you're worse than my followers."

"We can't help it if we're fangirls," he joked at her as they clinked their glasses together and sipped on the wine. "So, the Golden Globes are coming up in a few weeks. I'll have to go to L.A. for it."

She nodded. "You're a presenter?"

"Yeah. I don't always enjoy those things, but with the last movie out this year, they're starting the promotion process early. Would you want to go with me?"

Grace almost choked on the sip she had just taken from her drink. "You want me to go to the Golden Globes with you?"

"Of course, I wouldn't want you going with Chris Pine. You're mine now, Captain Kirk." He winked at her, giving a small kiss.

"I don't know." She never wanted to be thrust in the strange limelight. It seemed so formal. So official. "Walking a red carpet? That's…scary."

"It's not too bad. You could see my house. I'll get Zach to set up something with a stylist for you to get a dress. You might even revel in getting pampered." They moved toward the table and enjoyed dinner, but he wouldn't pressure her to go and told her to think it over.

The night progressed and Evan sat in bed while Grace took a shower. He needed to read through another script that Zach had given him. He had yet to find what he wanted to direct. As he reached for the script on the nightstand, her phone chimed beside him.

He glanced at the message that came in on the screen and saw a text. He scanned the contents and froze, wondering how long Grace had kept important information from him. She came out of the bathroom smiling, freshly showered with her wavy hair draped over her shoulders.

"Grace." He held out her phone. "You have a text message from Alan." She stopped in her tracks, her brown eyes widening in fright. "He's your agent, right? When were you going to tell me about this?"

She gulped and moved forward, snatching the device from his hands, her expression turning suspicious. "You're snooping on me?"

"No, the phone went off and I saw what it said."

"You shouldn't have touched it, Evan." They stayed silent as she looked down and read her message.

"Grace, he's saying he needs an answer about the memoir. You told me publishers didn't want it." He kept his eyes on her and then scratched his jaw, shaking his head in disappointment. "You lied to me."

Warning flashed in her eyes as she lifted her head. "I didn't lie, Evan. I got the offer a few days after I talked to you."

"That was in December. Why didn't you tell me? And he says they're offering more money. What's going on?" He sat forward, his forearms resting on his knees as he awaited an explanation.

"I told you I wasn't sure I wanted to publish." She walked away from him, attempting to clean the top of her dresser and refusing to glance his way. He was already taking it as a sign that she wasn't up for discussing more with him.

"How much are they proposing?"

"Does it matter?"

"Yes. What did they offer?"

She barely moved her head to look at him through the mirror. "A lot."

"And you haven't said yes?" He laughed out of shock as he got out of bed and moved to her. "Grace, this is it for you. This is exciting!"

"I told you I'm not sure I'm publishing."

"Why?"

"It's too personal."

He stared down at her as she busied herself. "Look at me, Grace."

"I don't want to talk about it."

"We have to."

"Can we not?"

"I think you're making a big mistake. You're afraid of your parents, of what they'll say, of what others will think about your story, but nothing ever came of playing it safe, babe."

She made a face and dismissed him, trying to pull down the emotions that were hitting her. "That has nothing to do with it."

He grabbed her arm and turned her to face him. "Look at me, Gracie. It has everything to do with it."

She shoved him away defensively. "You're one to talk, Matthews."

"What?"

"You're a hypocrite. Let's analyze you for a change. You haven't said yes to the John Whitford project. Why?"

"Gracie—"

"No. You're terrified that you might tank in his blockbuster. Or is it that you'll get more critical acclaim than you want? Which is it, Evan?"

"That's not what this is—"

"Isn't it? Why aren't you taking the role? You're stalling on what could be the biggest move of your career. Why?"

He stayed silent, looking at her directly. His jaw ticked as he finally tilted his head toward her. "I said yes to it." He clasped her face in his hands as she froze. "Mike was trying to get more money, despite me not giving a flying fuck over a few million more. Sometimes

Hollywood deals take a while, princess."

She wriggled away from him and moved toward her bed, annoyance flaring. "Well, aren't you just Mr. I'm-so-perfect-I-always-do-the-right-thing Matthews?" She rearranged her pillows and crawled in sinking down on the mattress.

"We're not done talking, baby. You need to figure this shit out."

Grace growled at him and sat back up. "Why, Evan? What do you want me to tell you? That I'm frightened? Fine, I admit it. I am." Her voice shook as it filled the room. "My parents already hate me as it is. The guilt I feel is still so overwhelming at times, I feel like I can't breathe. They're going to be able to read and relive every single detail about it, and know exactly what was going on in my head the moment their precious boy died. What he looked like, what he felt like in my arms, the shit I went through afterwards. The spiraling depression and fear and anger and hurt and blame, and how they abandoned me. I was so alone and I wanted to crawl into a hole and die. How could I inflict that on them? It's just more pain and suffering to add to their lives, and to put it out into the world and let others know it's there, in public, for anyone to read isn't fair to them."

He sat near her, gathering her in his arms as she tried holding back her tears. "They didn't abandon you, Grace. Your mom still tries to talk to you. I'm sure it would be difficult for them to read, but it'll also give them an insight to your life."

"Please, I can't, Evan. Don't make me face it. I can't

face them."

He braced her head and tilted it up. "Do you want to tell your story, Grace? Yes or no?"

She sniffled and closed her eyes, avoiding tears. "I don't kn—"

"Yes or no, Grace?"

"I can't."

"Grace, don't hold back from your chance at success, baby," he whispered in her hair as she tucked herself against his chest. He cradled her to him, his heart breaking for her. He wanted so desperately to fix things for her, make it better. If only he could find a way.

Chapter Twenty-Two

Damn treadmill. Grace puffed as the speed picked up. The Golden Globes were fast approaching, and she had decided to attend. She just hadn't told Evan yet.

Of course, completely last minute, Grace figured she would exercise. A few pounds lost would do some good, especially around her derriere. Evan wasn't too happy when she talked about losing weight, and he adamantly showed her how much he loved her body the way it was. She liked when he did that, plus he was a total ass-man.

Her ponytail bobbed in the air and she kept her eyes focused on him. He was right all those months ago when he said she would appreciate him even more when he was naked. She did, but he also looked pretty damn good working out in front of her. Evan heaved weights up in his arms as he worked on the art that was his body. He was damn sexy.

Grace panted, her heart beat strong, but along with that, her body throbbed in want of him as she watched his wonderful form lift two times the amount that she weighed. She loved when he became Neanderthal on her, taking charge and being all virile. It was exactly what she had craved in a man.

She smiled as he winked her way. The girl on the machine next to her giggled and waved. *Not for you, but nice try*. Grace wasn't usually a jealous type, but felt irked by the pretty woman who stuck her chest out and gave her boyfriend the *fuck me* eyes.

Evan walked over and stood in between her and the other girl's treadmill. The pretty brunette slowed her machine and said hi to him, and he nodded to her then leaned toward Grace, speaking to only her. "So, I saw you across the room and thought to myself, *I need to meet that woman.*"

She wanted to laugh as she grabbed her towel and wiped her sweat. "Did you now? What made you think that?"

"Your gorgeous ass."

Yep, total ass-man. The girl beside them gasped and Grace grinned. She stopped her machine and caught her breath. "You can't even see my ass."

"Well, I saw it earlier, and I think we're meant to be. Wanna go to the Golden Globes with me next week?"

"I would, but I'm washing my hair."

He grabbed her hand as she climbed down and he tugged her to him. She felt giddy as his mouth grazed over hers. "What can I do to convince you to go?"

She lifted her brow and whispered, "Sex. Lots and lots of it."

He chuckled as he kissed her lips once, then twice, and then again. "Let's get out of here, so we can get started on changing your mind then."

Grace move back to the treadmill to grab her things and saw pretty brunette staring at both of them with her eyes wide. Pride surged through her as she held herself up and thought, *"This man is mine, and he loves me."* She was certainly a lucky girl.

After a wonderful round of lovemaking, and telling Evan she had decided to attend the awards show with him, he left for filming. Grace worked on necessary duties for the day. One of the house's garbage disposal had stopped working. She had to make the proper phone calls, went over to see the neighbors, and started on paperwork. On top of that, the lawn maintenance crew hadn't shown up, and she had to call, telling them she would have to find a different company if they didn't adhere to their scheduled appointment.

After a full day of dealing with property work issues, she finally was able to sit down at her computer. She grabbed her phone when the chime went off. She read it, setting it aside, wanting to ignore her mother's frequent texts over the past few days.

Nancy: Grace, I would like to speak with you. Can I call?

Grace grimaced at the thought of having to actually talk to her mother. She couldn't remember the last time she heard her voice. Christmas and birthday cards were sent, but they got into their affable texting routine. What would they even begin to talk about? The weather?

Grace: Maybe tomorrow.

That should appease her mother for a bit. Before she knew it, the evening had arrived and Evan walked in looking drained. Grace set her work aside and greeted him, leading him over to the kitchen as she began to fix his regimented meal. Evan had a guide he kept nearby from his nutritionist, and Grace helped him out when she could. She had taken initiative tonight and cooked the simple meal.

"How'd filming go today?"

Evan sighed as he opened her bottle of Glenfiddich and served them both a glass. "It was tough. Physically, mentally. I sometimes want to just rip that costume to shreds."

Grace chuckled. "Well, you're almost at the finish line. Only a few more months and it's over forever."

"I can't wait."

"You still love it."

"I do. We've been training for the big water scene. So it's been all day spent swimming in this large tank. It's fun, but exhausting." She watched as he gulped the golden liquid, sure it would help warm his bones. He viewed his plate as she served it. "I can do that, you know."

"I don't mind." She kept her eyes on the food she'd fixed and smiled to herself, loving the idea of life with him. She could do it all forever if he wanted. "I never considered myself one to enjoy making meals for my man...but I've never had a man to make meals for, so it's all new to me."

He kissed her with affection and moved to the table, letting his aching body stretch out. "How's the writing going?"

"It's going. I've been preoccupied," she glanced at him with a wicked glare, "thinking about sex with you.

It really does take over the brain, doesn't it?"

"You have no idea." He pulled her to him and kissed her temple as she set his plate down. "I actually need to talk to you about something, Gracie."

Her phone sounded and she glanced at the screen. "God, what is her deal?" She texted a response, her fingers flying over her phone.

"What?" Evan began to eat his plain chicken breast, rice and broccoli. He looked edgy as he stared at her. "What is it?"

Grace shook her head, her eyebrows furrowing in contemplation. "My mom keeps texting me. She wants to talk. Like on the phone. We haven't spoken in God knows how long and she wants to now."

He shifted uncomfortably in his chair and grabbed his drink, swigging it again. He was restless as he played with his food. "I actually wanted to talk to you about your parents, Grace."

"Can we not? Every time we talk about them it turns into an argument."

"It's not an argument, we hardly discuss it." He lowered his frustrated voice and made it sound soothing. "If you sit down, maybe we can calmly talk about the issues."

"Why do you feel the need to analyze this, Evan?" Grace grabbed her glass of whiskey, downing it and gasping as it burned her throat. "Let's just drink and make love all night."

She moved to pour whiskey for him, but he stopped her. "I really want to talk to you, Grace. And I don't want you getting defensive before we really discuss it."

"Discuss what?" She took one more gulp, finishing what she poured and sat down next to him.

"I sent your parents the memoir."

Grace halted, her eyes widening in the realization of what he was telling her. The pit in her stomach began to grow, moving up and around and taking over her senses. "What did you do?"

"I thought it would be a good idea for them to read it." He reached his hand out to touch hers, but she recoiled. Betrayal pierced her heart. Evan sent her private thoughts to the people who had abandoned her and let her down. "Gracie, I did this for you."

She stayed silent. A wave of nausea took over. She felt ill, as the world around her spun and made her dizzy. It was as if the rug had been out pulled from under her feet, but she regained control. Hurt poured through her shaky voice. "How could you?"

He tried grabbing her hand again, but she flinched at his touch. His skin was no longer a comfort to her, but a danger. Evan was a traitor. He betrayed her, using her own words against her. He began to shift in his chair, unable to withstand her silence and anger she exuded.

"Say something, Gracie. Talk to me."

Refusal to glance his way only made the tension in the air thicken. She got up, the wooden legs of the chair scratching the floor in a loud scrape that echoed the room. Tears threatened to fall, but she wouldn't let them. Instead her cold, empty brown eyes set on his fretful blue ones. Only two words exited her mouth in a composed whisper. "Get out."

"What?" He jerked up from his chair and moved

toward her, which only made her withdraw. "Grace, come on. I did this to help you. Your parents would have eventually read it, and I just saved you the hassle of telling them. I gave the push you needed."

"Leave. Now." Her voice was low as she turned away from him.

He shook his head in defiance. "No. I'm not leaving you. Them reading this will help, Grace. Trust me."

The only way of getting away from him was for her to leave, and if that's what it took, that's what she would do. *Marla.* She would go there. Her body mechanically moved, but her mind was in a fog. She could only process, *keys, purse, phone. Keys. Purse. Phone.* It kept repeating in her head, lest she forget.

"Where are you going?" He followed her around the house as her breathing stayed steady. "It was for your own good, sweetheart. You're holding yourself back. Please, say something."

Grace reached for the exit of her own house, shrugging his arm off of her shoulder. He trailed behind her as she tried getting in her car, her shaky hand fumbling over the lock and finally opening the door. He slammed it shut, enclosing her between his arms. His forehead touched her shoulder. "Grace, don't go. Please."

"Move." Her voice was fixed and completely closed off.

"Don't do this. Talk to me."

"Move, Evan."

"No. Why can't you face this? What's the big deal? If they read it, they'll see your point of view." Silence.

"You have to get over this, let the fear go." He waited for her to say something, but she couldn't. The fury was taking root inside of her. She was unable to stop herself from saying something she would later regret.

Cold eyes met his as she turned back to look at him. "You're just like Kyle."

His body straightened up, his breath caught, and his voice became brusque. "I can't believe you just compared me to that asshole." He clasped her shoulders and turned her around, but she refused to look at him. "I didn't fuck you and leave you, Grace. You're being irrational right now. I'm going to forgive your idiotic accusation, and I don't ever want to hear you say something that ugly to me again."

Her eyes set on his, the vehemence in them unable to be held back. "You both betrayed me. What's the difference?" It was beyond words, beyond yelling, beyond giving him a piece of her mind.

He backed away from the glare, knowing he wasn't going to win. There was no way he would. "Grace… please. I won't give up on you."

She turned away again, got in her car, and hauled out of the driveway as quickly as she could. There would be no looking back now, knowing the one man she had given her whole self to, had trusted in, had been exactly who she thought he'd be. The one to leave her broken and hurting.

~

He had fucked up. Big time. Evan paced in Grace's

living room, running his hands through his hair and deliberating how he would ever fix the wreckage he had just caused. The act of what he did was meant from a good place. He truly thought he'd help get Grace over the nerves of sending the damn manuscript to her parents by doing it for her.

His worry level increased as he looked at the bottle of whiskey. He fought the urge to drown the feelings of inadequacy with liquor. Where had she gone? When would she get back? Would she be okay to drive? He clutched his phone tightly in his hand and stared at the screen.

He studied her picture in his contacts and pressed the call button. It jumped to her voicemail and he shakily spoke, "Grace, please, let me know that you're okay, wherever you go." He paused to swallow the lump of fear stuck in his throat. "You can't just not talk to me."

He hung up tried sitting down. Was she done with him? He wouldn't let her throw away what they had, not without talking to him. Even if she did try to justify breaking up with him, he wouldn't let her. No way in hell. He had waited too long for a woman like her, and she belonged with him. Without her he had nothing, her love absorbed it all.

He called again, then texted, then called. The clock on the wall crawled at a snail's pace, the quiet of the house making the pit in his stomach cramp. His food had been left uneaten, the remnants of it left on the kitchen table. And her scent. The smell of strawberries lingered in the air, on the cushions of the couch, in his running mind, and through his heart.

There wasn't much else he could do in the way of waiting. The headache he sported squeezed on his temples, but his appetite was non-existent. He wanted her back. He needed her back. She had to talk to him, yell at him, and tell him how badly he had messed up. But silence was the worst thing he could endure.

Chapter Twenty-Three

"I can't believe it. Fucking asshole," Grace sniffled. As soon as Grace had arrived at her friend's home, she poured everything out in a rage. After calming herself, Marla brought out the scotch, tissues, and chocolate. Grace snatched a tissue, wiping her nose, but she had barely cried.

"I knew he couldn't be that perfect." Marla patted Grace's shoulder affectionately. "He's a man, after all."

"I trusted him." Grace shivered, knowing things with him wouldn't work. "How the hell did he even find my parents' address?"

"I'm sure he has his ways, Grace. He's Evan Matthews."

"I don't *care* that he's *Evan Matthews*. He shits the same way everyone else does."

Marla winced. "Too much, Grace."

"I want him out of my house. I can't possibly go back with him living next door either. What the hell am I supposed to do?" The gaping hole in her heart made her want to break down into sobs, but she hated crying. She had spent too much of her life in grief.

Marla touched her hand. "You can stay here. I'll go by the house tomorrow and get you some clothes, your laptop, whatever else you need."

Small tears glimmered in Grace's eyes, grateful for

the help from her friend. Marla moved forward to hug her, but Grace shifted back. "Don't. I'll cry and I won't stop."

"I think this is the first time I've ever seen you close to it. I always thought you weren't human or something."

Grace gave a weak chuckle and wiped the corner of her eye. "I'm so embarrassed, Marla. The things I revealed in that book. I wasn't going to have it published. My parents..."

"Grace, I haven't read it, so I don't know what's in there, but babe, that was your life. Those things that happened made you who you are today. If your parents can't see past that, then screw them. The future Columbia-law-school scholar was their pride and joy, but you know what? You were Nathan's. He loved and cared about you."

Grace's chest felt like it was being pried open. That gaping hole was getting larger, and she felt like dying. Her eyes stayed down as she nodded in agreement, but it wasn't fully soaking in her head. "So, what's the point of you saying this?"

Marla continued. "Focus on what he'd think. And don't be ashamed of who you are, Grace. Of what you've lived through. It's all beautiful."

"You think Evan was right to send it?"

"I don't think it's that black and white. The way he went about this was completely fucked up. But still, he saved you the worry of having to tell them yourself. And you don't know how your mother will react." She shrugged and picked up a piece of chocolate, handing it to Grace. Grace scrunched her nose up and shook her head, so Marla then handed her the bottle of Scotch. Grace tipped it to her mouth and took a gulp. "Thatta girl. Drink yourself to sleep on the couch or you can go use the guest room. Just don't puke on my carpet."

The day was overcast and cold, and Evan was in a foul mood. He couldn't think about anything other than Grace. The fury in her eyes almost three nights ago was something he'd never forget. He wanted to hold her in his arms, run his hands through that gorgeous brown hair, gaze into those dark eyes and see the look of love in them. He wanted to comfort her, tell her everything would be fine and it would all work out for the best. But he wasn't so sure at this point if everything would work out and that scared him.

The more he tried calling and getting denied, texting without a reply, the more he became a grouch. His concentration was shot, and lines that were supposed to come easily just didn't stick. His listening skills were shit, so his cues kept being dropped. It came to the point where Charles, their director, pulled him aside and told him he needed to get himself together.

Evan had always been professional, and one thing that needed to be done was to leave problems at home and away from work. He felt ashamed for having been scolded, and he apologized as he tried to regain focus and get his lines done, but it wasn't happening easily.

Charles called for a break, and Evan entered his

trailer, sitting on the couch and staring at his phone. He scrolled through his photos and studied pictures he'd taken of Grace. One of them dancing together near her record player, another of them cuddled on the couch, one of her sleeping. He remembered when she woke from the sound of the photo being taken. She tried to tackle him, demanding he erase it, but he'd never. He cherished the memory too much.

The door swung open and Josh walked in saying nothing. He sat across from Evan and leaned his forearms on his knees, his fingers clasping together. Glacier blue eyes stared keenly at him. "What, Josh?"

"You what? You've been acting strange the past few days," Josh stated briskly. When Evan didn't answer, Josh's lips pressed together before he let out a laugh. "You fucked it up, didn't you?"

Evan's eyes pressed shut as he pinched the space between them. "Don't."

"You fucking fell in love and what did you do?" He pushed the sleeves of his Henley up, the cords of his muscles tightening as he shook his head. "What are you going to do to fix it, mate? Hmm?"

"I don't know. I don't know if I can fix it, Josh." He proceeded to tell him what he did, and his friend leaned back, giving a drained whistle. Evan tried to defend himself. "But, isn't she just being unreasonable?"

"No, you fucked it up. Don't know how you'll come back from that."

"She was going to publish it." His justification seemed weak when he spoke it out loud. "It would make their way to them eventually."

"No, no it wouldn't, Evan. This girl," he put his hand out as he tried to make his point, "she was so guarded you had to lie about losing a poker game to get to know her. Then you went, without her permission, behind her back, to find her parents and send something to them that she was quite sure she never wanted them to read."

"But they had to if she was going to publish."

"That's the thing though, Evan. She got offers and she turned them down because she didn't want them to read it."

"Because she was scared."

Josh laughed in frustration. "So why was it your job to get her over that?"

"Because…I love her. I want her to have a relationship with her parents."

"Why does it matter to you so much? Zach doesn't talk to his parents."

"His parents are assholes."

"So are Grace's, apparently." He looked at him questioningly, his eyebrows raised as he waited for the answer. "Why does it matter, Evan?"

"I want to marry her." Evan's eyes stung as he looked up at his friend's shocked face. "And I want her to have a relationship with her parents because I know one day she'll regret not having her father there to give her away at our wedding. Or not having her mom there to see how wonderful her daughter is. Or what it would be like to know their grandchildren one day. I want my future to be with Grace. She thinks they blame her for Nathan's death, but I know they don't."

"How do you know that?"

"I just know. Grace alienates people. She's great at pushing away those that try to love her. She's doing it to me now."

"Evan, she didn't alienate you until you made her."

"What are you talking about?"

"This girl let you in and she loved you, and you broke that. Can't you see what you did wrong? You aren't her savior, mate, you're the man she loves."

"But I needed to do it. She's missing this amazing opportunity, and I know she wants it. Her parents might've given up on her, but I won't. And I'm going to try to fix this."

"She doesn't need to be fixed. Maybe she doesn't need anyone right now."

"Everyone needs someone, Josh." He smirked at him knowingly. "Even you, bro."

Josh gave a slight nod and leaned back. "Just be there for her when she's ready, I guess." His eyes motioned toward the door. "Charles told me to tell you to get the fuck out of here. Rest up and be ready for a long couple of days ahead."

Evan knew he had to clear his head, attempt to catch some sleep, eat something, and find some way to win Grace back.

~

Evan stood, hands on his hips as he awaited the door to open. He shifted his stance and knocked raptly, his hand moving toward the bell and ringing it three times in a row. The sounds of scuffling could be heard along with footsteps. He bowed his head and then let his voice ring out. "I know you're there. Open up, Marla."

"Hello, traitor." Marla stood with a large knife in her hand, her body blocking any chance of Evan getting inside her home. He moved his head, trying to see if he could catch a glimpse of Grace. "Grace told me to tell you that she's not here."

Evan's steely eyes locked onto Marla's. The apron she wore had a vintage paisley pattern on the dark blue material, and Evan could smell Mexican spices wafting in the air. His eyebrow rose in speculation. "So she is here?"

She gave a sly grin. "Yes, but she obviously doesn't want to see you since you're a moronic *traitor*. Accept that, and she'll call you when she's ready. Why don't you go and hold your breath until then?"

"I need to talk to her. Please."

"We're busy. It's Taco Tuesday."

His pressed lips upturned slightly as he saw a glint in Marla's eyes. Evan leaned forward, speaking softly. "You think I was right to do what I did. Admit it."

"I don't admit anything. I stick with my best friend. She's hurting and she's pissed off at you. So I'm pissed off at you too."

He gazed down at his shoes, defeat coursing through him. His heart twisted mostly in pain, but partially in relief. She at least felt something. It would be worse if she didn't care at all. It might've been a selfish notion, but he wanted to know she missed him at least a fraction of as much as he missed her. "I didn't mean to hurt her, Marla. I was trying to make it better."

Marla's bourbon-colored eyes softened with pity, her defense breaking. "I know you love her, Evan." His gaze met hers again as hope peppered in. She put her empty hand out to calm him down. "I understand your intentions and where they came from, but it's going to take some time for Grace to realize it on her own."

"But—"

"No. Don't interrupt." Marla gave an irritated sigh and pointed the knife at him, making sure he wouldn't speak before she continued. "Once she figures it out, she'll be able to forgive you, but she needs her space right now."

His voice faltered as he looked away. "I miss her."

Marla shrugged. "Tough shit. Be patient."

He nodded and turned toward his car. He could be patient. He could wait a lifetime for her. His heart belonged with her, and he'd never ask for it back.

Chapter Twenty-Four

"Grace? It's your go."

"Hmm? Sorry." Grace shook herself out of the daze she was in and switched out two cards. Poker wasn't helping her forget the man who had taken her heart and killed it with a grenade launcher. She once again looked at her hand and knew it was shit. She had no chance of winning. Now it was a matter of whether she'd bluff. Marla and Jaime concentrated on their own cards, evaluating and adjusting as necessary.

One week. It had been seven agonizing days since she had last been in the presence of Evan Matthews, and it hadn't gotten easier. That night played in her mind on repeat. She thought of different ways she could've handled the situation. Yelled? Punched? Cried? No, Grace had stayed silent, and those feelings were beginning to root and fester and turn into something ugly.

She was angry—angry at him, at her parents, and at herself. She should have known better than to open up to someone like him. He had charmed his way into her heart, and now left her aching. But the truth was, she also still desperately loved him, and wanted to believe he acted with good intentions. It wasn't the intentions that upset her, it was the fact that he went behind her back and did it without asking.

"Fold," Jaime groaned and threw her hand down on the table.

"Marla?" Grace asked.

"I raise." The redhead smirked. "You have to call your mom back the next time she tries to get in touch with you."

Grace levelled in her chair and narrowed her eyes in annoyance. "Why the fuck would you even up the ante like that, Marla?"

"Why don't we just keep to the chips, ladies?" Jaime suggested with a careful countenance.

"No, I've seen Grace the past seven days moping about. She's not writing, she's not eating, and she's definitely not showering."

"Ew." Jaime grimaced. "You've got to fix that, Grace."

"I've showered." Grace raised her eyes to Marla and set them keenly. "Fine. If I win, you have to go on a date with Josh."

"Ha!" Jaime pointed to Marla as she made a squinted face. "You so want to."

"I loathe gym rats." Marla groaned as she studied her cards. "Let's go back to the chips."

Grace laughed, "Nope."

"I re-raise. You have to talk to Evan."

Grace became immobilized as her eyes widened with fright. "I can't do that. That's really cruel."

Jaime meekly responded, "You'll have to eventually talk to him."

"Don't have a good hand, Grace?" Marla sneered playfully.

Grace lifted her chin in defiance. "You have to tell your boss Cameron to fuck off the next time he tries to hit on you."

Marla gasped. "That's my career, Grace. You can't bet something like that."

Grace eyed her skeptically. "Then what?"

"I don't like this. Let's just drop it."

For once, Grace didn't mind. She nodded and threw her cards down on the table. Although it was fun for a bit, the repercussions of their wagers didn't bode very well for either of them.

"What did you have, Grace?" Jaime lifted the cards and laughed. "You were bluffing the whole time?"

"Yeah, I'm good at it, aren't I?" Grace stretched her body and yawned in exhaustion. She wasn't sleeping well. She felt depressed and her group of girls were helping her get through her disappointments on a Saturday afternoon. At least she thought so until Jaime added, "Almost as good as Evan."

"What does that mean?" Grace's heart started to flutter at the thought of him. She didn't want to have those reactions, but couldn't help her curiosity as she waited for more information.

Jaime closed her eyes then faced her straight on. "Um, well, remember when we first met him and played poker?"

"Of course."

"Well, Evan pretended to lose so you could win the game."

Grace's air fled out of her lungs as her mind jumbled with confusion. "What are you talking about?"

"He had a straight flush that night. He made me promise not to tell," Jaime confessed.

"Bastard," Grace whispered harshly. She then tried ignoring her tears as she began to put the cards and chips away in violent movements. "Why should I be surprised, right? I mean, he did betray me after all. And why didn't you tell me?"

"Grace, you really suck at dating." Marla laughed as she picked up the dishes from the table. "You needed a little push with Matthews."

"I date. I go out. You guys just wanted me to date *him* because he's a movie star." She felt herself becoming defensive and had to calm herself before she got too angry. Evan had tricked her.

"No, that's not it. You just keep yourself too guarded," Jaime contended as she helped clean up the rest of the dishes and handed them to Marla. "Evan wanted a way to know you, and he took the opportunity presented. Admit it. You would never have let him take you out on a date, or gone to Boston with him if he was just asking."

Grace shook her head. "I don't know what you mean." She did though, and it was about to be reiterated to her.

"Telling yourself it was a bet you were fulfilling made you less scared in getting to know him. You were protecting yourself by saying you'd keep to that bet, but right now you had no problem calling it off with Marla."

"I wasn't winning right now. Of course I called it off. And I tried getting out of Evan's stupid bet. I don't know why you're on his side anyway."

"I'm not on his side when it comes to what he did with your memoir, but he did what he had to do to get to know you better. It was the only way."

"She's right, you know," Marla said softly. "You don't seem to grasp happiness for yourself too often, Grace. You deserve it."

Tears threatened to fall over as Grace tried to understand what they were telling her. "I was happy. I was fine before Evan showed up. All he did was prove how all men are assholes."

Marla laughed. "That's my line, honey. Not yours. And you were lonely."

"He's not an asshole," Jaime corrected. "He did what he did because he loves you."

"Look, I appreciate your concern, but how would you feel if Dean took your journal and gave it to your parents when he knew there was stuff written in there about them?" Grace's temper began to flare the more she spoke. "That's what I thought. It would suck, wouldn't it? Evan took that and gave it away to them."

"Grace, sorry to say this, but I think you're being a bit of a coward." Marla said as she sat down and chewed on a brownie she had made from scratch.

Grace gaped at her. "Excuse me?"

"This isn't a journal. You're turning down a lucrative book deal. It could make your career. No more property managing, no more scraped up old Honda, no more scrounging for cash. You get to tell your story and help others, and you're not taking the risk because of your parents."

"So, obviously, Marla's on Evan's side, too." Grace's voice was strained as she tried to keep control of her emotions.

"It's not about sides. It's about you doing what you were meant to do. Evan pushed you toward it, and you won't even talk to your mom. She's calling you for a reason, and you're too chicken to find out why."

"I don't want to talk about this anymore. I'm going to take a nap." Grace made her way to Marla's guestroom and lay there thinking over everything. She reached to her phone and saw it void of texts and calls. Her mother stopped bothering her, Evan had cut his contact with her, and she had nobody to blame but herself.

She felt prickling in the back of her eyes and tried to ignore the feeling of her heart squeezing tight. She missed Evan beyond what she could admit to herself. He was her constant, her safe zone, the man she thought would perhaps be her forever. But happily ever after didn't exist, and she knew the risks she had taken in falling for him. She had kept her promise to Nathan, but she was also breaking it, and she was confused as to whether that was a good or a bad thing.

~

The air brushed against Grace's skin caressing her face as she leapt into the clear water below. It hit her with a cooling effect, its ripples taking her in, surrounding her. She felt weightless, tranquil, as the water framed her. Her eyes opened and she spotted a hand waiting for her to grasp it. She contemplated whether to grab hold or stay put. It was more peaceful down here, and though she couldn't breathe, she found solace in surrender. It would be easier to submit. Eyes that matched the water stared directly at her. Nathan. *He shook his head and gripped her, pushing her up toward the surface as he stayed behind. She tried to cry out, reaching back for him, but when she saw him again he looked different.* Evan?

Grace gasped as she startled awake. Her shaky breath calmed down and goosebumps covered her skin. Her blanket had fallen to the floor, and she felt her body chill from the cold air around her. She sat up and glanced at the time on the alarm clock nearby. Her nap lasted over three hours. There went her sleep schedule. It was early evening, and Grace could smell something heavenly drifting from the kitchen.

Marla was a goddess when it came to cooking. It was too bad Grace hadn't been taking pleasure in food over the past week. Marla usually forced her to eat, so it wasn't a surprise when she heard a knock at her door.

Marla peered in, her eyes concerned as Grace sat on the edge of her bed and ran her hand through her messy hair. "Grace? You have a visitor."

The tone of Marla's voice hadn't gone unnoticed. Grace shook her head, her brows furrowed in curiosity. She knew it wasn't Evan. There was no way Marla would do that to her. "Who is it?"

Her lips mouthed the words as she stayed in the doorway. "Your mom."

Grace's eyes widened as she stood up and violently responded in a harsh whisper. "What? Are you kidding me?"

Marla shook her head. "She's in the living room," Marla responded quietly. "I only recognized her because you both look similar. Anyway, she seems pleasant. She's out there waiting for you."

"Give me a moment." Grace's breathing accelerated at the thought of seeing her mom. What would she say to her? What would she do? How would she react? She moved to the vanity in the corner of the room and looked herself over in the mirror.

Untidy hair, pasty skin, no makeup, bags under her eyes, she was a mess. Her mother wouldn't approve. Grace looked over her warmups and Texas shirt and stood up tall. She needed to put on her suit of armor—steel herself, get ready to fight, and be who she was. Evan was right about her. She was resilient, and she would get through this just like she got through most of her life, fighting for what her heart believed in.

Grace tried to remember not to fidget as she made her way over to the living area. The windows let in streams of the setting sun, and in front of one of them stood Nancy Clark. She could only see the back of her as she approached, but she was still as thin and regal as Grace remembered. Dressed in some fancy designer blouse and slacks that probably cost more than Grace's car, Nancy was always one to keep up with the Joneses. She was a lawyer's wife, after all. Grace wondered what her father would think if he saw her now, and wasn't surprised about his absence.

Grace stopped midway from the window and chewed on the bottom of her lip. She clasped her hands in front of her to keep from moving around. It wasn't until she cleared her throat that Nancy turned and gazed at her daughter. Sixteen years changed a person, but she had seen much of her mother preserved with cosmetics and plastic surgery. It wasn't an overabundance of it. In fact, she was just as beautiful as ever.

The mossy green color with the flecks of yellow and brown dispersed through Nancy's eyes were unerringly like Nathan's. What stunned Grace was the look that radiated through them as her mother studied her. It was kind, and loving. "Hello, Grace." Her voice had changed. It was softer, more soothing, like the sun warming your skin when you exited a freezing room.

"Mom. How did you know where I was?"

Nancy's full lips turned into a smile as she moved closer. "Evan was staying at your home. He told me where I could find you."

Evan had met her mother. It was an odd thought. Her eyes roamed over Grace, her head tilting and surveying her. Grace held her breath, trying to keep her tears at bay. She wished she could hug her mother, feel comforted by her, but years of bitterness kept her from falling into her arms. It wasn't like she was one for warm hugs as she grew up. Nancy and Thomas weren't the affectionate type.

"You've become such a beautiful woman, Grace."

To say Grace was taken aback by that comment was an understatement. She couldn't find it in her to believe that comment coming from her mouth. Especially when she wasn't dressed up in the proper attire. "What?"

"You're lovely, darling." Nancy moved toward her and tried to touch her arm, but Grace recoiled out of habit. Nancy's hand fell down and she shook her head as she tried regaining her poised demeanor.

"What are you doing here?"

"Maybe we should sit, Grace."

Grace motioned toward the couch, each one of them taking a seat on the end and facing toward one another. She waited as her mother looked at her with a sense of tranquility that was unfamiliar to Grace. Her mother was always uptight, worried, tired. This wasn't the same woman.

"Where to begin…" Nancy let out a shaky laugh as she set her purse down beside her. "I want to say that first of all, I don't expect anything from you. I know your father and I were…distant after Nathan died."

Grace inhaled, her chest already starting to feel as if a ton of bricks were sitting on top of it. She listened as her mother continued in a soft voice. "And you were so detached from everything, we thought you were upset at us."

"I was," Grace snapped out and remembered to hold her tongue.

"We didn't handle it well. Obviously, nobody can ever handle losing a child."

"Or two."

Nancy's eyes began to water. "We thought we were giving you what you wanted, Grace. We tried to talk with you, but you pushed us away. It felt impossible to help you. We had just lost our son, and I couldn't stand the way I was losing you too."

Grace rolled her eyes, trying her best to keep in the anguish that was beginning to resurface. "When you think your parents hate you because you killed their son, that's reason enough to pull away."

"We never felt that, honey." She shifted her body closer to Grace, but all it did was make her tense up more. Nancy figured out very soon that it wasn't a good idea to try to touch her. "And we never thought less of you because you wanted to pursue your dreams."

Grace's eyes fell like a laser in on her mother's. "'*Why can't you be more like Nathan? Why are you always disappointing us? Why can't you do something practical?'* Any of those lines ring a bell? They were all said to me by either you or Dad." Nancy closed her eyes as Grace continued. "What is it you want, Mom? Don't worry I won't publish the memoir if that's what you're here to ask about."

"We had no idea, Grace. No idea how bad it was for you. We did what we thought was best for you." Tears began to trickle onto her flawless skin as she reached forward. "I came to ask for your forgiveness, Grace. Although, your father and I might not deserve it at this point."

Shock crossed over Grace's features as she tried taking in what her mother was telling her. Never had she thought this was the trajectory her parents would go. "You..." Grace tried to steady her trembling voice, "you can't just think that everything is going to be alright. Sixteen years is a long time. I don't know either of you anymore."

"I understand." She paused and gave a hint of a

smile. "But we're both very sorry, and we hope to get to know you better."

"Why isn't Dad here?"

"He's here, at the hotel. He wants to see you, but I wanted to test the waters with you first. He read your book as well. You can publish it, Grace. It's a wonderful piece of work."

"I don't need your permission," Grace said defiantly. She hugged her arms around herself, the knowledge of her parent's remorse beginning to crack the cement that held the obstruction around her heart.

She didn't have time to dwell on it much longer when her phone rang. *Evan?* Hesitant to grab her phone, she wondered what she would tell him. He had been right. Her parents wanted to know her better, were asking for a relationship. But could she let them in?

"You can answer," her mother urged.

The ringing stopped and Grace stayed seated, unsure of her next step. She had no idea how to behave in front of her mother, what to talk about or share. The life her parents built for themselves in California was so foreign to her. She began. "How long are you in town?"

"Only a few days. We weren't sure you would see us."

Grace's phone began ringing again, and she excused herself as she went to the guestroom to retrieve it. The number was unfamiliar, but it had a Los Angeles area code. She was tempted to let it go to voicemail, but something prompted her to answer.

She spoke and waited as she heard voices on the other end. "Hello?" Grace waited as she heard Zach yelling in the background. "Zach? Evan?"

Marla peered into the bedroom and looked curiously at Grace as she waited. A faint voice sounded on the other end. "Grace..."

"Josh?" Grace perked up, and she knew something wasn't right. "Josh? What's going on?"

A tiny escape of distress left Josh's mouth. "Grace, something's happened."

A chill ran over her body as her breathing hitched in her chest. "Josh, talk to me. What happened?" Only breath could be heard on the other end. "Josh? Hello?"

Shuffling was heard and a strong voice came from the end of the receiver. "Grace?"

"Zach? What the hell's going on?"

"Evan's had an accident. He's on the way to the hospital."

Grace covered her mouth as her heart slammed against her chest. "Is he okay? Please tell me he's okay. Zach...What happened?"

"They were shooting a water scene, and his costume got caught. They performed CPR. He was out for a while."

Grace felt her heart ripping into shreds, the fear taking hold of her. She couldn't lose him. "He was unconscious? Is he okay?"

"I don't know. I have to go, Grace. We'll be at Brackenridge Hospital, okay? Call me when you get there."

Before she could say anything else, the line had been cut, and Grace stopped herself from crying. Marla stood near her as Grace's voice shook in a murmur. "I need to get to the hospital."

Grace moved out of the room, and Marla and her mother followed behind. "I'll drive," Marla said, grabbing her keys and purse as the three women scrambled out the door.

They piled in the car and stayed silent before Marla broke with a soft voice. "What happened, Grace?"

She chewed on her thumb, her eyes closed as she whispered. "Evan's been training for an underwater scene. I don't know what happened…" She couldn't say it. A hand reached over and squeezed her arm, and though she didn't look, she knew it was her mother. Grace closed her eyes and held her jaw tight. She needed to be strong, to not lose her cool, because Evan would be alright. He had to be. She would never forgive herself if he wasn't.

Chapter Twenty-Five

Evan sat on the bleachers of a stadium, the sunshine warming his skin and the breeze cooling him in the most perfect way. He was the only one around, except for scores of football players huddled around on the field below in navy jerseys. He sat back and enjoyed surveying the world around him. The colors were vivid, as if they had their own life, and he felt serene. Joyful. Loved. He was curious where that feeling came from as he watched the players set into position. He thought he'd seen this game before, as if he was reliving a moment in his life. He just couldn't recall when.

Evan turned when a voice popped up beside him. "Can I sit?"

"Sure, man."

A guy with jet black hair and a face that radiated a sense of heroism scooted onto the bench and sat with his large forearms resting on his knees. Well over six-foot-two and two hundred and thirty pounds of pure muscle, he had the perfect physique for a football player. He was larger than Josh.

"We've got a great team this year." His voice was smooth, familiar, and Evan felt at ease, as if he knew him.

"That's your team?"

The guy nodded. "Yeah. Quarterback."

Evan chuckled. "What are you doing up here then? Shouldn't you be down there practicing?"

"They can do without me for a bit." He sat back and smiled, looking up at the sky, then at Evan. "It's a good life, isn't it? When you live what you love."

Evan reflected for a moment and then nodded. "It really is."

"Not everyone gets the opportunity to follow their heart. They're too scared of being judged. They worry about failing, or getting the shit knocked out of them."

"Failing's a part of life," Evan said assuredly. "And we all get the shit knocked out of us some way or another. It's unavoidable."

Evan's eyes stayed out on the field as he listened to the sounds of tackling, whistles being blown, and coaches yelling. He wished Grace was there with him. Not because she liked football, but because she would love the feeling of pure peace he was experiencing in that moment. After some time of silence, the stranger stood up. "I'd better get over there. I still have to change. Nice talking to you, Evan."

Evan nodded and glanced at him, peering into dark green, luminous eyes. He finally had to ask. "Do I know you?"

"I know you." The guy grinned and extended his hand. "Captain Drew Abrams, bro. Love those movies."

"Thanks." Evan laughed as he gripped him in greeting, a half shake and clap. He looked down and noticed a tattoo of an oak tree on the back of the stranger's hand in between his finger and thumb. The leaves were floating up from the branches, transforming into doves.

A loud sound caught Evan's attention and he bounced his eyes toward the field. Nothing seemed out of the ordinary. "I didn't get your name." He turned back and the stranger was gone. Chills ran through Evan as he felt his chest begin to cave. A pressure grew over his heart, and a stinging began deep within his lungs. He opened his mouth as everything around him was fading. The brilliant blue sky inked with black, and his vision blurred. He closed his eyes, and opened them again, the world around him vanishing into a blur. His breath—he couldn't catch it. Then he felt nothing but pain. Agonizing, torturous, blinding pain, as the world went pitch dark, and he was gone.

"Evan Matthews!" Grace rushed toward the front desk as she entered the hospital and asked the receptionist for directions. The woman held a straight countenance as Grace tried to recollect her breathing. "Please, tell me where he is."

"Ma'am," her voice was soft, but condescension leaked from her tone, "I have no record of an Evan Matthews in this hospital."

Marla stepped in and asked, "Where would someone be directed if they were looking for a near drowning victim? Perhaps brought into the emergency unit?"

Grace's trembling fingers attempted calling Zach for the tenth time but she kept getting his voicemail. She tried Josh and he didn't answer. And Evan? She couldn't call him. If she heard his voice on his recorded message she would lose it, worse than she was beginning to lose control now.

She didn't have anyone else she knew who could tell her where he was. No information left her utterly helpless. She could feel her pulse growing stronger, throbbing as much as her heart. Short, shallow breaths were escaping her and she felt a sense of disorientation. "Please…I know he's here."

"I'm sorry, there's no Evan Matthews here."

"I know he's here," Grace's voice picked up as she slapped her hand flat against the granite countertop. Her mother stood behind her and squeezed at her shoulder. "Tell me where he is!"

"I am going to have to ask you to lower your voice, please." The lady pressed her lips together and Grace knew she wasn't going to give her the information. She was nobody to him now. She had left him, and she was regretting it more than ever.

Her control was slipping, and a numbness began to take over her body. She felt hot, sweaty, and dizzy as she began to pant. "You don't understand. I need to see him! Tell me where he is! Tell me! Please, I beg you. Please."

"Grace," her mom's soft voice tried to soothe her. "Come on, honey, we'll wait."

"No! No, we won't wait, Mother! I can't…" Tears began to slip out and she was suddenly sobbing as her voice carried throughout. "I can't lose him. This can't happen. It's not happening to me, not again."

"Grace, come on…" Marla and her mother tried to pull her away, but she shrugged them off, not accepting of their touch.

"No, tell me where he is! Tell me! I need to see him. He can't leave me. I can't be without him!" She continued yelling at the receptionist as they tried to placate her.

Her mother turned Grace, grabbing her and cupping her cheeks in her hands. "Grace, look at me, sweetheart. You need to calm down. Breathe. You'll see him, he'll be okay."

"Mom…" She broke down and began to wail as she clung onto her. "I can't be without him. He can't leave me. He can't."

The grief was taking over, and all feelings of expectations for her life, the pride she had held onto, the feelings of failure or anything else just didn't seem to matter. It all fell away, and all she cared about was being in the presence of the man she loved so desperately. She'd give everything to be in his arms, to have him hold and kiss and love her.

Her mom held onto her, rocked her tightly, stroking her hair and cried with her. Both of them leaned onto each other for support. Both of them were reliving a traumatic experience they never wanted to repeat. Yet here they were, and Grace needed her mother, but she needed the man who was a part of her life now, who she couldn't live without. She needed Evan.

~

"Grace?"

Zach's voice was a lifeline as she stood from the chair in the lobby of the hospital. She hurried toward him. "Zach, is he okay?"

"He's getting tests done. We haven't heard anything else yet."

Grace hugged him. "I couldn't get to you."

"I'm so sorry. I wasn't getting service on my phone. I knew after some time that you had to be here by now. The media just found out about the accident and reporters are trying to find out as much as they can. We have him under a fake name. Come on, I'll take you upstairs."

He glanced back and nodded at Marla. "That's my mom," Grace said as they made an introduction and all headed toward the elevators. "Zach, how could this happen?"

"It was just a crazy accident. He was doing this stunt where he had to dive in and stay under for some time. They rehearsed so many times, and it was fine, they had rescue divers nearby. But today, it just, was a freak oversight. He couldn't get the costume off some side latch."

They stood in the elevator and waited as it accelerated slowly. "How long was he out?" Grace asked anxiously, trying to keep herself from losing control again.

"Not long. They figured it out pretty quickly. He was just tired, Grace. I'm sure that, on top of the lapse in judgment, made for a bad combination."

"He wasn't getting sleep," she acknowledged as it

dawned on her that their fight had caused him stress.

"No, Grace, don't go there," Marla warned her as they approached the waiting room.

Grace's mother stopped her in her tracks and held onto her arm. Her green eyes peered into Grace's with precision. "None of this is your fault, Grace. Nathan dying was not your fault and Evan's accident wasn't either. Do you understand me?"

"I just hope he's okay." Grace nodded. She glanced into the waiting room and saw Josh sitting in the corner, his head resting in his hands, along with other people who seemed to be a part of the filming crew.

"Josh feels pretty shaken up by everything. He's not good with feeling out of control," Zach said softly before they entered the room. "None of us have seen Evan yet. I chartered a flight for his mom and Hilary."

They walked in and sat beside one another, and it felt as if hours passed before a doctor finally approached. His dark eyes seemed friendly, and Grace could only hope that meant good news.

"He's going to be fine. We're keeping him in for observation." He was confident in his assessment, but Grace needed reassurance.

"But what about water in the lungs? Organ failure? Head trauma? How is he?" Grace asked a slew of questions, feeling overprotective as they all hovered around him.

"Lung problems could arise after a twelve-hour span, so that's why we're keeping him here overnight. We took x-rays and he seems to be okay from injury. He came in already awake and alert, so brain damage isn't a concern. He did have hypothermia, so he's getting rewarmed and we checked the oxygen levels in his blood. We're watching his heartbeat and hoping pneumonia won't be an issue, which could be common with near-drowning victims. He's just fatigued."

"Can we see him?" Josh finally spoke, his assessing glacial blue eyes focused on the doctor.

"Yes, but one at a time. He keeps asking if Grace is here."

Grace's head lifted and her eyes began to water. She looked over at Zach and Josh, and they nodded. Josh's soft voice spoke. "He needs you, Grace."

Grace entered the cold, dark room. The smell of antiseptic filled her nostrils as she peered across and saw Evan lying still in the propped-up bed. The nurse closed the door behind her and Grace quietly glided toward him, her eyes assessing him as he slept. His skin was pale, his lips had an underlying purple-blue tint, and she had to hold back jumping into his arms and kissing him, begging him to never let her go.

His chest lifted and fell in regular rhythm as his closed eyes fluttered. An IV was hooked into his arm, and blankets covered his body in an attempt to keep him warm. Grace pulled the chair beside his bed and she sat down, never letting her eyes leave him.

"I'm sorry for everything, Evan," she whispered as tears flowed down her cheeks. He needed his rest, and she didn't want to disturb him, so she just stared, grateful he was there. "You were right about it all. I was so stubborn. My mom and dad want to know me again, and I do want to know them. I've missed out on so much by closing myself off, but I'm not doing that anymore."

She gazed at the ECG machine, the lines steady. "You're my heart, Evan. You're everything to me, so you better be okay. I love you."

She bent forward and grabbed his hand, raising it to her lips as she kissed it. "You only ever going to tell me that when you think I'm asleep, doll?" his voice croaked out softly.

Grace's eyes landed on his and she laughed through her tears as she kissed him. "Evan, you scared me."

"Sorry, baby, but how else was I going to get you to forgive me?"

"This is worse than your losing a poker game on purpose," she cried.

He winced as he tried to laugh, "Guess Jaime ratted me out. Remind me not to give her tickets to the premiere."

"Not funny, Matthews." Although it was great to know that he was joking after a near-death experience, Grace was still in shock over the events. "How dare you almost die on me? I won't ever allow it again." Tears prickled up and poured over as she brushed his hair back from his forehead. "What happened, Evan?"

His brow crinkled in concentration as he shook his head. "I honestly don't remember much, Grace. The last thing I recall is getting in the water then waking up gasping for air."

Her lips peppered kisses over his hand as she clasped it in hers. "Are you in a lot of pain?"

"Nothing millions of your kisses can't cure," he

winked.

"Stop trying to be adorable. I'm trying to be angry at you."

She reached forward and touched her lips against his as he gave a small moan of happiness and pleasure. His hand moved a strand of her hair away from her face. "Did you see your mom, Gracie?"

She nodded and kissed his temple. "I did. And I think everything's going to be fine. As long as you promise to be."

"I promise, as long as you don't ever leave me again, Gracie."

She shook her head. "Never. I'll never leave you."

"Promise? Even when I piss you off?"

"Promise. Rest, Evan." She smiled as he closed his eyes. "I'm so in love with you, by the way."

"I already knew that, but it's always nice to hear. Even when you think I'm sleeping." She chuckled as he grinned, his eyes still closed. "I'm in love with you, Gracie Lynn. I'm keeping you. Forever. Get used to it, doll."

"I think I can get very used to that idea, Evan."

Epilogue

Grace hunched down brushing off dust and debris from the headstone of Nathan's grave. Taking her time, she arranged the fresh bouquet of hydrangeas. Evan sat down and helped. He had seen such a difference in his girlfriend since having left the hospital. She had agreed to a new publishing contract and had sold the rights to her memoir to be produced into a film—with his production company, of course. Who else could care for telling her story on the big screen like he could?

That success gave her the ability to write full-time and look for someone to take her place as property manager. She was also starting to talk to her parents more. It was a slow process, but Evan couldn't be more proud of her.

"Hey, bro, we're here," he stated gently as he wiped away dirt with a small cloth. Grace giggled, and Evan's heart jumped with joy at the sound. "Your sis and I finally got our shit together. I don't know how you ever put up with her stubborn ways."

He sat behind her as she leaned into his chest, her head resting near his. "You love my stubborn ways."

"I'm the one that's meant to put up with them."

"Nathan would've loved you."

"It's weird, I feel like I knew him or something. Can't really explain why." They were silent as the wind picked up, and they huddled closer together. Evan kissed her on her temple and spoke softly. "What was that promise you made to your brother, Grace?"

"The night he died, I told him I didn't believe love existed, and I definitely didn't trust men anymore." Evan wrapped his arms around Grace's waist, pulling her closer to him. "He sat beside me and told me all the wonderful things love could offer if I waited for someone who would value me."

"Smart guy."

"He was. He was an old soul trapped in a jock's body." They both chuckled as she linked her fingers with his.

"He was a jock?"

"Yeah, he loved football. Playing was his favorite thing in the world." She rested against his chest and let her hands trace the top of Evan's. He glanced down and his eyes caught on something. He pushed her long sleeved shirt up and stared at a drawing on the back of her hand of an oak tree with doves flying from the branches. The memory flooded in of a football player with the green eyes, and the tattoo on his hand.

"Grace, what…" His voice trembled as he looked at the intricate sketch. His fingers traced over the tree. "Why did you draw this?"

She smiled as she nodded. "I used to doodle on my hands all the time when I was young. Nathan hated it and gave me a hard time. I like oak trees though. They symbolize strength, endurance and protection."

Evan stayed still, the shock coursing through him, as if lightning had struck and left him with the aftereffects.

Grace comfortably continued to open up to him, finally answering the question Evan had wondered. "Anyway, he made me promise that I would wait to give myself fully to the man I knew loved me so much that my happiness meant more to him than his own. Someone who I would love just as much. And to always —"

"Follow your heart," he finished for her.

She straightened up and looked back at him, smiling wide. "Yeah. How'd you know that?"

Evan couldn't contemplate how to tell Grace of his dream, whatever it was he had experienced when he remembered meeting the stranger with the same tattoo —the stranger he knew had to be her brother. "This is going to sound so crazy, but I think I met him when I was unconscious."

Grace's eyes fixed on him. "What do you mean?"

"This drawing," he pointed to her hand. "It triggered a memory. I met this guy in a navy football jersey, and he talked to me about how great it was to live what you love."

Tear-filled, Grace gave a small chuckle. "He had a football scholarship to Columbia. And he always used to say to *live what you love*. That was his motto. How did this trigger your memory though?" She asked as they studied the tree drawn on her hand.

"The football player had a tattoo of that exact drawing."

Grace's breath hitched as tears streamed down her face. "I drew it on his hand the night he passed away."

"Do you think your brother's still watching out for

you?" Evan asked sincerely.

"Well, he brought me you," she beamed.

"You've kept your promise," he assured her as he cupped her jaw, bringing his lips toward hers.

"I know I have," she confidently responded as the breeze blew in around them. "Loving you helped me heal, Evan. It was meant to be you."

Heartache and tragedy—those were inevitable in loving someone, in losing someone. But beauty was also present in them. It gave gratitude for the moments truly lived, and even in an ending, it lasted forever.

"I followed my heart," Grace said, her eyes on Nathan's grave. "I kept my promise."

THE END

Acknowledgements

It's difficult to even begin this, there are so many to thank, and I apologize if I left anyone out. Thank you to my wonderful parents for supporting me throughout all the crazy endeavors I've attempted. My sister Gina for pepping me up when I felt down and for helping me set up timelines and plots. David for helping me with my computer setup. And Elliot for distracting me and making me laugh when I needed it. To my grandma for her many prayers, as well to the rest of my family. To my dear friends—Marla, Jaime, Carrie, Laura, and all the others who have been part of this crazy process—thank you for putting up with me (and letting me use some of your names). All the encouragement and support has meant so much to me! Jennifer, thanks for helping me figure out crazy things I needed to fix and helping me with ideas. Renee, thanks for being my cheerleader and loving Evan and Grace. I couldn't ever have done it without you all. Lissa Taylor, thank you for the cards!

Melissa Rheinlander, what can I say? You changed the course of my entire career, helped me find a purpose, and taught me so much about this crazy, beautiful book business. Danielle Sanchez, you rock, thank you for all your support. I'm forever grateful and always in awe of Julie Kenner. Julie, thank you SO much for taking the time to advise me. I've learned so much from you, and it means the world to me that you spent time helping a newbie. K.L. Grayson – I miss you so much, thank you for answering all my crazy questions and being one of the first to read my first loooong story. Tee Swan – thanks for the late night pep-talks, "you got this" chats, and help with my wonderful beta readers whom I love – you girls know who you are. K.P. Simmon – for reminding me of my goals and how to get there. Anna Todd and R.K. Lilley thank you for allowing me writing time with you ladies. I enjoyed every second. Erin Noelle, thank you for helping me fix my writing quirks! Regina Wamba, you are an insanely talented woman, thank you for bringing my vision to life. Ripp and Monica were perfect! Jeff Senter for formatting my book and being patient with my tons of emails, thank you. Amy Daws, thanks for taking my calls and helping me out so much! To all the authors I've had the pleasure of meeting - I have esteemed every single ounce of counsel and support. I commend all that you brilliant writers do. Emma Hart, thank you for wanting to read my book and encouraging me. Rachel Van Dyken, thank you for being awesome. To my Austenites back home in McAllen— it all started because of a little book we chatted about that became a big book and I decided to make us a little fan page where we could talk about our favorite character. I miss our brunches. Bloggers, thank you for all the work you put in and the love and devotion you have toward reading. I know how hard you work, and I appreciate it! Readers, thanks for letting me share my words with you. I hope you enjoyed Evan and Grace as much as I enjoyed writing them.

About the Author

Anissa Garcia earned her Bachelor's Degree in Speech Communications and English. She held an array of jobs including Public Relations Manager for Barnes and Noble. Wanting a change of pace, she attended The American Academy of Dramatic Arts, and trained full-time in theatre for two years. After working in Hollywood as an actress and casting assistant, she relocated to Austin, Texas and began writing freelance for Cosmopolitan and other magazines. When not writing stories, watching movies, or drinking a latte, she loves to daydream about romantic fictional men.

– CONTACT ANISSA GARCIA –
authoranissagarcia@gmail.com
www.anissagarcia.com
Facebook | Twitter | Instagram
Tumblr | Snapchat | Pinterest

Made in the USA
Lexington, KY
18 September 2016